Cease to Exist

by

Ian Rodney Lazarus

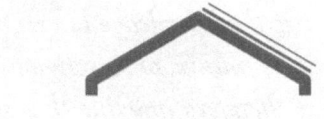

For Anthony, Myles and Emmalee

"**M**an *finally has the knowledge to get into the genetic code created by nature, or as religious people would say, by God. One may therefore imagine that scientists could create a person with desired features. This may be a mathematical genius, or an outstanding musician. But this can also be a soldier, a person that can fight without fear, pain, compassion, or mercy.*"

VLADIMIR PUTIN, 2017

1

Howard Steele was a selfish, misogynist pig. He was also one of the wealthiest men in the world. As the market for electric vehicles began to overtake internal combustion engines, Steele developed a cheaper battery with a lower carbon footprint than the Tesla. He followed this by building a network of innovative charging stations that would rival the coverage of Electrify America; customers would pull their car on top of a large plate that would wirelessly charge the battery positioned on the bottom of the vehicle.

Steele was a pragmatic industrialist; while everyone fully expected him to introduce an electric vehicle, he would never go there. For him, any market where subjective elements of design would influence buying behavior was a fool's errand. By the time he was found floating in the pool of his Malibu home, he had an estimated net worth over $100 billion.

Steele had been divorced three times before marrying Natalie Spencer, a successful actress who had been married before and had a daughter, Denise. While Steele insisted that Spencer sign a prenup agreement, he agreed to adopt Denise and serve as her guardian in the event of Natalie's death. The family was intensely private and shielded from the paparazzi by Steele's entourage of security, even as Natalie suffered from a particularly aggressive form of breast cancer and made several trips to Cedars-Sinai Medical Center in Los Angeles for chemotherapy. News outlets finally revealed that Natalie Spencer succumbed to the disease when Denise was only twelve.

The years following her mother's death were difficult for Denise. Her stepfather was abusive, and it was later suspected that he sexually assaulted her, but no charges were ever brought. She developed bipolar behavior on entering high school because of the never-ending drama in her life. Steele had her committed to a mental institution, claiming she was agoraphobic, thereby deflecting any attention from his role in her condition.

His significant philanthropic donations to a psychiatric hospital undoubtedly facilitated Denise's eventual placement there. After several years it was determined that Denise was healthy enough to rejoin society. Steele hired a caregiver for her so that he could maintain his distance. He was ready to move on.

After Steele died, Denise became the only beneficiary of his fortune. Shortly afterward, her aide mysteriously disappeared. And shortly after that, Denise disappeared. She would not resurface again for twenty years.

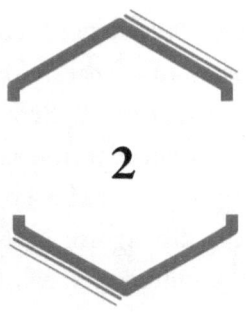

2

"**H**ana, dul, set, net..."

Kim Ji-Sung counted to himself as he lay as flat as possible in the cold, brittle grass on the North Korean side, watching the searchlights pass lazily back and forth across the frozen river representing the border with China. Ji-Sung could see thousands of stars tonight when the searchlights moved out of his view. He was, after all, far from any city centers in a country where reliable electricity was a privilege of only the Party loyalists. As he exhaled, his breath shot forth a frosty mist that penetrated the darkness all around, then just as quickly disappeared. As he shuffled forward, the stiff, near-frozen ground cover crunched under his feet.

Twelve others, consisting of three families, huddled a few yards back in the bushes, taking their instructions from Pastor Chun Ki-Won, often referred to as a modern-day Moses for his bravery in smuggling North Korean families across the border. It was estimated that thousands of people had entered China through Ki-Won's "Underground Railroad" since he started his operation in 1995. The families tonight included children ranging from five to fourteen years old.

On crossing, they would take off and shove their outer garments in the bushes to reveal colorful, pastel-inspired coats typically seen on the streets of Seoul. They were already carrying fake South Korean identity papers and had spent the past week gorging on donated food to gain weight and fill their cheeks to distinguish themselves from the emaciated faces of impoverished North Koreans. They would pose as tourists as they made their way first to Yanji, twenty kilometers from the border, then on to Harbin via train, which would put them 525 kilometers from Mongolia and ultimate freedom. Kim Ji-Sung would be going only as far as Harbin.

Unlike the refugees fleeing human rights abuses and poverty in North Korea, Ji-Sung was exactly where he was supposed to be as a member of the Reconnaissance General Bureau, or RGB, North Korea's intelligence agency. For this operation, the government of North Korea would conveniently ignore Article 47 of its criminal code outlining the punishment for defecting, to pursue the greater good of spying on China's biomedical laboratories and using the services of Pastor Ki-Won to do so. Besides, China had become quite skilled at ignoring international laws and norms by capturing North Korean defectors and repatriating them, so there was a good chance these families would be returning to North Korea. Most of those sent back would face harsh punishment in labor camps. Many would die.

Ji-Sung had orders to find and integrate with Won's Underground Railroad and to cross into China with them. His mission was to collect information about a Chinese operation code-named "Shiva." The Hindu god Shiva was known as the god of destruction, a god that would ultimately destroy the universe in order to recreate it. The Supreme Leader had been previously advised that the Chinese were creating an indestructible army within its bio-laboratories, a prospect that was irresistible to the Leader and a secret worth stealing at any price.

Ji-Sung was a perfect candidate for the mission: He had earned a degree in the biological sciences at Pyongyang Medical University and was later handpicked to join the RGB because of his "excellent genetic profile." There he was trained in martial arts, North Korean spy craft, and assigned to multiple covert operations. By the time of this mission, he had over fifteen years of field experience and displayed an understated confidence that his superiors admired.

Ji-Sung had not seen any Chinese or North Korean border guards for the past two days. According to Chun Ki-Won, this stretch of the Tumen River was the best place for the refugees to cross; even when the river was flowing it was shallow enough to cross on foot. Also, this was one of the last remaining gaps in a border wall that North Korea had been building since the beginning of the COVID pandemic. And with this being the night of the new moon, conditions for concealing their crossing would be ideal. Ji-Sung would wait until the searchlight had reached the far end of its range, then make his way across the river.

The ambient temperature was now about ten below zero Celsius, and winter was giving way to spring later than usual. He felt confident the ice on the river would not breach. As he pushed himself off the ground, he remained hunched over. The grass felt spongy under his boots as he navigated through the brush and approached the banks of the river. The others were transfixed on his movements. He stepped lightly on the ice and quietly made his way into Chinese territory.

A few moments later, when the searchlights once again reached their farthest point from each other, the three families, along with Ki-Won, successfully made the crossing as well. They were all in China now.

"THE UNITED STATES DISTRICT Court for the Southern District of New York versus Richard Anthony O'Brien," the court clerk bellowed while looking down at her notes. She made eye contact with Richard's attorney to signal his turn to approach the long, thin tables opposite the judge's bench. It was about 10:30 in the morning.

"Mr. O'Brien, how do you plead to the charge of aggravated assault?" asked the judge.

"Guilty, your honor."

Impersonating a federal officer is a Class E felony punishable with up to four years in prison. Sentencing guidelines varied; some jurisdictions would lean toward lighter sentences of about one year. Richard O'Brien's lawyer, James Rosoff, was confident that, under the circumstances, his client would be able to avoid jail time and merely be subject to probation. Rosoff was recommended by other agents in the FBI that found themselves in legal jeopardy.

"Here's what I recommend," Rosoff said as the two met prior to the initial arraignment, "in addition to emphasizing that you assisted in capturing a suspected terrorist, we will plead guilty to aggravated assault in exchange for the prosecution dropping the charge of impersonating an officer.

"Come again?" Richard replied.

"Okay, hear me out," Rosoff said, excited to pursue such a creative line of defense. "This isn't without precedent, he said, "in 2011, a man was charged with impersonating a police officer. He was wearing a fake police uniform, he detained a woman, forced her to buy him food at a 7-Eleven store, then demanded to strip search her in a motel under the premise that he was searching for drugs."

Richard continued to stare at Rosoff, wondering just how much control he really had over the situation. Besides, it seemed Rosoff was on a roll.

"I know," Rosoff continued, "I am not making this up. The woman feared the consequences of disobeying the man, but since it was his first offense, the court was more lenient than it perhaps should have been. His felony charge was reduced to a misdemeanor. Richard, this will potentially allow you to keep your job."

Richard's decision to steal his girlfriend's FBI credentials to capture a suspected terrorist, even though he was at the time just a low-level FBI employee, was not his brightest move but, as he later told his friends, "I may be crazy, but I'm not insane." At the time, there was no other way to capture the suspect on American soil. As it turned out, the rogue Israeli agent was captured in Canada, which was good enough. This was a case where breaking the law was the best of many bad options.

As several other cases were being heard, the judicial equivalent of horse trading was occurring in the back of the courtroom and the hallway outside. Because cases were being heard back-to-back, it was difficult to find any place where some quiet deal was not being negotiated. Richard had earlier watched from the back of the courtroom as Rosoff whispered to the prosecuting attorney about a proposed plea bargain. Heads were nodding; the prosecutor understood the system was so backed up with repeat offenders that Richard's case was a mere distraction. Rosoff placed his left hand on the prosecutor's shoulder, then presented his right hand to make it official. The other attorney obliged, and the handshake followed. The deal was done.

The judged looked down at her notes. The pause, to Richard, felt like an eternity. He did not realize that he was holding his breath.

"Mr. O'Brien, this is a serious charge, but in light of your service to the State of New York, and indeed, the rest of the country, the court looks with sympathy at your case. I sentence you to forty hours of community service and one year of probation." The judge tapped her gavel on the bench, then looked down at her notes to see what was next on the docket.

"Thank you, your honor."

Richard breathed a huge sigh of relief. The reduction of charge from impersonating an officer to aggravated assault meant that he was convicted of a misdemeanor, not a felony. As James advised, a felony conviction would make it impossible to continue his work for the FBI. A misdemeanor would not. In various courts, aggravated assault could be treated as a felony, but Rosoff understood the stakes and earned his fee by ensuring his conviction was classified appropriately.

Richard turned to his attorney, beaming.

"Thanks, James, nothing personal, but I hope our paths don't cross too soon."

"Oh, I've heard that one before," Rosoff replied, letting out a soft chuckle. "Well, it's been a pleasure working with you, Richard, and I wish you the best of luck at the Bureau. Where are you off to?"

"Not a hundred percent sure yet, but I think it's about time for a change of scenery."

The two men walked out of the courtroom and down the steps outside just as Sarah Goodman rushed up to the building. She saw Richard first. The sun was shining, and the city was alive with activity.

"Richard!" she called out, somewhat out of breath. "I'm so sorry, I got stuck in traffic!"

While Sarah had promised to be by Richard's side and to assist if necessary in his defense, he understood that planning to be anywhere on time in New York depended largely on traffic conditions. And as the worst-case scenario was behind him, he was not about to make Sarah feel guilty for being late.

"It's okay, it's over," he replied as the two met, grabbing each other's hands and nearly embracing as if they were in a rom-com episode. Richard turned to wink at Rosoff, who smiled and continued on his way.

"So they accepted the plea?" Sarah asked excitedly.

"Yeah," Richard replied. "I'm free and clear. For now."

"Oh, that's wonderful. Let's go celebrate!"

RICHARD AND SARAH SAT opposite each other at the Mille-Feuille Bakery on Broadway. A tiny flagpole with the number "5" sat on the small café table. It would be replaced moments later with the coffee and baguettes they ordered. New York locals and tourists buzzed past them constantly, but they didn't notice. Sarah gazed at Richard like a schoolgirl with a crush. Richard rubbed one hand over the other as if he were polishing them. It was time for him to level with Sarah.

"They are sending me to the Academy for agent training," he said finally.

"Richard, that's wonderful. You'll make a terrific agent. I'm so happy for you."

"Well, the offer was conditional," he continued, his voice cracking a bit as he prepared to reveal the rest of the headline. "I'll be based out of the field office in LA."

Sarah looked confused. This was not how the Bureau operated in her experience.

"Conditional? Really? Why?"

"To be honest," Richard said, embarrassed that he was messing up the whole reveal, "I put in for a transfer, and this was what they offered."

Sarah's eyebrows narrowed as she tried to decipher the story behind the story. She looked quizzically at Richard, waiting for more. A fire engine and several police cars came racing past the bakery, sirens blasting, but Sarah remained unfazed.

"Look, Sarah," Richard said, leaning in, "the past few months have been really difficult, I don't know if I could have handled it if not for you. But my parents found I was a fraud, I let my brother down, and a girl that cared for me committed suicide." This was not the time for Richard to add that his girlfriend Courtney was carrying his baby. "I've let a lot of people down, and I've made some enemies here. Basically, I need a fresh start."

Sarah's disposition had not changed. There was more to unpack here given how their relationship had developed during the mission code-named Utapeli. Sarah had finally allowed herself to have feelings for Richard after earlier swearing off intraoffice romances.

"Sarah, this should not change anything," Richard said. "It means we will accumulate more frequent flier miles, that's all."

Sarah's smile returned tentatively as she began to accept the news. Richard knew she would not readily leave her position at the FBI field office in Detroit where she had the highest level of seniority apart from the local special agent in charge. But she had no right to deny him the opportunity he earned.

"Okay, sure," she replied, finally. "This will be interesting. An agent. You're going to be an agent!" she exclaimed. "When do you start training?"

"I leave for the Academy on Sunday for classes Monday morning," he said.

Sarah looked at her phone. Today was Thursday. They had the weekend.

"YOU'RE GOOD TO GO, sir," the dockhand said as he stepped off the boat and onto the pier.

This was something John Kinkade had heard many times. An experienced sailor, he had come to regard the all too common "good to go" send-off as cause for alarm; there was almost always *something* that required a little more attention on the boat before it left the dock. He remembered the time a dock hand had sent him off with those words just before hardware that held the sail to the hull broke free as soon as the sail caught wind. As the sail whipped around violently, the heavy steel block that would normally be welded to the hull was flying free about five feet to the starboard side of the boat, on the end of the sail, and nearly knocked him out as it flew toward him. From that point on, "good to go" was a signal that he had to double-check *everything* on the boat before leaving the dock. Kinkade stepped on the boat and conducted his own inspection of the lines, fittings, and hardware all around the twenty-seven-foot Catalina. The last thing he always checked was the head.

"Okay, thank you," he said finally, "see you in a few hours."

John Kinkade had been looking forward to this sailing and diving trip for some time. Raised in Southern California and now a U.S. representative from the Thirty-Eighth

Congressional District, he was not able to indulge in his hobbies as much as when he was younger. He tried to make the trip to Mission Bay in San Diego once a month because he maintained a membership with a local sail club that would charge him dues whether he rented a boat or not. The Catalina was his favorite boat because it was something he could easily navigate on his own, and he was generally on his own due to the demands of his job and the spur-of-the-moment nature of his trips to San Diego.

Kinkade continued to work down his checklist mentally as he caught the line from the dockhand and was released from the pier. The engine was idling nicely, the mainsail was waiting to be hoisted, the jib was furled, and there was essentially no traffic ahead of him. He motored slowly out of the channel until clear of the channel markers. Then, he raised the mainsail. No drama so far.

He steered the boat to the left to pick up the wind coming out of the south. He raised the mainsail, and once he was certain that he could pick up the wind and depend on it for his source of power, he turned off the motor. The immediate silence that followed reminded him of why he loved sailing so much. The boat quietly cut through the water, and all he could hear was the sound of the small waves created by the hull as it sliced through the ocean's surface.

The ride out to his favorite dive site would take about twenty minutes. Once he was on the right course, or "tack," he opened the jib to gain extra speed. Both sails filled marvelously, and the boat charged forward even faster. The boat leaned to the left as it took in more wind, and as he adjusted the tiller, he was able to tilt the boat so far that water nearly rolled right into the boat.

He consulted his phone for the coordinates of Temples and entered them into the boat's GPS: N 32°42′206″ and W 117°16′264″. Temples was the name he gave to his favorite dive site, about a half mile off the coast of Point Loma and in the middle of a kelp forest. While the unfortunate effects of climate change meant you could never count on kelp anymore, Temples remained where it was the last time he visited it, providing not only a surreal experience, but multiple options for slowly working your way back to the surface.

He pulled in the jib as he approached the designated spot and lowered the mainsail after that. He allowed the boat to coast forward as he left the stern, made his way to the bow, and opened the locker where the anchor was stored. When his GPS indicated he was in the right spot, he threw the anchor overboard. He was sitting on top of about fifty-five feet of water between the surface and the sea floor. It would be a shallow dive in comparison to others in the area.

Kinkade paid out a fair amount of line to achieve the desired scope so that the anchor would set properly on the ocean's floor as the boat drifted back. After he was satisfied, he returned to the stern, a bit winded from having to lift the anchor and its chain from inside the locker. He sat down, closed his eyes, and welcomed the silence that the isolation offered him. The boat rocked gently, and all that he could hear was the sound of soft waves slapping the side of the hull. With the sails down, the sun warmed his face.

After a few moments, Kinkade reached down to unzip the bag at his feet, and he proceeded to gear up for a dive. Diving alone was not ideal, but he had visited this reef hundreds of times before moving out of San Diego. He was a confident and competent diver, and he really had no choice because it would be difficult to find a dive buddy without creating a potential media spectacle. No, he thought, it was far simpler to go it alone. Kinkade put out the red and white dive flag signaling that a diver was below. He donned his wetsuit and buoyancy compensator, the vest that allowed him to add air from his tank so he could float on the surface.

He then sat on the boat's edge to put on his fins, put his regulator in his mouth, adjusted his mask, then looked behind himself one last time before falling backward into the water. His entry made a splash, and the boat bobbed in the opposite direction. It was a wonderful feeling to be in the ocean again, about to start his favorite dive.

Kinkade followed the anchor line from the boat, slowly edging his way down to the bottom, equalizing his ears during his descent. He wanted to ensure the anchor was secured and would not drag on the bottom. He also wanted to attach a spool of line to it, which he would use to find his way back to the boat. This would not be so important if he were in a group or if there were someone on the boat looking out for the divers below. But since he was on his own, it was prudent. After finding the anchor and ensuring it was set, he attached his line to it, and proceeded into the Temples area.

Kinkade used that name for the area because the long, slender, and naturally sculptured stone pillars reminded him of the Indiana Jones movie *Temple of Doom*. The unique structure was unlike anything he had seen along the coast of Point Loma, the stretch of coastline that became the southernmost point of California. In addition to the surreal surroundings that resembled an abandoned temple, aggregations of kelp bass, California sheepshead, and garibaldi darted across the site. Occasionally, a giant sea bass, or GSB, would slowly cruise by. Lobster was abundant, too, although Kinkade was tired of catching lobster that were, according to regulations, too short to be taken.

He charted a course underwater that essentially triangulated from his original position. This was important to avoid tangling his line that remained attached to the anchor. For nearly forty minutes he weaved his way around the kelp, taking pictures with his GoPro: a reclusive octopus hiding underneath a boulder, a large school of surf perch resting in place, and a curious sheepshead that had followed him for most of the dive. He had taken about twenty-five pictures by the time he realized he was shivering from the cold. He began reeling in his line and heading to the anchor.

On arriving at the anchor, he carefully removed the hook that connected his line to it and stored the hook in a pocket on his BC. Once that was done, he found the chain to which the anchor was attached and followed it, expecting to find the rope that would lead to the boat. That rope typically would be vertical to the sea floor. Not this time. When Kinkade finally found the rope attached to the anchor's chain, it had been cut and was lying on the seabed. He was without a line to return to his boat.

Kinkade did not panic and continued to regulate his breathing. He presumed there was a reasonable explanation for why his anchor line was no longer attached to his boat, and he was a competent enough diver that a "blue water ascent" without the benefit of a line was not difficult. He proceeded to the surface, careful to ascend no faster than one foot per second to avoid any risk of injury from an air embolism.

Kinkade was accustomed to the fact that on these ascents it would not be uncommon for the dive boat to be several yards away from where he came up. In fact, nearly every time he surfaced, he would not see the boat at all, at least not until he turned his body around and found it behind him. So, when he surfaced this time, he did not panic when he did not initially see the Catalina. But he didn't see it when he turned around either.

He tried to remain calm, and regulated his breathing as he floated on the surface. If necessary, he could make his way to the shore about a half mile away. As he considered his options, he inflated a safety marker so other boaters in the area might find him. Within seconds, he heard a boat motor, the sound increasing as it approached him from the west.

The boat was a sixteen-foot Boston whaler operated by a woman who was also out on the water on her own. She slowed the boat as she approached Kinkade. The safety marker Kinkade had inflated made clear that he required assistance, so the woman came directly up to him, shut off the motor, and threw the step ladder off the side, allowing him to climb aboard.

"Are you okay?" she asked as Kinkade reached for the ladder.

"Yeah, thanks," he said, nearly out of breath as he climbed aboard.

"Here, let me help you," she replied, holding out her hand to collect Kinkade's fins so he could climb aboard more easily.

"Thanks," he said, again struggling to climb aboard with the weight of his tank behind him, trying to appear composed. "My boat seems to have taken off without me."

"Yeah, well, that's clear," the woman replied. "I don't see any boats around here."

Kinkade eventually got onto the small boat and collapsed to the deck in the corner, sitting cross-legged. He released the scuba tank from his shoulders so he could at least sit up straight. He stared at the woman, finally realizing she was alone.

"Hey, what's a pretty girl like you . . ."

The disgust on the woman's face made clear that Kinkade's small talk was not appreciated.

"Look," he said, trying to recalibrate the conversation, "I really appreciate you picking me up. My name is John Kinkade. And you are . . .?"

The woman did not answer, she just gave Kinkade a blank stare. Then, as she snapped out of whatever thoughts were occupying her mind, she picked up a speargun that was lying on the deck.

"Is this yours? I found it floating on the water not far from here."

Kinkade looked at the gun, pointing straight at him.

"No, it's not, but please don't point . . ."

The woman pulled the trigger. The spear punched through Kinkade's wetsuit and pierced his heart. The force of the shot caused his body to fall backward against the stern. The spear remained sticking straight out of his body, like a flagpole. He lay paralyzed, his eyes fully open and looking skyward as life drained from his body.

The woman casually left her seat behind the wheel of the boat and cut the line that attached the spear to the gun. She hoisted and pushed Kinkade's body backward so that it was lying on the edge of the stern. His eyes were still open and displaying the shock of being murdered. Because the scuba tank was behind the body, the woman easily guided Kinkade's limp arms through the vest again and locked the rig as it was before he came aboard. As she ran her right arm down his left, she popped the clasp of his Rolex Submariner and allowed it to drop to the deck.

She checked the lead weights in the vest to ensure they were sufficient for the corpse to sink in the water. Then she took the hose from the BC and blew a few breaths of air into it. This would ensure that Kinkade would glide along the bottom of the ocean floor without being over-weighted. The southwestern current would take him into Mexican waters by the end of the following day. Even if there was anything left of him after the sharks and other creatures feasted on his dead body, Mexican authorities would never be able to identify him and probably would not bother to try.

The woman hoisted the body again by pushing her shoulder under it, the spear still sticking out from Kinkade's chest, and rolled him over the side. A loud thump and splash followed as the boat rocked in both directions. He sank immediately.

The Catalina sailboat would be discovered in the very early morning hours of the next day, banging up against the rocks off Zuniga Point near the entry to San Diego Bay, not far from the end of the jetty, its keel lodged into the rocky substrate, ensuring it was not going anywhere. Had the boat not slammed into the jetty, it also would have ended up in Mexican waters. The Harbor Police came alongside the boat and rafted against it so they could board. There was no sign of a struggle on the boat, no sign of foul play, and no sign of Kinkade anywhere. All they found was his Rolex Submariner.

3

"Wait, wait, shhhhh!" shouted Emma. "Here it is..."

Emma Lee and her lab mate Justin Egrin leaned into the laptop that was playing the original *Jurassic Park* in the molecular research laboratory at the Salk Institute in San Diego.

Richard Attenborough played the role of the park's famed founder, John Hammond, who says passionately,

"I don't think you're giving us our due credit. Our scientists have done things which nobody's ever done before . . ."

To which Ian Malcolm, played by Jeff Goldblum, quickly replies:

*"Yeah, yeah, but your scientists were so preoccupied with whether or not they could . . . that they didn't stop to think if they **should**."*

"Yes! Yes! I love that man!" Emma screamed, leaning back on her stool, looking to the ceiling, and clapping her hands. "Did you see him in *The Fly*?"

Justin simply smiled. Emma's lively personality was one of the things he enjoyed most about working in the lab.

Emma Lee was always fascinated by genetic engineering, and she was living her dream by working now at the Salk Institute. On this evening, she was preparing therapeutics for an experiment aimed at eradicating targeted cancer cells in laboratory mice. She was in the fifth year of a PhD program at the University of California at San Diego, a close partner to the Salk Institute. Unlike Emma, Justin was not pursuing a PhD. His lab tech job was as far as he would likely go in his career.

Emma came to the United States from Harbin, China, the capital of Heilongjiang, China's northernmost province. Harbin was built on the backs of Russian immigrants and engineers who constructed the eastern leg of the Trans-Siberian Railroad. Emma's father was a Russian rail worker; her mother worked in the textile mills. As her parents witnessed the limits of careers available to young women in China, they eventually decided to send her to Los Angeles that she could establish residency and attend university. After graduating from UCLA, she enrolled at UC San Diego as a doctoral candidate. Nobody would notice that she was older than the typical student.

As is often the case with lab work, there were many moments of hurry up and wait in the routines that Emma and Justin were performing. Whether it was incubating a sample, running a centrifuge, or waiting for an analyzer to complete its work, there was ample opportunity to simply chill, and watching classic science fiction movies was Emma's favorite accompaniment to that requirement.

This was one of the growing number of labs where CRISPR experiments were conducted. CRISPR (clustered regularly interspaced short palindromic repeats) represents the fastest growing segment of the gene-editing industry, expected to exceed $8 billion in 2026.

The existence of CRISPR sequences in bacteria was discovered in 1987, but their potential to become the predominant engine of gene editing was credited in 2012 to Jennifer Doudna from the University of California at Berkeley and Emmanuelle Charpentier from the Max Planck Institute in Berlin. These distant lab partners would win the Nobel Prize in Chemistry eight years later for creating what is often referred to as "genetic scissors," a process whereby an enzyme known a Cas9 literally cuts a DNA strand, replacing it with a genetic modifier. It was as if geneticists discovered the equivalent of a word processor's cut, copy, and paste function. The approach quickly led to several dozen clinical trials to treat sickle cell anemia, leukemia, blindness, and cancer in which Cas9 was used to cut out genetic sequences and mutations that give rise to the disease. If you were interested in human genetic engineering, there was no place more exciting than those labs experimenting with CRISPR-Cas9 tools.

"I've got to use the john," said Justin, who tapped the space bar on the laptop and put his feet on the floor, allowing the stool to slide back from behind him. "I'll be right back."

"Sure," Emma replied, putting her hands on her hips while sitting up straight on the stool, shoulders back, rolling her neck, and stretching her spine. "I'll check the samples."

Justin walked down the length of the lab and its long white countertop crowded by microscopes, pipetting equipment, flasks, and petri dishes. As he went out the door and into the hallway, Emma leaned forward to watch him disappear. She knew Justin would not be hurrying back because on his return he had to cut off the heads of laboratory mice that had received the experimental drug several weeks ago and squeeze the blood from their headless bodies for analysis. Fortunately for Emma, her duties did not include using the tiny hand-operated guillotine designed specifically for this gruesome task.

Emma hopped off her stool and moved quickly to Justin's desk at the back of the lab. In his top drawer were the keys to all other labs in the building for which he had clearance as a full-time lab technician. Emma quickly found the key to the liquid nitrogen storage and removed it from the key ring. She laid it on the desk surface, under the fluorescent desk lamp. Next, she took a quarter from the bottom of her left lab coat pocket and set it next to the key to properly scale the photo she was about to take. She withdrew the phone from her other lab coat pocket and took the picture. She put the key back on the keychain, placed it back in the drawer, and returned to the stool. She was one step closer to stealing the samples.

BY THE TIME THE REFUGEES reached the Harbin train station, Kim Ji-Sung no longer needed them as cover, as they had successfully evaded capture by the Chinese army when they were most vulnerable. They now sported Guess and Tommy Hilfiger-themed shirts but continued to look out of place with their worried and confused expressions. Ji-Sung could not afford to be seen with them any longer.

Had he been caught, Ji-Sung would have been spared any punishment and simply returned to the RGB. Now, he would allow himself to get separated from the group at the station by hiding in one of the toilets until he was certain his earlier companions were on the train bound for Mongolia. The station was busy enough that getting separated from the group was easy. The families were more concerned with faces they did not recognize than those they did.

For his part, Chun Ki-Won would be relieved that Ji-Sung had mysteriously disappeared. From the beginning, he was suspicious of him. Although he produced the right papers and claimed he was a coal miner with no immediate family to join him, his clean, smooth hands and unblemished complexion were simply too pristine to fit the role. He was handsome, well-fed, and groomed his hair. He did not fit the profile of a coal miner or any man desperate to risk his life by choosing to defect.

Ji-Sung looked past the layer of filth accumulated on the mirror in the men's toilet. Staring back at him was a tired but resilient man in his 'thirties with a thick furrowed brow over a pair of dark and serious eyes that, taken together, signaled "you had better take me seriously." He wore a brown leather jacket that was a gift from his wife when he joined the agency. He dug into one of its pockets to reveal a wad of Chinese yuan wrapped in a tight roll. He threw open the door of the toilet and stepped into the street. The sun was rising, and several taxis appeared for those passengers who could afford a ride.

Ji-Sung looked back at the station. It was an unremarkable building, utilitarian in design and less impressive than the Pyongyang station near his home, which was adorned with elegant chandeliers, murals illustrating the industrious working class, and giant portraits of the Supreme Leader. For all the talk of China's dominance in Asia, it did not seem to invest heavily in making its transportation hubs very comfortable, he thought to himself.

He hailed a cab and handed the driver an address, choosing not to speak and risk the fact that his accent might betray his identity. The cab drove off toward the Harbin industrial complex, the epicenter of genomics research in China.

QUANTICO, VIRGINIA, about thirty-five miles southwest of the nation's capital, is home to the largest U.S. Marine Corps base, the Naval Criminal Investigative Service, and the FBI Academy where new agent trainees, or NATs, undergo twenty weeks of rigorous training. The facilities and vibe are not unlike a college campus, housing approximately 28,000 military and civilian personnel on a secluded, wooded area of nearly one hundred square miles.

Approximately 30 percent of those who enter the Academy either do not finish it or fail to pass various tests or examinations, which include legal theory, informant development, interrogation, surveillance, investigative techniques, defensive tactics, and fitness and firearms training. For many NATs, the highlight of their experience at the Academy is Hogan's Alley, a town square with its own fake bank, shops, hotels, and restaurants and where agents practice real-life conflict scenarios.

One week into his stint at the Academy, Richard began to have second thoughts. He felt very confined, living in conditions reminiscent of the tiny dorm rooms he occupied as a student at the University of Michigan. He was older than most NATs and accustomed to a more vibrant lifestyle than would be tolerated on the base. On top of this, the number of hours spent in web-based training on subjects ranging from policies and procedures to sexual harassment made him restless. He missed Sarah and desperately wanted to get high.

There were two bright spots, however. First was his roommate, Jeff McAuley, who came to LA years before from the east coast. Another Irish descendant, Jeff had the disposition of a native New Yorker combined with the cool demeanor of a West Coast beach bum. He also had a seemingly unlimited supply of surfing trivia which he loved to weave into conversations. He was destined to return to the LA branch after graduation, so Richard would be heading out there with at least one friend on whom he could count.

The other bright spot was firearms training, which was to begin at the outset of the second week. If an agent could not carry a badge and a gun, Richard thought, what was the point of the whole thing?

"You had an affair with another agent?" Jeff asked once the two started sharing backgrounds. "Good on ya, man! Ha! How did you keep that on the down-low?"

"We were just getting into each other when I got busted," he replied, still not entirely clear if the relationship had legs.

"You got rolled?!" Jeff was beginning to think that perhaps Richard was on a completely different level. He understood Richard was already an FBI employee before training, so the idea of him getting in trouble with the law was unexpected.

"It's a long story," Richard added. "But basically, I took her badge because I was trying to help capture a terrorist that was at Dulles, about to catch a flight. He was involved in that plot to bomb Tel Aviv, you know, the one that was detonated in the desert instead. After it was all over, I got tagged for impersonating an officer."

Richard decided not to explain that Isaac Shulman, the man behind the plot, was actually a former agent of the Mossad determined to con the world into thinking that Iran and Hamas were behind the whole shitshow. Part of the problem was that Richard wanted to put the trauma of that experience behind him, especially the part about the woman who had been his girlfriend before the Shulman incident. She had committed suicide while carrying their baby. The other problem was that the FBI tagged the case as top secret to prevent the whole story from reaching the media, which could have precipitated retaliation from right wing or antisemitic groups. Now that he was on the path to becoming an agent, it was good practice for Richard to learn how many details it was safe to share and when to keep his mouth shut. Jeff was giving him a lot of practice.

Jeff had heard through the grapevine that Richard was involved in the Utapeli operation and didn't want to badger him about it. But now that Richard had raised the topic, it was fair game.

"Dude, haven't you heard that there is no such thing as free will?" Jeff said. "You had no choice but to steal the badge!"

"Come again?" Now it was Richard who was confused.

"We don't have the freedom we think we have," Jeff continued. "We are a product of our environment, our genetic makeup, and signals we receive that fire neurons that drive our behavior. We may *think* we are making choices, but in reality, those choices were *made for us*. You couldn't help yourself, man!"

"Yeah, well my neurons exercised their free will, but I'm the one that got caught," Richard replied.

4

Harmony's iPhone started playing Alicia Keys' "Empire State of Mind," the ring tone she set for her alarm. Her arm emerged from under the white sheets while she lay face down, her head buried in her pillow. She grabbed the phone lying next to her head and silenced the alarm. It was 8:30.

This was early for Harmony, but she had plans to meet her friends for breakfast at a coffee and acai bowl joint a few blocks away. She rolled off her bed, her knee landing on the floor because the mattress lay directly upon it—she had never invested in a frame or box spring. The sunlight was shining brightly through her sheer curtains, causing the natural wood floor to reflect its rich, caramel stain.

The room was a messy testament to the life of a Generation Z twenty-something, but at the same time it was so bereft of any furniture—just a mattress, dresser, and chair—that it looked like the perfect place to simply hibernate. In a corner of the room just outside her closet was a stack of boxes containing merchandise she was expected to promote online: mascara, a cashmere sweater, several varieties of jeans and shoes, and a new type of curling iron that would supposedly repair split ends. Several boxes were open, the products hanging halfway out of them.

She grabbed her phone and dragged herself to a tiny bathroom just outside her bedroom in the apartment she shared with two other roommates. She stood in front of the mirror and leaned in, critically examining her complexion. She had bright blue eyes under narrow, crescent-shaped eyebrows, pouty lips, satin smooth skin, and stringy brown-blond hair parted down the middle. She could have been a model had she not been so entrepreneurial and determined to control her own professional trajectory. She was also too politically enlightened to submit to the stigma associated with modeling. In other words, she wanted to be respected for her opinions, not her looks.

Harmony Hutchins was one of the first of the Generation Z cohort and a very early influencer on Instagram. She was so successful in monetizing her presence on Instagram that with just a small allowance from her parents she was able to sustain herself in the apartment she rented in the coastal community of Manhattan Beach. After removing her retainer, she plopped down on the toilet, dragged her panties to the floor, and started to pee. She opened her phone to check her Instagram feed to see if she had any recent activity on her latest post.

Harmony typically promoted women's makeup and apparel, but she also used her significant following on Instagram to post about her political views and conspiracy theories. One of her favorite targets for criticism was the for-profit "Center for New Beginnings" in Whittier, one of the less affluent cities in LA County, where she joined a growing number of people who suspected the institution of abusing patients. Her first exposure to this story was watching an investigative reporter from KCBS-TV attempt to interview the administrator of the institution and get pushed back at the door by security. The reporter was looking into the welfare of homeless men taken off the streets and sent to the facility for a mental health evaluation, but who then subsequently disappeared. There must be an easier way to breach this place, she thought to herself at the time.

Looking at her feed, she was disappointed that the new knee-high boots she modeled in a post two days earlier had barely gained one hundred likes across 155,000 followers. This would disappoint the supplier, and she would have to consider a second post. She wondered: *Would I gain more followers by promoting more stories or more products*? She scrolled back to see if her last post about The Center for New Beginnings was getting traction. It read: "What is going on inside CNB?" under a picture of the hospital, and suggested that if they had nothing to hide, there was no reason to deny access to the reporter.

The Center for New Beginnings had a complicated history. It started out as Los Angeles County Rehabilitation Hospital operating under the charter of the LA County Department of Health, but budget cuts, losses from care of the indigent, and epic mismanagement drew criticism and pressure from the public for privatization of the facility. During the height of the recession in 2001, the hospital's CEO was found in his office, hunched over his desk, gun in hand, and with a bullet hole running from one side of his skull to the other. The death was ruled a suicide even though the ballistics report showed the bullet entered his skull from the right side, but the deceased was left-handed.

In the summer of 2003, the county finally bowed to pressure to issue a request for proposal from regional health systems and private investment groups to take over the hospital. A private equity group acquired the hospital the following year, and for a time at least, the hospital remained out of the headlines.

Harmony's post about the hospital had nearly as many likes as her post about the knee-high boots and far more activity in the comments. She thought to call her brother, an analyst with Fox News, to see if he could help her understand how to assess the question of "product vs. story" more effectively. Then she remembered—the products pay the bills.

Harmony pulled up her panties, flushed, and turned toward the mirror. She had so much natural beauty and such disdain for makeup that, after brushing her teeth, she simply applied some eyeliner that she received from a supplier. She went back to her bed and fell down on her behind, reached for the jeans she wore last night, and pulled them onto her legs. She stood and jumped twice while yanking the waist of the jeans up, then slid over to her closet and grabbed an oversized sweatshirt. The shirt's neckline was so large that one side would float down her right arm, revealing the tattoo that she commissioned on the back of her shoulder a few weeks before. It was important to Harmony to put this on display.

The tattoo represented the culmination of a lot of introspection following a bad breakup during which Harmony felt disrespected and mentally abused. Although the tattoo artist had a butterfly in mind, Harmony demanded a three-headed dragon. The majestic image was in flight, rising from her right shoulder blade, its necks reaching toward hers. No more than a few inches in length, it was a dramatic statement that Harmony felt put her on the same footing as Daenerys Targaryen, the beautiful but badass queen from *Game of Thrones*. The tattoo would remind her that she was not taking any more shit from the narcissist men who would typically pursue her.

Harmony pulled on her deck shoes, pushed her phone into her back pocket, and headed out the door.

JACK REEVES STARED at the monitor on his desk at KCBS-TV on Radford Avenue in Studio City. It was a little after 9 in the morning. His desk was so littered with documents from leads and stories he was following he would be hard-pressed to find his phone beneath all the clutter. While the senior staff enjoyed window views of Wilacre Park or the Hollywood sign, Reeves's view was of the 101 freeway. Three years into his stint as an investigative reporter, Reeves was still chasing the story that would get him the exposure and airtime to get noticed by network executives and, someday, an anchor desk.

He was continuing to look for information that would get him access to the management at The Center for New

Beginnings. He refreshed the page on Google that he had opened the day before, and "What is going on inside CNB" was presented about halfway down the page. He leaned in to look more closely at the link. Instagram? Really? Without better options, he clicked through to see the post by Harmony Hutchins a few days before.

She's cute, he thought as he clicked through to see Harmony's profile pic. "And damn, she likes a lot of products."

He sent her a message introducing himself, then got up to refresh his coffee.

"I KNOW, RIGHT!?" JASMIN blurted out as her friend Cindee shared how difficult it was to dump her most recent boyfriend. They had been dating for three months, and he was cheating on her already.

"They want it both ways," Harmony added.

Cindee had a habit of finding men who were constantly working on finding their next ex-girlfriend.

The three young women were seated at a small table outside the coffeeshop, waiting on their acai bowls. The sun was shining, and the sky was clear, offering another typical Southern California morning. Harmony's dragon was peeking out from under her top as she leaned toward the table, just as she intended.

"What did you finally tell him?" Jasmin asked.

As Cindee continued to describe her most recent breakup, Harmony quickly checked her phone to see if any new activity required her attention. While this was not considered the best etiquette among friends, both Cindee and Jasmin realized that the phone was Harmony's connection to her career, and that at this time of day she was never off the clock.

"Hey, check this out," she interrupted, presuming that her news would be more interesting than the end of one more casual fling. "Remember that reporter from CBS that was denied access to that hospital in Whittier? He just pinged me."

"Oh wow, that's . . . Reeves, right? Jack Reeves?" Jasmin asked.

"Oh, he's cute!" Cindee added. "Hey, you ought to be more than friends!"

"Well, one step at a time," Harmony replied as she clicked the prompt that would connect the two. "He looks like he is old enough to be my dad."

The fact was that Harmony did not see the age difference as a problem. After witnessing the romantic entanglements of her friends, she vowed that at least for the next few years, she would choose the path of sexually-safe promiscuity: she would sleep with whoever she found attractive, so long as they wore a condom, and as long as she dictated the terms.

HARMONY WAITED OUTSIDE the bar's entrance for Jack Reeves to show up. She had already calculated how to arrive about fifteen minutes late. She was not expecting the possibility that *he* would stand *her* up. Now, she wasn't so sure. She resolved to give him five more minutes when an Uber swung up to the curb and he stepped out. She recognized him instantly.

Jack Reeves was as handsome as a major news network would require: tall, slim, broad shoulders, and pitch-black hair that just might have had the gravitational pull of a black hole. He had the serious face of a Shakespearean actor but the casual demeanor of a rock star. He wore an azure blue suit with a white shirt, no tie. When he spotted Harmony outside, he flashed a broad smile that made her forget he was late.

"Hey Harmony, Jack Reeves. Sorry I'm late. I had to meet a deadline to submit a story that they probably won't even run!"

Harmony smiled tentatively. "It's okay. I just got here myself."

She was instantly attracted to Reeves, who, unlike most men, did not look her up and down to assess her value as a potential sexual conquest. The fact that Reeves was nearly twenty years older than her was irrelevant; Harmony preferred older men who were simply more refined than young and immature alternatives. She would spend the next thirty minutes looking for clues to determine whether Reeves was, in fact, sponge worthy.

Jack glided his arm out to the far right to guide Harmony inside. A host met them at the entrance.

"Can we get that table over there, in the corner?" Reeves asked.

"Sure," replied the host. "Please follow ... wait, aren't you ...?"

"Yeah, thanks," Reeves cut off the host. "We'll just follow you."

Again, Reeves put his arm out to the side as if to signal to Harmony that she should go ahead. Within moments, they were seated opposite one another. They ordered a couple of martinis from a male waiter who either did not recognize Reeves or could not care less. The restaurant was busy, and most LA locals wouldn't be impressed that a reporter was in their presence.

"So," he continued, "thanks for agreeing to get together. Hey, I'm a big admirer of your work."

Harmony laughed. "My work? You mean hawking shitty products that I don't use?"

"No, no, I mean the stories you post online, they're really good. You are a good writer," he replied. "How did you get interested in the hospital?"

"To be honest," Harmony said, "it was your coverage of it. I mean, it doesn't matter that they are homeless people, it doesn't make sense for a single person to simply disappear. How do these people end up at this hospital in the first place?"

"It's something the cops call 'code 5150,' that part of the California Welfare and Institutions Code that permits the police to commit someone to psychiatric evaluation, against their will if necessary, for up to seventy-two hours. Remember Amanda Bynes? She got tagged for walking down the street naked, poor thing, and was taken in under 5150."

"Oh, yeah, I read about that," Harmony replied. "I wonder whatever happened to her."

"Yeah, I'd have to ask our celebrity desk. Anyway, the homeless are sitting ducks to get picked up for this," Reeves continued, "and they are particularly vulnerable anytime they are in the path of law enforcement. But if there is nobody to collect them after the seventy-two hours of evaluation and observation . . ."

Harmony was not listening to Jack Reeves at this point. All she was thinking, as she stared at his lips moving, was *I could totally fuck him.*

Then she snapped out of it. Her attraction to older men was undeniable.

"Who is in charge of this place?" she finally asked.

"According to the facility's business license, the administrator's name is Dennis Spence," he replied. "Here's another weird thing. In addition to my being unable to meet with him, there are no pictures of him online, nothing in the news, nothing on social media. He's like a ghost."

"Wow, is there anything I can do to help?"

"Just keep doing what you're doing," Reeves said. "Keep asking the tough questions. Help me keep pressure on Spence to be more transparent."

"Oh, I can do that," Harmony replied as she took a small sip of her drink.

"Great," Jack said as he raised his martini glass to his lips, turned it nearly upside down, and quickly emptied it. "Look, I'm really sorry, but I've gotta go. I have to get back to the studio for the eleven o'clock running. They have me doing a story on the poaching of lobsters off the coast of Catalina Island. Apparently, you are not allowed to take lobsters that are less than three and one-quarter inches from the eye socket to the start of the tail. And get this—you have to measure them underwater before taking them out of the water, or you risk a $250 citation from the Department of Fish and Game. Exciting stuff, you know."

As he got up, he flashed that million-dollar smile down at Harmony, who was still sitting, half-shocked that her date was over already. She was not used to men behaving this way toward her.

"Hey, speaking of lobsters, would it be okay if I took you to dinner one of these days, you know, so we can compare notes on how things are progressing?"

Harmony was not sure if this was a proposed collaboration or a request for a date concealed as a business meeting. But one thing she knew for sure: It didn't matter.

"Okay," she said, deciding the premise of the offer would be revealed later.

"Great," he said, "I'll be in touch."

"Wait, don't you need my number?" Harmony asked.

"What kind of investigative reporter would I be if I had to ask YOU for your number?"

With that, he smiled again and left the bar.

Harmony had barely touched her drink.

EMMA LEE SAT IN THE corner of her apartment at her small desk, a lamp concentrating light on the firm but thin sheet of plexiglass that lay there. Leaning over the desk, she opened the iPhone picture she took of the lab key, then dropped a quarter on her phone; it made several turns before resting near the middle of the glass. With her index finger and thumb, she slowly expanded the picture until the quarter in the picture matched the size of the quarter on the phone. Then, she took a screenshot and sent the image to a printer sitting on the edge of the desk.

When the image of the key and coin popped out of the printer, she placed it under the plexiglass. She recalled this part of the training she had received to be the most difficult. Slowly, she traced the image of the key on the glass using a carbide tungsten cutting tool.

Using firm pressure, she paid particular attention to the dips along the length of the key's image. The tool rolled along the image, cutting into the glass. As she returned around the back of the key to the smooth portion along the top of it, she realized she had been holding her breath the whole time. Finally, she reached the point at the tip of the key where she had started the cutting process.

Lifting the tool and setting it down, Emma raised the glass toward her and, with the eraser-end of a pencil, she gently tapped the center of the image until the new plexiglass key popped out and landed on the top of her desk. She took the copy and wiped it down with fine grit emery cloth to remove any burrs, sprayed it generously with WD-40, placed it in a Ziplock bag, and sprayed more WD-40 into the bag. She may only get one shot at this, she thought, and wanted to be certain the key remained lubricated and would pass smoothly into the lock. Emma turned off the lamp, grabbed the hoodie that was draped over the chair, and stuffed the baggie into its pocket. She looked at her phone. It was 11:40 p.m. The lab would be essentially deserted.

BECAUSE OF THE SALK Institute's affiliation with the University of California in San Diego, it wasn't uncommon for students to come and go at all hours of the night. Some students had to tend to experiments that required attention at a particular hour. Others worked during the day and could only conduct their research at night. Then there was Emma Lee, who was not supposed to be there at all.

"Hey, Emma," said the security guard as she entered the building. "Wassup girl?"

"I forgot my notebook for class tomorrow," she replied. "I'll only be a minute."

"Take your time," the guard replied, smiling. "You're good. Nobody here but the rat ghosts from experiments past."

Emma signed a log maintained of all visitors throughout the day as the guard turned his attention back to the movie he was watching on his phone. To create plausible deniability, she wrote "1:55p" on a new page instead of "11:55p," and the guard was too busy watching his phone to take notice. Certainly, there would be other entries that could make this appear out of order. But Emma understood "the liar's dividend," that a lie told often enough can push the truth out of the conversation.

She went to the back of the lab facility where the liquid nitrogen freezers were located, their samples frozen to −196 degrees Fahrenheit. Several warning signs made clear that entry was forbidden for unauthorized personnel. The hallways were abandoned in either direction. Emma quickly inserted the counterfeit key, turning it gently to prevent the plastic from breaking into the lock. There was some excess oil in the bottom of the plastic bag if she felt resistance and wanted to lubricate the key again. It wasn't necessary. As she turned the key, she simultaneously turned the door handle. She could feel the mechanism moving. A quiet click signaled the door was open.

Once inside, Emma moved quickly among the ten shiny stainless-steel freezers. They were shaped like massive Weber-style barbecue grills, five on each side of the room. Each had a separate logbook documenting the contents inside and an integrated digital display showing time, temperature, and humidity. Emma had been in the room with Justin before; she knew exactly the freezer she needed to open. It was the middle freezer on the right side of the room.

She put on gloves, then carefully lifted the large, round lid attached to the base via a vertical hydraulic post. As the lid rose straight up, a cold fog emerged, hissing from inside before quickly dissipating. A series of small tubes, no bigger than a person's pinkie, became visible in a rack attached to the lid and organized in a perfect circle around the diameter of the opening. Once fully extended, the lid had risen about two feet and revealed five rows of tubes on trays attached to a rod running down the center.

Each tube on the outer ring was accompanied by five more behind it, leading to the center rod. Using tongs, Emma carefully removed six tubes at random locations and put them into the left pocket of her lab coat. From her right pocket, she removed six tubes containing an inert liquid that she put in place of the tubes she removed. She slowly lowered the lid, then returned to the entrance of the secure room. Slowly opening the door, she checked in both directions, then walked to the lunchroom where a refrigerator contained employee meals. Inside was her YETI-brand insulated lunch box she had set there earlier that day. She placed the tubes in a tube stand within the box, which contained a layer of dry ice, and left the facility.

The exchange was complete.

5

"As agents, you need to see what others cannot see and discover what lies beneath the surface of situations you investigate," said the instructor, Heather Anderson, a member of the Academy faculty with a PhD in psychology. "But if you cannot be honest with yourself first, you cannot expect to get the truth out of anybody else." Henderson scanned the crowd of NATs in her auditorium and saw a group of weary but obedient young soldiers, thirsty for as much knowledge as the Academy could dish out but not entirely sure where they were heading next.

Anderson continued, "Who can tell me, when do you know a person is lying? Harris?"

"If they are shifting in their chair?" Mickey Harris ventured.

"Good," Anderson replied. "What else? What if they are not sitting down? Kramer?"

Matt Kramer went next. "If they shift their eyes or attention, or if their pupils dilate."

"Okay, let's talk a bit about interviewing techniques. Who can tell me about mirroring? O'Brien?" Anderson knew this was a part of their online training, so it was fair game. Richard felt confident offering the answer because he saw Sarah Goodman use the approach brilliantly while interviewing Basheer Aktar, one of the accomplices in the cybercrime and terrorist activities that became the FBI case known as Operation Utapeli.

"In mirroring, you repeat back aloud the last statement of the suspect. You rephrase it as a question to get them to expand on it, you know, to offer more information than perhaps they intended."

"Very good," Anderson replied. "Okay, then, we are going to be pairing you up this afternoon with other NATs, not your roommates, but other trainees that will be interviewing you to see how much information they can extract, something material that is not already in your personnel file with the Bureau. If the interrogator senses you are not being truthful, this will be recorded as well. Feel free to mix it up as you engage in this exercise. In other words, mix truth with lies." Anderson paused to let the implications of the exercise sink in. It was clear that several students were feeling quite vulnerable.

"You need not feel threatened by the exercise," she added, "and I am here to assure you that nothing revealed in these conversations will go into your file. Let's see how much of your past that perhaps you'd rather not talk about will come out. Class dismissed."

Anyone observing this lecture would assume that the students were silently replaying their past to identify any risks that might be revealed in the upcoming exercise. The look of pain on their faces spoke volumes. Richard was not sure he would survive this one.

DENISE STEELE NEVER had a boyfriend, never drove a car, and never socialized with others. It was very likely that the trauma inflicted by her stepfather, followed by treatment in a mental institution and later abuse from her male caregiver, all contributed to Denise's world outlook, which was consumed by despair, fear of betrayal, and general xenophobia.

It wasn't a surprise that Denise drugged her stepfather before she dragged his body and rolled it in the pool, nor that she later drugged her caregiver and left him to suffocate in the woods. What was surprising was how dispassionate she could be about how she disposed of these men, as if they were nothing more than a perfunctory homework assignment.

One of Denise's most valuable tools was the wolfsbane she grew in her garden, a plant she toiled to produce in its most potent form. She learned about the dangers of this living organism from watching *You* on Netflix, a thriller in which lovers use the plant's extract to paralyze anyone they consider a threat. Also known as aconite, this toxic plant will, in small amounts, temporarily immobilize the cardiac or respiratory muscles. Any more than a few drops and you've taken flower power to the deadliest interpretation possible. Denise's experience with wolfsbane drove her interest in biologic sciences, especially microbiology, physiology, botany, and genetics.

After the mysterious disappearance of her caregiver, she retreated to the suburbs of Los Angeles and obtained degrees in pharmacology and medicine from UCLA. However, whereas most medical school graduates go on to a residency program or primary care practice, Denise did not. Instead, she initiated masculinizing transgender therapy to exchange her female identity for one more empowering, at least that's how she justified her decision to get the treatment. The process would take at least two years to complete, another reason why she was hardly ever seen in public back then. Psychologists would later try to explain her behavior as relating to the trauma she experienced as a child at the hands of powerful men. This would reveal how little we understand about gender dysphoria and identity conflicts that occur in some people.

Exactly what Denise did with her free time was a matter of speculation for her neighbors. A clue, however, was provided when she published in the journal *Genetics* an article titled "Germline Engineering Will Displace Evolution of the Human Race." The arguments in the piece were articulate, compelling, and terrifying.

JUSTIN UNLOCKED THE molecular research lab in the Salk Institute at 9 o'clock. He would be alone most of the day, as many PhD candidates were notorious for sleeping in, arriving late, and working all night. Others may have been serving as teaching assistants at the UC San Diego campus or working day jobs to help make ends meet. Whatever the case, Justin would not expect to see anyone in the lab until after his lunch break.

He set his Starbucks coffee on the long counter and opened the appliance beneath it that resembled a dishwasher. This was used to sterilize equipment, and the upper shelf contained the handheld guillotine that Justin would use to cut the heads off lab mice to draw blood from them. The guillotine was red painted stainless steel, with a handle that moved the blade up and down. The bottom of the frame was V-shaped; the animal's head would lie in the center of the V. Anybody who suggested they enjoyed this part of the job would have to be sick or lying, Justin thought to himself. He pulled the device from the sterilizer and set it next to the sink where he would begin the worst part of his day.

The unfortunate mice that would lose their life today had been injected with a tumor-targeting reagent using the CRISPR process. This experiment was aimed at a tumor responsible for triple-negative breast cancer, or TNBC, which has the highest mortality rate of all types of breast cancer, occurs most frequently in women under fifty, and can be passed down through generations. The disease attacks three vital receptors that support the immune system, with devastating effects. Using CRISPR formulations injected into the mice, the therapy effectively "knocks out" the protein responsible for the tumor's growth. The experiments being run at Salk and other laboratories would transition to human clinical trials upon successful completion of studies on laboratory animals.

Justin collected the ten mice that had first received human TNBC cells and then received the CRISPR injections a month later. CRISPR interactivity with its targeted cells is expected to occur almost immediately, so only a few days after the CRISPR injections, the mice are decapitated to study their blood and to determine whether the therapy worked as intended. After taking blood from a now headless mouse, Justin would place a sample on a slide, cover it, examine it for the presence of TNBC cells, then record the findings on a spreadsheet that would be analyzed by another member of the team. The process would take him the entire morning.

By 11:45, Justin had completed the routine on all the animals and started to clean up the bloody mess in and around the sink. As he did so, he worried that he botched the analysis. What bothered him was that so few mice responded to the therapy. In fact, by no definition would the experiment be regarded as a success. Justin did not understand that some of what he thought was a CRISPR reagent intended to knock out the TNBC tumor was an inert saline solution.

HARMONY WOKE EARLY again, but it was not because she had plans for breakfast. She could never sleep well in any bed other than her own, especially one properly supported on a box frame and a couple of feet off the floor, like the one in Jack Reeves's bedroom. It was 8:45 in the morning, and

Jack was in the kitchen of his Culver City apartment, the smell of gourmet coffee wafting its way toward her.

She took the time to survey the surroundings that were barely visible when she saw them after their dinner date last night. And besides, she was very much enjoying the fun and games that her date served up, which included some of the best sex she had in a very long time. Now, she could see how meticulous her date was, in an apartment that looked like it belonged in a fashion magazine.

She wore only the panties from the night before and noticed a crisp, white business shirt hanging on a wooden valet not far from the bed, just outside a walk-in closet full of dark suits. She quietly moved in the direction of the shirt and put it on. While it covered her behind, she only attached the middle two buttons so that Jack could enjoy a partial view of her chest. She moved to his bathroom to straighten her hair and use the toilet. Before leaving, she squeezed a tiny bit of toothpaste on her index finger and pushed it back and forth across her teeth and gums. She then took a sip of water from the faucet and swished this around so that her breath was passable. She spit the water in the bathroom sink and washed it down. She was ready for him.

"Hey, how did you sleep?" Jack asked as she made her way toward him.

"Great," she replied, moving close enough to constitute an invitation. Jack got the message and pulled her even closer, kissing her a kiss as if he fully intended to pass the audition. Harmony let him take as long as he wanted with her in his arms. Eventually, he loosened his grip and she fell back slightly. The two stood facing each other in front of the kitchen sink.

"Wow," she said, "you're good."

Jack smiled. "Would you like some coffee?" he asked, reaching for the pot.

"Sure," Harmony replied as she hopped on a barstool next to the kitchen island.

"So," she said, "why no girlfriend?"

Jack smiled again. "It's hard, you know, a lot of people in this town are not very authentic. They dress to impress but there is not much there underneath it all. Also, I've got to be honest, I can be a bit of a dick sometimes."

Harmony could not resist. "Well, the bit of dick I've seen so far is pretty damn amazing."

Jack laughed. "Well, thank you, I was shooting for 'spectacular.' No, seriously, I'd love to see you again, but I've got to run. Help yourself to some food if you're hungry, and I'll call you later, okay? I've got to head down to the studio. It seems some of those poor souls that were poaching lobsters on the far side of Catalina actually drowned last night."

Harmony had heard about these stories before because her father was an avid diver, especially during lobster season, and he would force the family to hear all about his catch, especially the ones that got away. Unfortunately, undocumented immigrants and adventurous teenagers would also dive for lobsters without the proper training or equipment and try to sell them. Many tried to simply hold their breath while diving and suffered shallow water blackout, others went deep and ran out of air or surfaced too quickly and suffered from an air embolism that burst their lungs on ascent. They never expected how hard it was to catch a lobster that did not want to be caught, or how dangerous it could be to dive at night when conditions were rough. Every year it seemed a few people would drown trying to catch something you could buy in the grocery store for about $12.99 per pound. It hardly seemed worth it.

"We are trying to persuade the Department of Fish and Game to increase enforcement and to prevent these drownings," Jack added.

"Okay," Harmony replied, winking, "you go and make the world safe for lobsters and the people that hunt them. I support that movement one hundred percent."

Jack leaned back to kiss Harmony again. As he did, he got a peek at her perfectly shaped breasts hiding behind his shirt. *A beautiful and intelligent woman with a terrific sense of humor*, he thought to himself. *Yes, this one I'd like to see again.* But he'd been down this road before, with disappointing results. Then there was the matter of the age difference, a matter he readily elected to defer for later consideration. He disappeared around the corner and left the apartment.

As Harmony heard the door slam, her first instinct was to snoop: to look for Jack's current or previous love interests, skeletons in closets, or unexpected items in his medicine cabinet. She caught herself because, first, that was not her style and second, she wanted to start from a position of trust. She admired Jack for his courageous journalism, and he was certainly the most dynamic man she had met in a long time. So, she stayed put on the barstool alongside the kitchen counter and took another sip of her coffee while reaching for her phone with the other hand.

It was time for her first provocative post of the day. She felt a sense of inspiration in the apartment of a new man in her life. And he gave her the information she required to take her own investigation to the next level. Opening a new post on Instagram, she typed:

"Dennis Spence, what and why are you hiding?" and attached an image of The Center for New Beginnings.

Harmony dropped her phone on the counter and hopped off the barstool for another cup of coffee. As she was pouring the coffee, her phone pinged. It was common for "likes" to come in almost instantly when she posted product, not so often when posting a story. This was a good sign. She decided to enjoy a couple of sips of coffee and glance at the apartment's features. The living area had the standard sofa facing a big screen TV with a coffee table in between, copies of *Men's Health* and *GQ* stacked on top of each other. There was a smart mirror against the wall with an exercise mat and some dumbbells below it. And on the wall behind the sofa, framed pictures of Jack's major stories and pictures of him with famous people. She was about to look out the window at what she expected would be a terrific city view, then remembered to check for likes and comments on her post.

The ping, however, didn't indicate a comment below the post, it was a private message from a profile she did not recognize. It read:

"I have information on Dennis Spence that I want to share with you."

Harmony stared at the message. This was new. Should she ignore the message? Should she tell Jack? LA certainly had its share of kooks and people looking for attention. Is this one of them? She considered the matter just a few seconds more, then replied.

"Okay." One step at a time. There was a good chance this would be the end of the conversation. She stared at her phone, waiting. Another PM came back:

"Meet me at the corner of Motor and Park Ave, tomorrow, 5pm."

Harmony looked up the address on her phone. It was the southeast corner of Carlson Park, just east of the 405 freeway. She felt she could easily make the commitment and then back out if she got cold feet.

"How will I recognize you?" she asked. Again, she watched the phone, now with anticipation.

"I know what you look like from your posts. See you tomorrow."

And that was that. She had a lead. The only problem was this was not the reason why Harmony maintained an Instagram profile nor why she became an influencer. But she had an opportunity to further expose the hospital and to potentially assist Jack in his assignment. She set aside any thought that she might be walking into a trap.

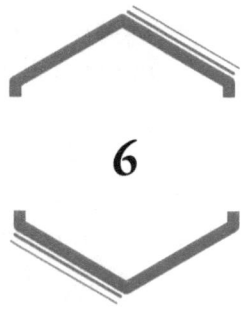

6

Denise stood in front of the mirror in her bathroom. Leaning in, she gave her face a quick examination, then stood back to take the rest in. Her brown hair was now short, and the features that made her feminine were giving way to a more masculine look, but it was clear she had a long way to go to complete her transformation. Her breasts had flattened and lost their shape, and her arms were becoming more muscular. At five-foot-six, she would remain shorter than most men but no less determined to be taken seriously.

Emma Lee stared at her phone as she contemplated the call she was about to make. Her relationship with Denise had grown more complicated since the start of Denise's transgender therapy. She cared for Denise, a connection that grew stronger since the two were lab partners in the pre-med program at UCLA. At that time, both were older than the typical student, and both were very much alone in a very competitive environment.

Denise was not the easiest person to be with, but Emma demonstrated the patience and compassion that would keep the relationship durable. Also, she *needed* the relationship to work. When Emma called, Denise was carefully examining how her skin tone was changing. She pulled at the skin covering her cheeks, noting how the texture was becoming coarse, with signs of acne at the top of her cheekbones.

"Hi, how are you feeling?" Emma started out, keeping the message generic enough that it would not presume anything.

"I'm okay," Denise replied. "But the drugs make me really tired."

"Did you get the vials? Did they arrive okay?"

"Yes, thanks." Denise was never particularly good at small talk, even with Emma, her only friend in the world and the only person for whom she could feel an enduring love.

"Denise, do you really think this is a good idea? You are already on a lot of drugs."

"Emma, my mother died from this despicable disease. Like I've told you before, from what I've been able to piece together of my own genetic makeup, I'd probably get it as well. Your lab is the only one that has produced an effective CRISPR solution. I am taking it."

Emma had misgivings about stealing the samples for Denise, but in the interest of what was considered "the greater good," it was decided by the agency that she should proceed with the it.

"And what about the phalloplasty? Are you still serious about this?"

"Of course," Denise snapped back. "I am also looking at doing a FOXL2 knockout."

Emma had learned to no longer be surprised at Denise's commitment to complete her gender transformation. The FOXL2 gene was involved in establishing gender identity, and when "knocked out" by introduction of a disrupting force like CRISPR would trigger the ovaries' somatic cells to convert to the equivalent cell types ordinarily found in the testes. It would mean that instead of hormone replacement therapy, the transformed gonadal tissue would begin to produce the hormones congruent with the desired gender.

Emma was aware that in China there was a near obsession with the creation of a procedure to perform the exact opposite. China's one-child policy, introduced in 1979, created a significant imbalance in the country's gender demography—at one point it was as large as 35 million more men than women. Had Emma not been sent to the United States, she would likely have been assigned to one of these laboratories.

As the two women continued to talk, the dynamics of their mutual deception remained the same: Denise needed Emma to obtain CRISPR samples to further her research into extending human life. She had discovered that the asexual reproductive properties of plants, combined with CRISPR agents of human DNA, could suspend the aging process when administered to her patients. Emma needed Denise to continue that research and to discover the secret to everlasting life so that at the appropriate time, she could steal it.

KIM JI-SUNG ARRANGED to be dropped a quarter mile from Harbin Bio-Splice Laboratory Company Ltd. as the sun was starting to set. He would walk the remaining distance, allowing him the opportunity to fully view his planned entry and possible escape routes from the facility. The laboratory was a five-story rectangular building, spartan by design, with slender vertical windows around its perimeter on the top three floors. It was surrounded by a small forest, but due to the time of year, it would not supply him with much cover. Nevertheless, he could use it to gain an approach to the facility that would be less visible than walking through the parking lot.

He left the road and made his way through the trees. The ground was a combination of mud, leaves and patches of ice that were now melting. As he approached the building from the rear, he saw an exit door near a dumpster and loading dock. He knelt to observe any activity. He checked his watch. Soon there might be people leaving the facility at the end of their shift. He moved closer, selecting some trees that were close enough together that he would not be seen by any casual observer.

The sun began its descent below the horizon, turning the sky bright orange, just as someone exited the facility. The man was wearing a loose, one-piece blue uniform and carrying a lunchbox. Ji-Sung presumed this was someone working in maintenance or as a janitor. He was good enough. As the man walked unsuspectingly toward his car, Ji-Sung approached him from behind.

"Ni hao!" he yelled at the man while waving and smiling as he approached, as if greeting an old friend. The man had reached his car and had been about to get in when he turned to face Ji-Sung. He was confused because Ji-Sung did not look familiar. As the two came together, Ji-Sung continued to smile, holding out his left arm as if he would embrace the man. As he came face to face with the man, he slung a blade into the man's side with his right hand and grabbed him around the neck with his left, pulling the man into his chest. With all his strength, he pulled the knife up so that it ripped a six-inch gash in the man's side, causing him to spasm and blood to spurt out in three directions, as if a dam had sprung a leak. The man was considerably larger than Ji-Sung, who had to pull him backward toward the trees where he could be laid down far enough from the building that he would not be discovered, at least not until the following day.

Ji-Sung had hoped to wear the man's one-piece uniform, but it was now torn on one side and drenched in the man's blood, so that was out. Instead, he took off his coat to cover the man as best he could. He took the man's security badge, which was clipped to his breast pocket. He fished through the man's other pockets and removed his cell phone. He then took his cell phone and stuffed it into a secret pocket inside his pants. If he were captured, it would be the dead man's phone that they would presume was his own.

Ji-Sung turned his attention back to the door near the loading dock. It was much darker now, and he could walk from the forest with little fear of being noticed. He waited fifteen more minutes just to be certain he hadn't missed any security on the grounds. As he did, he noticed many employees leaving the facility, getting into their vehicles, and driving away. When the last of these people disappeared from the lot, he walked briskly toward the door, wearing the security badge that would enable him to enter the building. There were still a few cars left in the lot.

Once inside, he found himself in the corridor to the immediate left of the interior part of the loading dock. His instructions were specific: Obtain any documents that might summarize the activities of the facility, collect any samples that were easily stolen, and take pictures of everything else. He presumed he would have to get to the upper floors where the laboratories and administrative offices were likely to be.

He took a quick look at the posters lining the walls of the corridor. Typical stuff, including instructions to employees for safe handling of radioactive materials and instructions on how to safely evacuate in the event of an emergency. A door in front of him had a window that revealed another hallway, providing clear separation between the loading dock and the rest of the facility. That door also required use of the dead man's security badge. Ji-Sung realized that in passing through this door, his vulnerability rose significantly. He opened a utility cabinet in the hallway between the two doors. Inside was a wide floor broom, the perfect accessory for his mission.

The first thing he noticed on passing through the second door was the lack of windows on the floor, as if it was sublevel. The round, protruding doorknobs let off a dim glow from what little light was available. This made him wonder if there was indeed a sublevel, and he made a mental note to check later. He listened for any activity on the floor. It was quiet. As he looked ahead, there was a hallway straight ahead with several rooms on each side and hallways to the right and left. The floor consisted of shiny white linoleum, and the air smelled of disinfectant. At this point, very bright fluorescent lights built into the ceiling tiles left no shadows anywhere. There were no stairs or elevators that he could see from his vantage point, so he proceeded quietly straight ahead, pushing the broom in front of him in the event somebody popped out of a room.

At the far end of the hallway he found stairs next to an elevator. He decided to take the stairs as high as they would go. If there were any specific technical data worth gathering, he thought, he would find it there. He quietly made his way up several flights of stairs, then entered the sixth floor. The entire space was a huge laboratory with a series of modules around its perimeter. The room was impressive for the volume of technical equipment it housed: microscopes, centrifuges, pipetting machines, and other equipment that Ji-Sung did not recognize.

Ji-Sung looked past the lab equipment, which any lab would predictably have, for whatever in the room might silently call out for his attention. In one of the center islands, or cells, he saw a series of very large glass containers nearly filled with a yellowish liquid. As he approached, he noticed that some jars contained what looked like a partially developed human fetus. Other containers contained fully developed babies. He understood that if Bio-Splice was experimenting on humans, it would violate every ethical and moral norm in the scientific community. He took pictures of each jar and the notes on each container.

He made his way to one of the desks where a series of drawings were hanging on the adjoining wall. The images resembled the Vitruvian man, a famous rendering by Da Vinci demonstrating the proportions of the human body, with a circle encompassing the body and just touching the feet and hands. In this case, however, the images looked like a perversion of that drawing, with some subjects barely resembling the human form. If this indicated the direction in which the Chinese were heading with their experiments, Ji-Sung would be bringing home valuable intelligence.

He sifted through material on the desk and came upon a document titled "5 Guiding Principles." He pulled it from the pile and laid it on the table for closer examination. As he pulled his phone from his pocket to take pictures, he read down the list:

- Accepts commands
- Competent to defend itself
- Regeneration of organs and limbs
- Significantly longer lifespan
- The whole is greater than the sum of parts

Ji-Sung carefully positioned the phone to capture the entire document and touched the shutter button. It was time to see if there was a basement. He entered the stairwell, broom in hand, and proceeded down.

Unlike the higher floors, the sublevel floor smelled musty and didn't have the bright linoleum or bright lights overhead. There was a hallway leading in the opposite direction from where he entered with fewer, likely larger rooms on each side. The floors were concrete, and the lighting consisted of a cable running the distance of the hallway along the ceiling, with an incandescent bulb every few feet. This suited Ji-Sung just fine as he felt particularly exposed and vulnerable elsewhere in the building.

He heard shuffling noises from one of the rooms, as if caged animals were inside, perhaps subjects of the experiments he was sent to investigate. He moved toward the door. There were warnings on the door suggesting only authorized employees may pass, and it was locked. He pulled out the single most important tool he took with him on the mission, similar in design to a Leatherman multi-purpose tool but specifically designed for picking locks and, if necessary, slicing up people who were in his way.

Ji-Sung selected the right implement from the tool and quietly inserted it into the lock with his right hand while using his left hand to shove the security badge into the door jamb where the door latch was locked in place. He pushed his tool into the lock while pushing the badge against the latch. A bit of juggling of the tool caused the door latch to give way. He was in.

The stench of animal waste hit him immediately. There were no windows and little ventilation. A series of bright fluorescent lights revealed a neatly organized environment. Large oxygen tanks, taller than him, were stored in the corner. As he expected, the room was full of cages of all sizes arranged on a series of shelves directly in front of him. The cages held a variety of small creatures: rabbits, opossums, rats, and mice. Each species was kept in a separate cage, and each cage had a card containing details on the contents: type of animal, when it arrived at the lab, and a feeding schedule.

Ji-Sung presumed these animals were part of the lab's inventory and that any subjects used for experiments were on the higher floors. He decided the sooner he could get to more floors, the sooner he would find what he came for.

As he was about to leave the animal room, he noticed a large, thick stainless-steel door in the corner that likely led to a refrigerated room. His training for the mission recognized that some of the most valuable specimens would be subject to refrigeration, but he had no good mechanism to transport them, so he would have to take pictures and hope that any documentation gathered would explain what he had found.

As he opened the large metal door, the room inside lit up automatically. It was very cold, and an immense fog flew past him and out the door he had left open. On either side of the room were large metal drawers, similar to a file cabinet but much bigger, reaching from the floor to just below the ceiling. There were twelve drawers on each side. He opened one drawer slightly to peek at the contents inside. He knew at that point: he was in a morgue.

Each drawer contained a human subject as indicated by the details on an attached card. Many of these were Uyghurs, he noted, a persecuted ethnic minority living predominantly in northwest China. Ji-Sung was not surprised to see them being used for medical experiments. This validated the intelligence that was widely accepted as fact based upon reports that had surfaced in Western media outlets.

Ji-Sung examined one of the cards that was at eye level. There were some markings he did not understand, but he was able to snap a picture of it while translating in his mind what he could:

Uyghur #5921. Male. Approx 32 years.
Injected with Z-32 on 22 June. Expired: 27 Nov.
Lab results on file Z-4294750

Ji-Sung pulled a handkerchief from his pocket with his left hand and covered his mouth with it. With his right hand, he pulled the door toward him. It slid easily on bearings, bringing the dead man out toward him. Ji-Sung was not prepared for what he saw.

The corpse was grotesque. The man's arms and legs were so swollen that muscle tissue seemed to have replaced the epidermis layer of his skin. The long strands of muscular tissue had pushed their way to the surface, as if the skin was carefully pulled away. Because the man's muscular tissue was about three times the circumference of a normal arm or limb, he looked like some creation from a monster movie, the kind that might appear in a classic Japanese horror film. Ji-Sung reached for his phone to take a picture of the unfortunate soul who lost his life to a sick experiment. He pushed the drawer back into the wall.

Ji-Sung feared the image of the corpse would haunt his dreams, but he knew he was uncovering valuable intelligence. He scanned the rest of the room for additional clues and noticed the drawers on the opposite wall had temperature sensors integrated above them. Each sensor read somewhere between minus 195 and minus 200 degrees C. He took a picture of one of the cards:

David Koch. Male. USA. Approx 79 years.
Cryopreservation initiated 22 August 2019.

Ji-Sung presumed this subject was frozen alive as part of a cryonics experiment. He would not make the connection to the immensely rich industrialist who, as the patriarch of the Koch family, was a great influence on conservative politics throughout the first two decades of the twenty-first century. It was reported that Koch died on August 23, 2019, but not long after the announcement he obviously disappeared from the headlines. Koch was seventy-nine and suffered from prostate cancer. He was the eleventh richest person in the world when his death was reported to the world. However, he was not technically deceased.

The Supreme Leader had an intense interest in preserving his body for resurrection once science had eradicated all major disease. Ji-Sung told himself he would be decorated and recognized for his ability to bring knowledge of this science back to the motherland. He took a few more pictures before finding his way out of the facility. He wanted to record the data on each card detailing the person inside. Since some of the names appeared to be of Western origin, there was likely more intelligence to be gained from this room.

As he positioned his phone for another shot, the steel door to the cryogenic morgue slammed shut. Ji-Sung rushed to see if it would open. He was locked inside.

He looked at the temperature gauge embedded in the door. It read minus 10 degrees Celsius. More fog began to form, and the temperature started to decrease further. Minus 15 degrees, minus 18, minus 20 ... the fog was making it difficult to read what was happening in the room.

Ji-Sung understood that every body will react a little differently to extreme temperatures. He did not know what that meant for him. In fact. the average human will collapse from hypothermia in less than ten minutes at temperatures below minus 20 degrees Celsius and die shortly thereafter.

Ji-Sung realized he was in trouble. He squatted down in the corner of the room, fog enveloping him, and passed out within a few minutes.

7

"I solemnly swear that I will support and defend the Constitution of the United States against all enemies, foreign and domestic; that I will bear true faith and allegiance to the same; that I take this obligation freely, without any mental reservation or purpose of evasion; and that I will well and faithfully discharge the duties of the office on which I am about to enter. So help me God."

The sound of 168 graduating students from the FBI Academy chanting the oath in unison reverberated within the Quantico auditorium. While 250 students entered the Academy, the program's rigors inevitably resulted in significant attrition. Richard was there, in the third row, reciting the oath with the other graduates. He had many doubts along the way but had finally fulfilled his dream of becoming a special agent. He was beaming with pride next to Jeff McAuley, who was likely just as surprised as Richard to have made it this far.

A powerful slap across the back of his shoulder snapped Richard out of his moment.

"Congrats, dude, we did it!" It was Jeff. "Let's throw back some beers, crank some tunes and party!" Although this day was one that both looked forward to with great anticipation, they never discussed how they would celebrate it.

"I can't tonight," he replied. He had chosen instead to share the moment with Sarah Goodman, who would be flying in from Detroit later that evening.

"I appreciate it, though. I'll meet you at Dulles for the LA flight, okay? You still okay for me to stay over until I find my own place?"

"Absolutely, bro, it would be an honor to have a special agent visiting me."

DR. GEORGE KOLINS, professor of microbiology at the UCLA Center for Law and Biosciences, leaned to the right as the UCSD program director whispered in his ear before walking off the stage. Kolins shuffled his notes at the lectern, then tapped the microphone to ensure it was turned on. It was effective in bringing the audience chatter to an end.

"Good morning," he said in a deadpan voice. "I was just informed by the program director that there is very likely a spy in the audience."

Emma Lee looked up from her phone and turned her head in both directions, startled. Many other students in the massive auditorium on the UCSD campus did the same. The partnership between the Salk Institute and the University of California at San Diego was well-known for its pioneering work in gene editing, and the promise of this technology had massive implications for how societies would further evolve. In the wrong hands, gene editing could trigger everything from the introduction of designer babies to immortal and invincible armies. The ethical implications were frequently debated by scientists and the organizations that funded them.

"I'm just kidding," the professor continued, converting the murmur from the audience into muted, nervous chuckles.

"But seriously, the results of our studies will inevitably be of great interest to those that hold the keys of power in various seats of government around the world. And so, we have a moral obligation to consider the *full scope* of consequences of our work. Of course, I am not telling you anything you don't already know."

Dr. Kolins served as a liaison to the Salk Institute and worked closely with programs across the University of California campuses to catalog the progress and implications of germline editing, a new frontier. The process focused on genetic alterations in reproductive cells, such as sperm and eggs, that would produce inheritable genome changes. The work in Emma's laboratory had not yet extended into this realm, but it was clear to anyone in the industry that this field would suck up all the funding and attention while it pursued new applications of the technology. The opportunity to hear Kolins, a guest lecturer to the various science programs across the UC system, was not to be missed.

"Let's take a quick look at where we've been recently and where the industry is going," Kolins said to an audience that was no longer looking at their phones but transfixed. Kolins picked up the remote from the lectern to introduce his first slide.

The first image to appear before the audience was a book cover, *The Time Machine*, by H.G. Wells.

"As far back as 1895, society has imagined a world where science could control the trajectory of evolution. In *The Time Machine*, a traveler to the future discovers that humans evolved into two separate species, a leisure class of Eloi and working class of Morlocks. Of course, fantasy and reality remained far apart for some time, which is why we have a genre known as science fiction." Kolins advanced to the next slide.

"The road to engineering genes actually began in 1972," he continued, "when a Stanford professor discovered a way to take the DNA from a virus found in monkeys and splice it into the DNA of a totally different virus. Scientists later discovered ways to make these artificial genes efficiently and to clone millions of copies of them. Thus, the race began to exploit this new and promising field."

"It took another fifteen years before scientists began to deliver engineered DNA into the cells of humans. The goal was not to edit existing genes but to create an effect similar to what was previously accomplished by medication therapy. Instead of treating a disease with drugs, the engineered DNA acted to counteract a faulty gene or supplement its capabilities."

"The first trial in 1990 was on a child with a genetic mutation that compromised her immune system and left her at risk for infection. Doctors found a way to get functioning copies of a missing gene into her blood, with the effect that she was ultimately able to live a full life."

The next slide showed an obscure story in 1999 from a Philadelphia newspaper. It read, "Gene Therapy has Fatal Consequences." In the article, the death of a young man due to a massive immune response was blamed on the use of unproven genetic therapies.

"Unfortunately," Kolins said, "tragedies like this set the industry back ten years as clinical trials were no longer being conducted."

"From 2015 to 2018, various governments around the world recognized the moral implications of gene and germline editing and prohibited experiments and clinical trials on human populations, calling for a closer examination of the ethical consequences of the practice." The slide on the screen showed a flat map of the world with red shading designating those countries across Europe and North America that had enacted legislation controlling the use of gene editing on human subjects.

"Then in November of 2018, a Chinese scientist by the name of He Jiankui modified embryos of two women, removing the genetic marker known as CCR5 and later implanting a modified embryo into the uterus of each woman. As far as we know, this was the first example of germline editing on human subjects." Kolins paused to verify that his audience was listening. They were not only listening, they were taking notes.

"The aim of the experiment was to eliminate the risk of HIV, smallpox, and cholera. One woman supposedly had twins; we don't know the outcome of the other pregnancy or, indeed, the health status of any of the genetically modified pregnancies. One reason why we have such little information is that Jiankui was sentenced to three years in prison shortly after going public about his adventures."

Kolins advanced to the next slide.

"Not even a year later, just across Torrey Pines Road at the Salk Institute, your own Juan Carlos Izpisua Belmonte extended the lifetime of laboratory mice by approximately 25 percent by injecting synthetic RNA that would isolate the portion of genetic material responsible for rapid aging, neutralizing it. While the results look promising for possible application in humans, it must be noted that the mice eventually died from drug-induced tumor and cell dysfunction. Nobody asked the mice if they would rather die with dignity of natural causes or from a drug-induced tumor."

A short series of chuckles emanated from the audience as Kolins advanced to the next slide.

"In 2020, researchers at Columbia University conducted an experiment on forty human embryos using eggs from healthy donors and sperm from a man with a gene mutation—a single nucleotide from a single chromosome—that causes blindness. Using a similar CRISPR technique as was used on the embryos in China, they attempted not to eliminate a portion of the gene, but to add the missing nucleotide. They then studied the fertilized eggs to see how many were successfully repaired. Guess what? The mutation was gone! Guess what else was gone? The entire chromosome!"

The audience again let out a nervous chuckle.

"Had the scientists not known the entire chromosome was missing, they may have had a false sense of security that the experiment was a success because the mutation was no longer present. And for three out of the forty embryos it was a success, they remained viable and fully repaired. But the others could not have been brought to term. I'd hardly call that a success."

He paused briefly as he scanned the audience.

"Look," he said, "For over a decade we have been using this technology on mosquito populations to control malaria. There have also been some very promising clinical trials to eliminate sickle cell anemia from isolated tribes in sub-Saharan Africa. There are absolutely some valuable applications of germline editing that can solve societal problems and improve the health status of populations. But beyond the ethical implications of CRISPR applications on humans, we still have a lot of work to do to understand how to make a *change* that is truly an *improvement*. I'd be happy to answer any questions."

Students began asking questions, but Emma did not hear them. She was preparing herself to ask the question that she was sent to put to the professor. She waited until a few other students had their opportunity, then raised her hand. Kolins pointed in her direction, and she stood up.

"Is it true that at UCLA you are experimenting with CRISPR to support regeneration and, potentially, biological autonomy?"

Kolins hesitated and looked a bit surprised by Emma's question. Some of the experiments were not made public, and this one in particular was quite sensitive. While humans had very limited capacity to regenerate damaged organs, the idea of regenerating body parts would have massive implications. But Emma's directive was to gather intelligence on Kolins's work in this area, and she felt confident using such a direct approach.

"Well, uh," he started out, looking to his right to see if the program director might rescue him. "I am not at liberty to discuss many of our experiments, but yes, we have had some success with this application on laboratory animals, not humans, of course." Emma nodded her head and sat down.

Kolins wasn't satisfied that his answer met his own high standard of ensuring his audience would understand the profound implications of his work.

"Look," he added, "there is a very significant difference between making people better and *making better people*. And this is why we have the field of bioethics, an area that picks up where this lecture leaves off." Kolins paused to let his statement sink in and finished with "thank you." The applause signaled the audience's abundant appreciation.

As people filed out of the lecture hall, the sun was just setting on the other side of Torrey Pines Road, a short distance from the Pacific coastline. In the distance, Emma could see hang gliders streaking against the mauve-colored sky. It would be hard not to be grateful to be in this place, at this time. The lecture at UCSD gave her insights into the pioneering work being done in the field of work that she loved.

She continued walking toward the west and the setting sun then pulled out her phone. As she walked, she sent a message to her handler in China via Threema, the Swiss equivalent of Signal and very popular in China because no user data is stored.

"They did it."

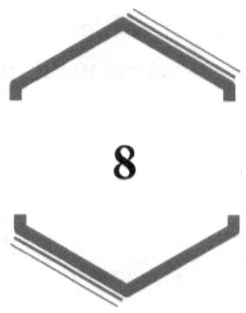

8

Harmony wore tight jeans and an oversized white T-shirt and had her hair in a ponytail. She had the bare minimum of makeup applied. She did not want to attract attention and vowed to abort the rendezvous if the person she was meeting looked at all threatening.

The Uber driver dropped her at Braddock Drive and Le Bourget Avenue. From there, she could look for anything unusual as she walked diagonally across the small park to meet with this supposed source on CNB. Although the temperatures in LA this day were in the mid-70s, Harmony found herself practically shivering from excitement. This was what a day in the life of Jack Reeves must be like, she thought.

She could see the corner of Motor and Park Avenue ahead of her, but nobody was there. As she walked toward the corner, she checked her watch. It was a few minutes after 5 o'clock, and the sun was setting behind her. Was she late? She continued to the corner.

"Hey, over here!" came a voice from across the street.

As Harmony continued toward the corner, she saw a woman, scarf over her head, leaning out of the window of a Nissan Maxima.

"Over here!" the woman repeated.

If Harmony was nervous before, seeing the woman relaxed her. She waved to acknowledge the woman and picked up her pace, reaching the corner.

"Come on over," the woman said. "I can't park here, it's reserved for street cleaning today."

As Harmony approached the car, she tried to get a closer look at the woman. She looked young but had a very hard face, as if she perhaps had plastic surgery. That would not be uncommon in LA, Harmony recognized, and the city was certainly full of cosmetic surgeries that went bad.

"Please get in," she said, "let's go someplace we can talk."

Harmony considered the park an excellent place to talk, but she could see the signs that prohibited parking on that day, and she did not consider herself in a position to negotiate. She walked around the car to the other side, opened the door, and got in.

The woman looked forward, put the car in drive, and slowly headed north on Motor Avenue, then turned west on Braddock Drive. Her driving was tentative as if she had little experience behind the wheel; they were traveling only about twenty miles per hour. The car itself was immaculate, and because it was a late model, Harmony assumed it was rented. Harmony looked over at the woman. She looked older than she probably was. Her hair was covered by a scarf, and she wore a white lab coat. Although she was wearing lipstick, it did nothing to soften her appearance.

"I'm Harmony."

"I know who you are," the woman replied, continuing to look forward, saying nothing further.

"What's your name?"

"I'm not telling you my name. I could get fired just for meeting with you."

Harmony could see that she would need patience to get what she came for. At least her contact appeared to be a harmless looking woman, driving slowly enough that she could open the door at any corner, and walk away.

"Where are we going?" she asked.

"I am a nurse at CNB," the woman said, ignoring Harmony's question. "I work in the psych ward."

Harmony needed a moment to take that in. A real insider! Now she understood why the woman was being so cautious. She decided to suspend her questions and to allow the woman to decide when to speak. She had so many questions and began queuing them in her head. The two remained silent for several blocks until the woman slowed down across from Veterans Memorial Park, only seven blocks from where they started.

"Let's go here," she said, parking the car across the street. By now, it was starting to get dark and there was little chance that either of them would be recognized in this part of town.

The woman opened her door to step out, waiting for Harmony to do the same.

"I, I can't open the door," Harmony said, trying several times to yank the handle.

"Oh, sorry, that door is broken," the woman said. "I need to open it from the outside like you did when you first got in. I'll go around and open it for you."

The woman stood up outside the car as Harmony looked forward, waiting. She made a motion as if she was about to move forward, then dropped her keys on the ground and kneeled to pick them up. As she did, she reached under the front seat to open the valve of the nitrous oxide tank hidden there. She threw the door closed and locked the doors with her electronic key.

As the gas hissed from the tank underneath the seat, a thick fog encircled Harmony and filled the car. Harmony could not see anything. She choked on the gas and frantically tried to get out first from her door, then reached across to the driver's side door. She tried to open the automatic windows. She tried to honk the horn, but everything had been disabled. This was not the first time the car was pressed into service for a kidnapping.

The woman watched dispassionately from outside the car. All she could see was a pair of young, slender hands pushing the window, trying desperately to escape. What felt like hours to Harmony was only about a minute and a half. By then, she was unconscious.

The woman lit a cigarette to pass the time. After about five minutes, she opened the door, allowing the gas to escape. Then, she propped up Harmony in the passenger seat, strapped her in, and drove her to The Center for New Beginnings.

"TAKE A DEEP BREATH, then slowly let half of it out, and hold what is left," Jerry O'Brien said to his son, Richard, who was at the time no more than ten years old. "Then, hold steady, take aim, and slowly pull the trigger. Watch."

Jerry knelt in the grass in the middle of their backyard in a suburb of Grosse Pointe, Michigan. His right index finger was resting on the trigger of the BB rifle, his left elbow balanced on his knee; the fore stock was cradled by his left hand. He took aim at a lead pencil sticking out of the grass at the end of the yard. Richard watched in amazement as his father shattered the pencil with a single shot.

"There, now you try."

Jerry O'Brien owned a successful construction consulting firm, but in his spare time he served as a lieutenant on the auxiliary police force of Gross Pointe, a role he took as seriously as if it were his full-time occupation. He cherished his work with the police force and brandished his badge whenever provided the opportunity. In reality, the most serious action he would see as a volunteer policeman was a complaint that a child shot a bottle rocket in the neighborhood that bounced off a homeowner's picture window. Gross Pointe was a quiet, upper- to middle-class community, and Jerry O'Brien was determined to keep it that way.

One summer evening the year before the BB gun lesson changed Jerry's world view. That night, as he sipped from a cup of tea at the kitchen table following his shift and while still in his police uniform, somebody broke into his den and stole everything that could be carried, even taking the family stereo. The humiliation of being burglarized while he sat in the other room and while his children were sleeping nearby was too much for Jerry. Richard's mom had been opposed to the notion of him ever having access to a gun, but she acquiesced following the break-in and allowed him to get a

BB gun. By the end of the second day of practice, Richard could shatter the pencil not just from the middle of the lawn, but from twice as far, at the other end of the yard.

Richard sat on the corner of his bed in his Brooklyn apartment and looked down at the marksmanship certificate that he held in his right hand, recognition he earned during FBI training a couple of weeks before. These days he was taking target practice with an FBI-issued Glock Gen4 9mm pistol, quite different from the days when he practiced with a BB rifle. But the skills his father taught him transferred to his current line of work. Dad would be proud, he thought, had he not died the year before. Richard took the certificate, folded it up, and shoved it into the inside pocket of the suitcase he was packing for his move to Los Angeles. As he did so, the bedsheets behind him were being pulled in the opposite direction.

"What time is it?" Sarah said, pulling the sheets again, and forcing Richard to stand up.

"It's nearly seven," he replied. "Sorry if I woke you up."

Although Sarah was considered an exceptional agent and ready for whatever the mission required, she also relished the opportunity to sleep in whenever possible. But she realized that she and Richard had some unfinished business. She pulled herself up to prop her back against the headboard.

"Do you want to talk about last night?" she asked.

What Sarah referred to was the aborted attempt at sex following his graduation from the Academy. Congratulatory phone calls from a series of people, mostly women, put Sarah in a bad mood, and Richard was unsuccessful in diminishing their impact. To make matters worse, he wasn't able to maintain an erection, which convinced Sarah that his mind was elsewhere.

"Hey, I'm sorry about that, it's my fault," he offered, "I guess I'm just excited about graduating and anxious about what happens next."

Sarah understood. She had been down that path herself. She'd have to give Richard a pass. He then put his left hand on the bed, leaned over to her, and gave her a kiss.

"I'll see you in LA, okay?" he said. She returned a tentative smile, turned her back to him, and pulled the covers back over her head.

Richard quietly stepped in front of a full-length mirror perched in the corner that he always had intended to mount and now no longer had the need. He gently touched the likely permanent scar on the right side of his forehead. He thought back to when his head was bashed against the bathroom sink at Dulles airport, his fifteen-minutes-of-fame moment that led to the capture of a rogue Mossad agent. He reassured himself that he was ready to make the not-so-insignificant leap from being a low-level employee of the FBI to a bona fide special agent. He turned back to the suitcase, flipped it closed, and zipped it up. He lifted the bag and gently closed the door to his bedroom. Sarah lay in bed on her side with her eyes open and heard the apartment door open and close.

"WE'RE NOT BUILDING organs, we're building hope."

George Kolins watched the CNN news story featuring Doris Taylor, PhD, from Texas Heart Institute in Houston. Taylor was describing how she was able to take a pig heart, clean its valves with baby shampoo, then adapt it for use in heart transplants by attaching the patient's stem cells to it. "We teach our legs to become more efficient," Taylor explained, "human stem cells will teach these hearts how to work in the human body. We will be able to build specific organs that will resist rejection because the recipient's stem cells will dictate their behavior." Taylor's research was capturing the attention and imagination of a segment of the scientific community that was obsessed with figuring out how to extend human life.

Kolins shut off the program, leaned back in his chair, and ran his hands from his forehead down his face until they rested under his chin. He exhaled loudly and looked up at the ceiling of his UCLA office, lost in his thoughts. He was in this subcommunity as well. However, he was also going through a costly divorce and trying to secure the funds to send his daughter to a private school while paying the mortgage on two properties. To say he was a bit distracted would be an understatement.

Kolins was in a race with Taylor's lab to commercialize the business of creating self-sustaining organs, also referred to as biological autonomy. Taylor's success and media attention frustrated Kolins because she would find it easier to attract venture capital, while he was constrained by the conditions of his grant. The dirty little secret of academic research went something like this: publish quickly, publish often, and publish before your peers know you plan to publish. Repeat as often as necessary until the unrestricted grants and venture capital flow toward you as if you are a massive magnet. Taylor understood this. She was winning.

Kolins understood it as well, but in his desperation to get funding he accepted a grant worth $5 million with several strings attached. For starters, he signed a very restrictive nondisclosure agreement and could not publicize his findings without the sponsor's approval, and his work would have to be conducted in a manner that would not attract attention. Kolins was too excited to receive the funding to ask many questions. He suspected the donor was a bio-pharma company based in China that was able to funnel money through an entity designed to support scientific collaboration, which offered the advantage of avoiding excessive regulatory interference.

Kolins was in a classic Catch-22 dilemma: He could not reveal that his work included experiments on human tissue from organ donors, for it would not only violate his NDA, it would land him in the middle of an ethical firestorm. On the other hand, he would never extricate himself from his financial nightmare without the outlet to celebrate his accomplishments.

Kolins returned his chair to its original position and reached for his computer keyboard, determined to break free from his mental masturbation. Before he could sign back into the university's system, his cell phone rang.

"George Kolins," he said.

"Dr. Kolins, my name is Emma Lee. I am a doctoral student at UCSD. I attended your lecture the other day."

"Oh, yes, how did you get this number?" Faculty members were notoriously guarded about giving their number to students, especially those not in their programs or classes. Emma ignored the question.

"Dr. Kolins, I am working on an article for *Fast Company* with one of my professors here, and I'd like to visit with you to discuss your work."

Kolins took a moment to respond. *Fast Company* was not exactly a scientific journal, and he could talk generally about the field without revealing too much about his work. This could raise his profile substantially without violating his agreement with his funding sponsor.

"Okay ..." he replied, slowly measuring his response and trying to temper his obvious enthusiasm.

"Can you fit me in tomorrow afternoon? Say three o'clock?"

"Yes, that would be fine. Come to the Terasaki Life Sciences Building. My office is on the third floor. The address is ..."

Emma cut him off.

"I know the building. Thank you, Dr. Kolins, I look forward to meeting you." Emma ended the call quickly.

Kolins stared at his phone as if it might offer him some answers on what just transpired. Maybe this article could be the beginning of his introduction to the world stage. Instead, it would put him squarely in the sights of the world's intelligence agencies.

9

The first thing Kim Ji-Sung felt was his right knee. His legs were mostly numb from the ice water, but the right knee was just above the water line. This was the only part of his body below his waist sensitive enough to feel the slight draft from the open bathroom window. He jiggled the right leg slightly, causing the ice cubes to bob back and forth, clicking against each other as they floated around the tub. If not for the blood in the water, he would not have thought to move the cubes out of the way, revealing the stitches running across his midsection.

He looked around the bathroom for something he might recognize. The white tiles running across the tub enclosure did not look familiar, nor did the long streaks of blood running across them and down to the top of the tub where he lay. It was a bathroom in somebody's home, but the surroundings suggested the owner was poor or disinterested in the room's attributes. Across from the tub was a white, slender pedestal sink, and behind it, a mirror with a long diagonal crack, the lower right corner completely broken off. The toilet took the form of a porcelain dish built into the floor, the type you would squat over, which was typical of the style found in the poorer villages, well outside the perimeter of Pyongyang. Except Kim Ji-Sung was not in North Korea, he was in Beijing.

He placed his arms on each side of the tub and tried to sit up. As he put weight on his arms, the stitches around his abdomen gave way, and blood began seeping out between them. The pain was so intense that he shouted in despair and slumped back. He moved the ice cubes away again to examine the slash. An amateurish attempt was made to stitch him up, but why? He was vaguely familiar with the urban legend that the Asian Mafia would drug unsuspecting people, steal a kidney for transplantation in the back alleys of Shanghai, and then stitch up the body so they would be less likely accused of murder. But this myth has been debunked many times and was generally seen only in the movies.

So, why am I here? he said to himself. His heart rate began to climb as he considered his predicament.

A buzz below the bathtub interrupted his train of thought. He turned his head to the left, looked down over the side of the tub, and saw a cell phone vibrating on the linoleum floor, twisting back and forth. Reaching down with his left hand, he picked up the flip-phone and opened it.

"How do you feel, Comrade?" said a voice speaking in Min, a Chinese dialect similar to the Korean language.

"What happened to me? Who are you?" Kim Ji-Sung replied, his voice trembling from the cold blood racing through his veins and the fear consuming his thoughts.

"Comrade, we need you to do something for us," the voice said. "If you succeed, you will be returned to your family."

Kim Ji-Sung could not imagine what was so important that some perpetrator would steal one of his organs.

"Why did you remove my kidney?" he demanded.

"We did not remove your kidney," the voice replied. "We inserted an explosive device."

"You what!?"

"We planted an explosive device that can be remotely detonated. We need to know we have your loyalty to this mission."

Ji-Sung was momentarily speechless. No amount of training had prepared him for this.

"Comrade?"

"What mission?" he said finally.

"All this will be explained to you in due course, but first comrade, tell me..." the voice replied, pausing before transitioning from Chinese to English, "do you speak English?"

Kim Ji-Sung's head fell back and nearly hit the wall behind him. He had studied English but struggled with it because of limited opportunities to practice. However, in that moment he felt that it best to tell his captors what they wanted to hear until he was in a better position to control the situation.

The voice repeated the question, "Comrade, do you speak English?"

"I do," he replied.

"Very well," the voice replied, "When you complete your mission, we will remove the implanted device and reunite you with your family. One of our people will be arriving soon to assist you with your journey to the United States. Good luck, comrade."

RICHARD GUIDED THE white, rented Ford Fusion into the parking lot at the FBI field office in San Diego at 8:45 in the morning. The meeting in San Diego was far from the home he was renting in Huntington Beach with McAuley, but this office had jurisdiction over the case of the missing Congressman John Kinkade since it was established that he was in San Diego when he disappeared. The issue of jurisdiction was a bit ambiguous in that it was presumed Kinkade was lost at sea, in federally protected waters, somewhere off the Point Loma peninsula. Had Kinkade's disappearance represented an isolated incident on *terra firma*, the FBI likely would have left the issue to local authorities. But Ben Klein, special agent in charge of the San Diego field office, saw a pattern that could not be ignored and established an agreement early on that he would handle the case and run operations out of the Los Angeles field office once his initial team was briefed.

Richard stepped into the lobby, where Klein was waiting for him.

"O'Brien," he called out as he walked toward him. "Welcome to San Diego." He extended his hand to Richard. Klein presented himself in the prototypical FBI uniform: navy blue suit, white shirt, black tie, and black leather shoes that were so shiny they reflected light in all directions. He was tall and thin; his hair was pasted down with abundant pomade. Hints of gray hair were a testament to his age, which otherwise was difficult to tease out because he was in terrific shape. He certainly wasn't giving out any clues since the mandatory retirement age for special agents was still fifty-seven.

"Thank you, sir," Richard replied. "I appreciate you giving me an opportunity to work on this case."

"The more the merrier," Klein replied. "But sorry we don't expect this to be nearly as exciting as your last adventure."

The case of the rogue Mossad agent Isaac Shulman had gained significant attention within the agency, making Richard something of a celebrity even though he was not an agent at the time he was involved.

"Follow me to the conference room," Klein continued, "and we'll grab you some coffee on the way. The briefing will start in ten minutes."

Richard walked into the conference room behind Klein, introduced himself quickly to the other agents present, and took a seat at a large, rectangular table. The conference room window faced west but instead of an ocean view it looked down on the I-5 freeway that Richard took on his to drive down from LA. Like most FBI offices, it was devoid of any character, much like the conference rooms in the New York offices, but cleaner.

Richard looked again at his newly adopted peer group: five white men and one black man, all likely in their thirties or forties, all in blue suits, white shirts, and ties that were either blue, black, or red. All looked toward Klein without expression, as if they were frozen. All that was missing were the Wayfarer sunglasses, he thought to himself, and he'd be in a version of *The Matrix*.

"Okay everyone, look, we've seen a dramatic increase in missing person reports in LA and San Diego counties since the beginning of the year," Klein said excitedly, "and for at least three of them, we've detected a pattern."

Klein fired up the projector in the room, and the first picture to appear was that of Congressman John Kinkade.

"You are all familiar with the Kinkade case. He's been missing for two months now, presumed dead as a drowning victim although the body has not been recovered. More on him in a moment." Klein advanced to the next slide.

"You may not be as familiar with this man. His name is Gil Kumar, a botanist at Berkeley who was nominated for the Nobel Prize for his work in applying CRISPR techniques in plant species. He disappeared several years before Kinkade."

Several of the agents began taking notes.

"Crisper?" said one of the agents quizzically.

"In simple terms," Klein continued, "CRISPR has revolutionized the industry of genetic engineering. It takes the mechanism bacteria use to fight viruses and applies it to fighting diseases in animals and humans. It has now developed to the point that scientists believe they can use it to create designer babies ... or extend life indefinitely."

The silence following Klein's "simple" explanation indicated that either the agents didn't understand it or were not certain they were in the right meeting.

"Finally," Klein added, advancing the projector again, "we have Paul Brooks. He went missing nine years ago."

"Why would you connect this missing person with the others when he went missing so long ago?" came a question from one of the agents.

"That's an excellent question, Robinson," Klein replied as he advanced the projector a final time, showing all three missing persons side by side. "What all these people have in common is a connection to The Center for New Beginnings in LA."

Klein went on to explain the levels of connection to the hospital for each person missing.

"Kinkade was responding to complaints within his community about the hospital and concerns they were poaching homeless people. He was pushing for an investigation by the state, and he had placed an initiative on the docket for debate in the next session of Congress. He had already lined up the necessary votes for sanctions against CNB and was buoyed by significant press attention to the matter. Kinkade was a competent sailor and scuba diver. On the day of his disappearance, the marine conditions off San Diego were pristine, with no significant weather events. The Coast Guard found the boat he rented, but no body. That is the kind of mystery you don't see very often. Our investigation is ongoing.

"Kumar was involved in doing research at the rehab hospital, running a series of clinical trials. These are generally very secretive activities as the clinical investigators want to protect their research and findings until they can be published. What is odd is that in ten years of research as a part-time employee there, he never published anything.

Then, he disappeared, and according to the hospital, he returned to India where he had family."

"Finally, Brooks was a contract employee that served as a temporary caregiver and home health aide for discharged patients. It got our attention when his parents reported him missing. The hospital claims he quit without giving notice."

By now all the agents were hastily jotting down notes while staring at the images on the screen, trying their best to memorize the faces.

"How do we get in there to, you know, look around?" came another question from the group.

"Obviously, we'd need a warrant, and we don't have probable cause or factual predication of any kind yet," Klein replied. "And there are some additional sensitivities to us being in that particular environment conducting an investigation."

Klein was referring to the strict safeguards on personal health information that governed the operation of healthcare facilities, especially in California. He did not want to blow his chance at breaking a case open only to be told, "that information is protected by the Health Insurance Portability and Accountability Act."

"At this point, we don't have enough to open an official investigation of this facility, but we *can* initiate an assessment." If anything, Klein was a man whose understanding of how to work the system was unassailable. He understood that FBI protocols evolved significantly since 9/11, which would allow him broad latitude, including surveillance, interviews, and even informant recruitment without having to file virtually any paperwork to justify allocation of resources.

"I'm sending two agents over there to meet the administrator and to get a feel for the place. His name is Dennis Spence," Klein said. "Felix, I'd like you to partner with Richard here and make that visit. No sense in Richard coming all this way for nothing."

Richard looked across to Felix Jordan, the sole black man in the room, and did his best to smile without making it look as if he was anything more than pleased to make an acquaintance. Both men knew that partnering to visit a facility was agency protocol for their protection, but this buddy system was only as good as the implied commitment each agent had to the other. Only an actual conflict would reveal whether that commitment was worth anything. Many agents would prefer to be free agents without the need to coordinate their schedule with anybody.

Felix was a large, stocky man who looked like he could have been a defensive back for a college football team. He allowed his eyes to roll in Richard's direction, but he did not betray any emotion being assigned to a rookie agent from the East Coast, as he would later describe Richard to his agency peers. Finally, he slowly turned his head in Richard's direction and gave a slight nod.

Klein observed the silent ritual of agent pairing to verify that his instructions were understood and accepted. He then continued.

"Let me be clear: We don't want to spook the guy, we just want to see how he responds to questions about our three missing individuals. Look for clues based on his responses and behavior. Try mirroring. Be alert but be careful. You won't be the first to go into a kissing booth convinced you wouldn't come out pregnant."

A few chuckles came in response to Klein's advice.

"What do we know about Mr. Spence?" Richard asked. He felt under some pressure to show he was fully engaged.

"Nothing," replied Klein. "And I mean, absolutely nothing. He doesn't have a digital footprint, and we cannot find any records on him from the state of California, not even a fucking driver's license, and no passport photo either. He's done an exceptional job flying under the radar, but that does not mean he's guilty of anything. Remember that. He's got the right to be invisible."

Klein appeared done with the topic.

As he was about to adjourn the meeting and dismiss the agents, an aide entered the room and handed him a small, pink slip of paper that was folded in half. Klein opened the paper expecting a message of an important call he would need to return. The expression on his face indicated otherwise.

"Well, men," he started out, "it appears we have another important development potentially affecting this case. Jack Reeves, a reporter from the CBS news affiliate in LA just contacted the agency. It seems his lady friend has gone missing."

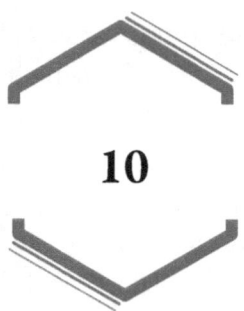

10

The bright sun rose above the city's skyscrapers, but Kim Ji-Sung did not see it directly. He was lying in an alley beneath a layer of crumpled newspaper. As he woke, his first instinct was to run his hands across his midsection to see if the stitches were still there, as they were when he was last awake, before he lost consciousness in the bathtub. He no longer felt the protruding threads of the hastily performed surgery, but his skin was coarse, bruised, and extremely sensitive. He remembered the phone call, the confusion he felt over the conversation with an unknown perpetrator, and the fact that promises were made if he were to complete some form of mission on behalf of the caller. Pushing up his body with his right elbow, he slowly perched himself up with his shoulder against the building behind him and swept the newspapers away to his side. He noticed several homeless men were in his company, lying not far from him behind what seemed to be a shopping mall.

He continued to push himself up until he was leaning completely against the building. He wore a weathered, green jacket over an LA Dodgers T-shirt and faded blue work pants, clothes he would never wear if given the choice. People were walking briskly past him in the general direction of the mall. He pushed his way forward in order that he might move away from the alley's residents and toward whatever was around the corner. As he began walking, he saw a river, and across from it, the most spectacular buildings he had ever seen.

Kim Ji-Sung had seen pictures of this place before; he was looking at the Huangpu River and The Bund, the historical and financial district of Shanghai that was home to some of the most creative architecture in China. Kim Ji-Sung had never been to Shanghai and it was a mystery to him how he ended up there at this moment. As he took in the view, he put his hand in his front pants pocket and found a small wad of bills. At least he could buy himself something to eat.

He continued walking toward the mall, while checking his other pockets. In his right-side pocket was a collection of documents, pushing against his chest. He pulled out a forged Chinese passport, an address in La Jolla, California and a plane ticket to Los Angeles International Airport on China Eastern Airlines for a nonstop flight leaving Shanghai at 10 that evening. He pushed the documents back into the pocket that held them originally. From his left-side pocket he pulled out a cell phone. Taped to the back of the phone was a USB memory stick.

Ji-Sung was a veteran agent and he understood instinctively that the memory stick would contain important details about his next mission. He also knew that the mission was controlled by a powerful agency that could destroy him if he did not succeed. But of all the potential next moves for him to consider, he concluded that nothing productive could be done until he had something to eat.

THE FORECAST IN LOS Angeles called for rain. At 7 in the morning, however, it was merely muggy and overcast. The gloomy conditions often burn off and give way to sunny skies. Today was not expected to be one of those days.

Richard waited outside Jeff McAuley's apartment complex as Felix Jordan pulled up in a black, late-model Ford Fusion, typical of the FBI fleet. He balanced a large, nearly overflowing file folder under his arm and nodded as Felix glided the car to the curb. With his free arm, he reached for the passenger side door.

"What the fuck is that?" Felix asked as Richard slid into the front seat, the folder's contents nearly falling out. While profanity was not tolerated at agency meetings, it flowed readily in the field.

"Just a bunch of unrelated documents I shoved in a folder. It's designed to intimidate a suspect. I saw it on an episode of NCIS."

Felix grimaced. Not only was he assigned a rookie, but a rookie who believes television could accurately portray the life of an FBI special agent. He tilted his head up almost imperceptibly and shook it slightly to indicate his disapproval. Richard was tempted to reply with a "look here, buddy" statement, but he understood his place in the pecking order and was anxious to soak up whatever knowledge he could about practical FBI techniques. Besides,

Felix looked like he could shut out anybody's lights with one blow.

The two sat silently for the first few miles, when Richard decided to break the ice. "Man, you are in terrific shape, what's your secret?"

Felix pondered the question for a few seconds.

"Well, apart from being a big motherfucker," he replied keeping a perfectly straight face, "I played left tackle at UCLA. You gotta keep the weight on while still being able to float like a butterfly and pound like a grizzly bear."

Richard gave a single nod while managing a smile. He could work with this guy.

The two continued in relative silence as they approached the institution. As they did, the skies darkened, and it began to sprinkle.

The Center for New Beginnings was on 240 acres of semi-rural land, about half the size of Disneyland. The enormous grounds provided an effective buffer between the main facility and the outside world. The facility sat in the center of the property at the top of a hill. Small gardens and benches dotted the grounds near the slightly inclined and winding road to the top of the hill. A grounds worker could be seen in the distance driving a lawn mower to a shed. The benches were empty.

It was an impressive campus, with a center building and two long wings off either side, creating a giant "C" shape. Behind the facility were more gardens and a farm where animals were housed in pens and barn-shaped structures. In front, the entrance was flanked by two pillars and a porte cochere that cars could drive underneath, which on this day would offer some shelter from the rain.

It would be difficult not to be drawn into the drama of approaching the facility, particularly with the rain falling somewhat consistently. Felix pulled under the overhang, put the car in park, then turned to Richard. "Look," he started out, "let's stick to the script here. We are on a fact-finding mission. We are not here to make a scene."

"Understood," Richard replied, clearly recognizing that, even without formal ranks, Felix was the agent with the most experience. Although at that point Richard realized he really did not know anything about Felix's background.

Inside, the agents saw an interior that looked spartan and dated, as if it had never been remodeled. The reception area in a cheap motel would have looked similar. A woman sat behind the counter, smiling.

"Good morning, gentlemen," she said with an air of professionalism that seemed a bit out of place at that moment. "I assume you are here to see Mr. Spence?"

"That's right," replied Felix. "We have an appointment."

"Yes, of course, we have been expecting you. Please, follow me."

The receptionist motioned the men to come behind the desk so they could access the hallways on either side of the main building. As they did so, a guard who had been sitting at a desk behind and to the right of reception stood up.

"Good morning, sir," he said, addressing Felix first, "we will have to ask you to leave any firearms here at reception."

Felix looked annoyed but not surprised. It was well-known to law enforcement that mental institutions and similar facilities were hypersensitive to the presence of weapons of any kind. Patients may overreact at seeing them, or worse, take advantage of an unsuspecting officer, assault him, and grab his weapon. Many officers did not understand the capacity of patients in a mental health hospital to represent a fatal threat.

Felix reached into his jacket and removed from his waistband his Glock 19M. He turned the gun around so the handle faced the guard, who took it and placed it on the table in front of him. The guard then looked directly at Richard, who similarly surrendered his weapon.

The guard placed each weapon in a separate bag. "These will be here waiting for you on your way out," he said as he placed them in his desk drawer and locked it. "Right this way, I'll take you to the administrator's office."

Felix and Richard followed the guard through a set of double doors. Richard instinctively started to observe and mentally record everything around him. He assumed Felix was doing the same. They were led down a corridor with various offices on each side. The walls on one side contained framed certificates, typical of a healthcare facility and dealing with accreditations earned and licensures. About halfway down the hall, the guard stopped just past a door on the left. He held his outstretched arm toward the door. The door had a plaque with the word "Administrator" on it.

"Here you go, gentlemen."

Felix and Richard stepped into another office with a receptionist's desk as the guard headed back to the lobby.

"Good morning, please take a seat," said the woman behind the desk. "I'll let Mr. Spence know that you are here."

The two men took seats against the office wall and continued their surveillance. The office was warm, with maroon, striped wallpaper and landscape oil paintings within massive wooden frames. There were no windows. A door behind the receptionist's large, wooden desk presumably led to the administrator's office.

The woman returned to her desk. "Mr. Spence will see you now," she said, standing and pointing to the door behind her.

Felix entered first, followed by Richard. A slight looking man in a three-piece suit was standing behind a massive desk, a window looking out on the courtyard was behind him.

"Good morning," he said. "I apologize for the mask, it's a requirement for those of us working with our patients."

The mask on Dennis Spence was indeed unfortunate; it made it impossible to establish a visual reference of a person who was already indistinguishable.

"Thank you," Felix replied as he and Richard took seats across Spence's desk. "My name is Felix Jordan, special agent, FBI."

"And I'm Richard O'Brien, special agent." Richard had waited a long time to be able to introduce himself in this manner.

Felix and Richard silently took in as many details as possible about the man opposite them.

Richard estimated that Spence was no more than five feet four inches tall. His suit was ill-fitting, as if he was underweight. His short, dark brown hair was immaculate, parted on one side. He had thin eyebrows and green eyes. He looked frail, but both agents knew not to underestimate him. While his facial expression behind the mask couldn't be seen, it was obvious that he was not in the mood to engage in small talk.

"Well, I assume you are not here to give me a parking ticket," he said, with a hint of sarcasm in his voice.

"No sir," Felix replied. "We'd like to ask you a few questions about people that have had some involvement with this institution. People that have since gone missing."

At that point Richard hoisted the file he had brought with him and placed it on his lap. The sound of the file landing caught Spence's attention, and he stared directly at it. If Richard had intended to intimidate Spence with that move, it worked. Spence continued to stare at the file.

Without adjusting his focus, he asked, "What people are you referring to?"

Felix leaned in ever so slightly to get a better look at Spence and to draw his attention from the file.

"So, most recently we have a young woman ..."

"I'm sorry, please excuse me a second," Spence interrupted as he pulled his phone from his vest pocket and quickly sent a text message.

"Sure," Felix replied, leaning back into the office chair.

"Please, proceed," Spence said, putting his phone on the desk in front of them.

As Felix observed Spence, something seemed off. Did he suffer from attention disorder? There was something awkward and quirky about him. He decided to pivot from his original line of questioning to something less direct, less threatening.

"Mr. Spence," he said, "what type of patients do you treat in this facility?"

Dennis Spence settled back into his chair, finally taking his attention away from the file.

"Gentlemen, are you familiar with the term dissociative fugue?"

"Dissociative what?" replied Richard, anxious to remain relevant.

"Fugue, dissociative fugue," Spence repeated. "It's a condition that is rarely reported but can occur for a variety of reasons. Several patients here suffer from this condition, which you may think of as a form of amnesia. It can often be reversed with treatment. That's an important part of what we do."

Felix immediately thought of shock treatment experiments that were highly controversial and considered unethical, but before he could resume his questioning, the aide that had been sitting outside entered the administrator's office.

"Mr. Jordan, there is a call for you," she said, interrupting the conversation. "You can take it in a spare office next door, you know, for privacy."

Felix appeared startled but was aware that his whereabouts were known to the chain of command and that he could be pulled from one case and put on another without being provided much advance notice. He wondered why he didn't get the call on his cell but got up anyway.

"Thank you," he said and followed the aide out the door and into the private office.

Richard's body was turned toward the door behind him as he watched Felix walk out. He snapped back to face Spence. As he did, Spence picked up the phone on his desk and pushed an extension.

"Anthony," he said into the receiver, "would you please bring some coffee in for our guests? Yes, I'll be right there, thank you, Anthony." He hung up the phone, reached for his cell phone, and stood up.

"Would you excuse me before we start up again?" Spence said, "we seem to have an incident with an unstable patient that I need to tend to very quickly. I'll be right back. Please, make yourself comfortable."

Spence slipped out a side door to the immediate right of his desk. As he left, a man walked in the front door, set down two cups of coffee on the table between the two guest chairs, and left.

Richard was now alone in his office, a bit startled at how conditions of the meeting had changed so quickly. On the other hand, he now had time to learn more about the mysterious administrator. He stood, grabbed a cup of coffee, and slowly walked to the far side of the office, looking for anything that might raise red flags.

Richard knew it was common for CEOs to post pictures with celebrities, high-ranking government officials, or others who would be recognizable. There were no such photos on the wall of Spence's office, just a few framed certificates commending the facility and its work. He slowly wandered behind the desk. On it, he saw a picture of two women in a warm embrace, taking a selfie. Richard grabbed the phone from his jacket pocket and took a picture of the framed photo.

"Did you find what you are looking for?" came a loud, stern voice from behind him. It was Dennis Spence; the space between his eyes narrowed in what was clearly an irritated state. His return through the side door caught Richard by surprise.

"Oh, sorry," Richard replied, standing straight up like a flagpole after having leaned over the photo frame. "Just standard procedure."

Exactly what procedure Richard was quoting would have put him in a tight spot if Spence were to challenge him.

"Please sit down," Spence said in a tone that indicated there was no other option.

Richard returned to his seat, grabbing the file he had placed on the coffee table and returning it to his lap.

Dennis Spence returned to his desk and stared at Richard. The space between his eyes seemed to return to normal.

"Everything okay with the disturbance?" Richard said, hoping to get the conversation back on track.

Spence didn't reply. He simply continued staring at Richard for what seemed to be an eternity. Finally, he spoke.

"You seem to have accumulated quite a file on our institution. What's in it?"

Richard opened the file and began moving documents from one side to another: a receipt from his dry cleaner, an old bank statement, and his apartment sublease.

"Oh, you know, just standard stuff, articles of incorporation, business license, community complaints."

At that moment, Richard realized he was looking at not one person on the other side of the desk but two men who were overlapping each other. As Spence stared at him, Richard stared back, trying to get the two images to collapse back into one. However, they remained fixed in position, vibrating slightly, one image overlapping the other, then moving slowly apart. Richard was familiar with this sensation from the various recreational drugs he used before taking the oath as an agent. However, he had never experienced the effects of N, N-Dimethyltryptamine, commonly referred to as DMT, a powerful hallucinogenic drug that occurs naturally in plants.

DMT is so dangerous that it is illegal to manufacture, possess, or purchase for recreational purposes, and it has no recognized medical purpose. It affects all the senses, confusing a person's thinking and ability to function. In aromatic form it can debilitate a person in just five minutes.

Richard's immediate instinct was to jump to his feet. He was in danger—he knew it with as much clarity as possible in a near comatose state of mind. As he jumped up, he lost balance and fell to the floor, hitting his head on the edge of Spence's desk on his way down. The contents of the file flew in all directions.

Dennis Spence slowly rose and walked around his desk to look at Richard, who lay face down on the carpet, arms and legs spread out. He stared at the papers on each side of Richard's body, the file folder peeking out from below his chest. Spence then stepped deliberately over Richard's body, and out the front door of his office. He walked directly to the front registration desk to complete the visitor's log indicating that Richard left the facility that morning at 8:45 a.m.

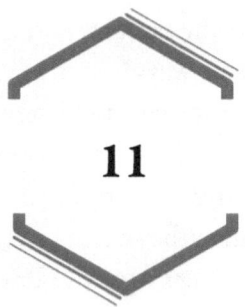

11

Felix Jordan slowly opened his eyes as he sat on the office floor, his back against the wall, legs spread apart, arms resting between them. Spots of blood dotted his otherwise clean white shirt. He was no longer wearing the suitcoat he had arrived in.

A woman was kneeling beside him, holding his wrist, and looking at her watch.

"How are you feeling, Mr. Jordan?"

Felix looked at the woman as she stood up. The back of his head was throbbing.

"You gave us a scare, Mr. Jordan, are you feeling all right?" the woman continued, "we were worried you had a concussion. Anyway, we've called an ambulance for you. You know you can't be too careful. They will be here any minute. Can you get up? Can you stand?"

The questions from the unidentified woman were coming too fast for Felix, who was still disoriented.

"Mr. Jordan?"

"What, what happened?" he managed.

"Oh, you were attacked from behind by one of our patients!" she said. "I'm one of the nurses here at the institution. It's a good thing Mr. Spence was able to

113

intervene and subdue the patient. Some of our residents can behave in unpredictable ways."

Felix was even more confused now. *Spence subdued a patient? How? He could not weigh more than 140 pounds.* A patient that could be subdued by Spence would have a hard time taking down a man the size of Felix Jordan.

"Where is my partner? Agent O'Brien?"

"Mr. O'Brien was here until just a few minutes ago. He was quite concerned about you. But once we called the ambulance, he said he was going to return to his office."

Felix looked at the surroundings, trying to piece together what had happened. The office was unremarkable. A cheap, brown desk had only a desk pad and phone on it, the handset was dangling from the side. There was a standard office chair; his suit jacket was lying across the back. He remembered walking into the room, but he did not recall the phone call that was waiting for him, nor did he remember removing his jacket. He instinctively ran his hand on the back of his head and felt a bandage.

"Now Mr. Jordan, don't mess with that or I'll have to redress it," the nurse said sternly. "I am going to get an orderly here that can help you into a wheelchair. Maybe we can get you out to the entrance before the ambulance arrives."

Felix was not listening to the nurse. He was still processing the scene. How could someone have snuck up on him without being noticed? And why did Richard leave the scene? That was just rookie behavior. He would have a word with him when he got back to the field office.

"You're a lucky man," came the voice from the hallway. It was Dennis Spence. "Now you know why we don't let you guys carry weapons in here. This could have ended very differently."

"I have some questions about what happened," Felix said.

"Sure. Once they have a look at you, we can reschedule with you and your partner."

With that, Spence disappeared, leaving Felix alone on the office floor.

FELIX JORDAN WENT DIRECTLY home after being discharged by the Emergency Department with what was diagnosed as a mild concussion. He had spent the better part of the day being poked, scanned, and tested. By the time he arrived back in San Diego, it was nearly 11 p.m. His wife had been texting him constantly, for hours, his teenage daughter was involved in some new drama with her boyfriend, and his son was about to miss returning home before his curfew.

It was Friday night and the last thing Felix wanted to do was to speak with Richard, although he did send him a text message asking that Richard confirm the story he was told at CNB. He never heard back, but his attention promptly moved to his own recovery, which he tried to accommodate with alcohol disguised as self-medication. He would submit his field report on Saturday and go to church on Sunday. Apart from that, he had no intention to think about work or Richard O'Brien.

But Sarah Goodman *was* thinking about Richard. The two talked every few days, and by Sunday, Sarah started to worry. She had sent him a "miss you" on Friday, but according to her phone, he never read the message. He also did not return her call on Saturday. As an agent herself, Sarah Goodman knew when to suspect something was wrong. And she knew Richard was uniquely capable of getting himself into trouble.

On Monday morning, she called the LA field office to see if Richard was there, prodding and leveraging her credentials as a special agent in the Detroit office. *He's in the field*, she was told. *On assignment in San Diego but coming back to LA shortly*, they said. It did not make sense to her. Her next call would be to Jeff McAuley, Richard's roommate. It was 12:30 Eastern Standard Time.

"Hi Sarah, Richard has not been in the office today," explained McAuley. "He went out on assignment with another agent on Friday, but the two were separated, and we've not heard from O'Brien. Mind you, it's only 9:30 here; maybe he's running late."

"Is the other agent in?" Sarah asked.

"Agent Jordan? Yeah, he's in with the boss."

"Well, did you see him this weekend?" Sarah asked, feeling a bit maternalistic.

"Honestly, Sarah, we run in opposite directions sometimes," McAuley replied. "He might have been in the apartment, but frankly, I wasn't around much."

Sarah imagined an apartment with two male roommates: broken potato chips littering the sofa, unwashed dishes in the sink, with empty beer cans and pizza boxes on the coffee table. She thanked McAuley, hung up, and went online to purchase tickets to LAX.

THOUGHTS OF DESPAIR began to creep into Richard's psyche as he saw the door close. He looked down at his feet. They were held to the sides of the bed with restraints. His right hand was restrained as well. All he could do was move his left hand to grab and eat the toast or drink the coffee that the nurse's aide had just left for him.

Remember your training, he thought, although simply forming thoughts was a challenge because he was obviously drugged. *Your training! Your training!* he thought again. He closed his eyes and tried to transport himself mentally back to the Academy and the program he attended on "Surviving Extended Detainment."

"When you are detained by the enemy, you will experience a range of emotions, on either end of despair," said the lecturer, an expert in field operations and combat strategies. "The key is to keep yourself on the positive end of that spectrum."

"The first step is to establish some form of mental awareness," he said. "The goal is to keep it simple. If you are being subjected to torture or drug therapy, you need a simple system for remaining *in the present,* so you are ready to take advantage of a situation where you might gain the advantage and possibly escape.

"I am going to give you one word that will be the foundation of this system: PACKMEN. How many letters are in PACKMEN?"

Although it sounded like a trick question, one of the NATs offered "Seven."

"That's right," the instructor replied. "And how many days in a week?"

"Seven," came the answer from another NAT. No one could argue with the simplicity of the questions so far, Richard thought then, sitting in the fifth row back from the lecturer.

"What we know from behavioral science is that it can be very difficult to remember the day of the week even when you are not in the stressful situation of being detained for an extended period. PACKMEN will help you keep yourself grounded. It's a simple game you will play every day."

Richard could see where this was going. He played similar games when he was smoking weed and could not remember the last thing that was said to him. During those intense highs, he felt the equivalent of a dog trying to chase his tail, desperately trying to remember what he said, thought, or heard so that he could continue to function in the presence of others without giving away the fact that he was not 100 percent there.

The instructor continued: "You'll find it easier to remember the letter representing the day, than the actual day. One letter. Each letter in PACKMEN is unique and not repeated so there is no risk of getting confused. Easy peasy. This will help train your brain when it would otherwise want to give up."

The instructor paused to gauge his audience. The NATs were highly intelligent and engaged in the topic, recognizing the value of the subject matter.

"Next, you'll remember one number. Once you've reached the end of the word PACKMEN, you'll remember the number of weeks you've been detained. If possible, you can etch roman numerals somewhere to help count the weeks, like John McCain did when he was a prisoner in Vietnam for five and a half years. So you only EVER need to remember one letter and one number. Dickerson, if I am on C2 today, how long have I been detained?"

Mickey Dickerson paused for a moment, then shouted from the back of the room, "Two weeks, three days?"

"That's right," the instructor replied. "Like I said, easy peasy."

"One last thing," the instructor said. "To give your brain even more exercise, after you establish the letter representing today, pick one emotion you are feeling, or one word that represents the day in general. Build out a sentence if you can during the week. That way, when you are free, you have a construct you can return to that will help during the debriefing with the agency and potentially reveal important intelligence about the environment you were in. And yet you only had to remember a few words."

"So in review, one word, PACKMEN, one letter and one number, and one-word description per letter. Think of it as a survival kit."

A question came from another NAT, "What happens if we are detained more than fifty-two weeks?"

The instructor hesitated, looking uncomfortable.

"You start to pray, instead," came the response from Jeff McAuley, sitting next to Richard.

Richard opened his eyes. The PACKMEN strategy was a perfect fit for his current dilemma. Today was P1, he thought to himself, and he needed one word starting with "P" to describe his emotions. He did not need much time to complete his assignment for the day.

"Pissed," he said aloud.

EMMA WAS THUMBING THROUGH her TikTok feed when she stopped at the image of an elderly man sitting cross-legged on the floor and reading a book aloud; he never looked up at the camera. The book was oversized and had a bright pink cover. He was surrounded by stuffed animals and in front of a bookshelf in what looked like a nicely appointed playroom for toddlers. The whole setup would be considered absurd if it weren't so effective at concealing its true purpose.

If you wanted to send encrypted messages on a dynamic social media platform that would leave no significant digital footprint and never be discovered, you would find no solution as effective as TikTok. The platform has been downloaded over 2.5 billion times, had over 1 billion active users, and was growing exponentially. At any given minute users could access the equivalent of 200 million hours' worth of video. A message to or from an agency's clandestine network could hide in plain sight on the TikTok platform, making it an effective complement to more common encrypted chat platforms like Signal or Threema.

It was inevitable that Emma's handlers would be determined to learn more about her message following the Kolins lecture. The secret to regeneration was, after all, the holy grail to sustaining the human condition, the first step to creating an indestructible army because the soldiers would be impervious to permanent injury. She knew without being asked that she would be expected to procure samples from Kolins's lab.

"We will send you an Angel, said the Wizard to Emily," the man said in Chinese. "You must assist this Angel to find the missing ingredients for our potion that we can wake the princess from the evil spell put on her. The Angel will need your help—the Angel is not one of us. Will you please help the Angel?"

Not one of us, Emmalee thought. She knew exactly what this meant. Her agency was sending her a captured North Korean.

RICHARD OPENED HIS eyes and stared at the four slender fluorescent bulbs above him, integrated into the ceiling tiles. *I'm still here*, he thought to himself. But did he sleep through the night? Is today P1 or A1? His body was telling him that today was A1, and he was in agreement. He surveyed the room, as sterile looking an environment as he'd ever seen. White ceiling, walls, and linoleum floor. A window over his left shoulder, with security bars on the outside to prevent escape. To his left, a sink and mirror were attached to the wall. To his right, a simple office chair next to an inside door that led to a toilet. He recalled vaguely having an aide helping him into the toilet the night before.

He looked down at his legs and noticed that he was no longer restrained. He swung his legs off the bed and decided to see if he could stand on his own. His legs were weak, mostly from lack of significant exercise lately, and his head was foggy, as if he was hung over from a night of partying. He was certain that he was not recently in the partying mood. As he stood, he noticed he was still wearing a hospital gown and a pair of slippers were next to the bed. He slipped them on his feet and walked to the door. It was unlocked. He walked into the hallway.

To his left was a short hallway leading to a corner. He did not want to walk around the corner, only to be taken back to his room or worse, punished for leaving it. To the right, the hallway included multiple doors that he presumed were rooms for other "patients." At the end of the hallway was light from outside the facility. It was an exit. This was the direction he would be heading.

Richard did not take the time to consider what was behind each door he passed. His room, 3B, was next to 4C, 5D, then 6E and so on. Each door had a tiny window with reinforced glass to prevent injury if it was smashed from either side. Richard would not be looking inside any rooms today, although most doors were at least partially open. Next to each door was a card hanging from the wall with notes from the staff responsible for whoever was inside. Richard would not be examining these either. Instead, he was singularly focused on reaching the exit.

He pushed open the door and found himself in the hospital's courtyard. The facility had two wings connected by a central administration area at one end. Richard surmised at this point that the administrative area must have been in the other direction of the hallway he entered, around the corner from his room. Across the courtyard he could see the other wing and, in the huge gap between the two, a parklike area with thin trails, small trees and bushes, and benches that patients could use as part of their daily exercise and meditation. Two diagonal paths crossed in the center of the courtyard, creating a giant X; the end of each X offered entry back into either end of each wing.

"Good morning, Mr. B." Richard was startled and turned around to see a young man in uniform behind him. "Good to see you up and about. We were worried about you."

Richard looked the man up and down. The uniform indicated the young man was some sort of security guard, but Richard did not recognize the company and had never seen him before.

"My name ... my name is Richard," he replied.

"Yes," the guard said, "we heard about that. It's okay, Mr. B, you're in good hands now. The staff will get you back on the right path soon, you'll see. Anyway, enjoy the grounds, and I'll see you around." The guard walked away toward the other wing, with Richard just staring at him, confused.

Richard gained enough confidence now that he felt he could safely explore the rest of the grounds and hopefully find someone who could explain why he was being held here. He started on the diagonal path toward the other wing and arrived at the corner connecting the far wing with the administrative building. A sign on the door to the opposite wing read "Authorized Personnel Only," but the other door into the administration building had no such sign, so Richard went inside.

He found himself in a large community-type meeting room with a variety of round tables holding half-finished puzzles and others with board games. On the side of the room were bins containing additional games, books, and blankets. Patients were roaming around, many acting as if they were in a mental fog. Some patients were sitting and staring out into space, others were rocking in place. One was standing and speaking loudly in an incoherent rant as if he were giving a speech to an invisible audience. A series of old arcade games and pinball machines sat unused on one side of the room.

The room had several windows facing the courtyard that provided a view of farmland in the distance, beyond the facility grounds. Several patients in wheelchairs were positioned at the window, staring into their own personal abyss. Most had blankets on their laps, their hands resting on top.

Among the younger patients Richard noticed something else: They all had a buzzed haircut, leaving their scalps visible.

Richard was immediately reminded of scenes from *One Flew Over the Cuckoo's Nest*. Richard became nervous. *Is that where I am?* This was most definitely NOT a good situation.

THE AGENTS FILED INTO the San Diego branch main conference room on Monday at 10:30 in the morning with a sense of urgency that signaled the critical nature of the situation: One of their own had gone missing. Ben Klein, Felix Jordan, and additional blue suits pulled up chairs to the large white table in the center of the room. The mood was serious, and all eyes were on Klein, who stood at the front of the room.

"Good morning. Our last contact with Special Agent O'Brien was on Friday. He had joined Agent Jordan here on a routine visit to The Center for New Beginnings in Whittier. Agent Jordan, please summarize the report you filed."

Special Agent Jordan could be forgiven for his embarrassment at that moment. As he recounted the incident, the assault, and losing track of his partner, he felt the gaze of his fellow agents and presumed they were judging him and holding him at least partially responsible. Jordan, on the other hand, felt completely responsible.

"When I regained consciousness," Jordan concluded, "I was told that O'Brien had left the facility, and I took that at face value. But I also checked the visitor log on the way out and saw him as having signed out. I later realized..."

"Okay, Jordan," Klein interrupted him. "Thank you." Klein was not interested in capitalizing on Jordan's guilt. It wasn't productive, and it wasn't the kind of leader Klein wished to be.

"What else do we have? Anybody?" Klein continued.

"Sir, we have a picture sent by O'Brien by text at about oh-nine-forty that day. It's a picture of two women, and it's on an office desk. They appear to be on a beach, you know, on vacation or something."

Jordan was not aware that O'Brien had the presence of mind to gather intelligence while in the office of Dennis Spence, and he leaned into the table. Perhaps he was a competent agent after all.

A voice came bellowing in from the speakerphone in the center of the room. "Do we know the identities of these women?" It was Sarah Goodman, who apart from Klein, had the most field experience in these types of investigations. She was participating remotely from an FBI satellite office within the Detroit airport as she waited for her flight to board. "Have you run them through FACE?"

FACE was an acronym for Facial Analysis, Comparison, and Evaluation, which the FBI used in its investigations. FACE utilizes an algorithm to reveal patterns not detectable to the naked eye. In the ten years since FACE was implemented, it had evaluated over 10,000 subjects with accuracy as high as 85 percent. Software upgrades continued to improve the platform.

"We have the photo in the biometrics division now and they will run it through FACE, as well as IPS, just in case," Klein said. IPS, the interstate photo system, was used mostly by local law enforcement, and it compared new photos to existing mug shots.

"Sir, I'd like to go back in there," Jordan added. "The longer we wait, the harder it will be to find him."

"Me too, sir," another agent said. It was Jeff McAuley. "Sir, we already passed seventy-two hours."

Klein was familiar with the significance of the seventy-two-hour mark. Although data was scarce, it was understood that the difficulty in finding a missing person grew exponentially after this time. Ninety-four percent of missing children are recovered within that time frame. Few survived afterward.

"I'm well aware of the situation," Klein replied. "That's why we are moving this operation to LA immediately. I've arranged with the director that we'll continue with the case from there. In the meantime, we will be securing a search warrant."

The team seemed dissatisfied with Klein's response, and as the words left his mouth, he felt the same.

"Jordan and McAuley, I want you to get over to CNB to initiate surveillance. Advise local law enforcement that we don't attract any unwanted attention."

Jordan and McAuley glanced at each other with looks of mutual commitment, then gave a brief nod back to Klein.

"That's all for now," Klein added. "I'll see the rest of you in the LA office at sixteen hundred hours. You better get moving. Traffic on the I-5 won't get any better from here on out."

RICHARD WOKE UP AGAIN staring at the four fluorescent bulbs in the ceiling of room 3B. He pushed his butt back and to sit up. But as he did so, he felt weak and disoriented, as if he was coming off an intense high.

Like a bad movie where a character awakens from suspended animation, Richard had many questions but few answers. A sense of desperation set in. Was he going crazy? Was he already crazy? Was he ever, in fact, an FBI agent? And what day was it anyway? A1? C1?

An aide walked into his room carrying a tray. The aide was wearing a clinic-type uniform. He was in his thirties, nearly six feet tall, fit, and probably capable of putting down most any disturbance.

"Good morning," he said.

"Why am I here?" Richard asked, hoping for a piece of the puzzle.

"You are here for your protection," the aide said as he laid the tray on an aluminum cart and wheeled it over to the bed.

"Protection?" Richard replied. "Why do I need protection?"

"Seriously?"

"Yes, seriously." Richard was losing his patience.

The aide finished positioning the tray over Richard's midsection. It contained a sandwich, soup, and water in a covered Styrofoam cup. He reached down to Richard's right arm, which was resting at his side, and gently picked it up, turning the wrist toward Richard.

"This is why."

Richard was horrified. His wrist had five stitches going across it, a telltale sign of someone who had attempted to take his own life. He just stared at his arm, confused. *How is it that I never noticed this before?*

"This is ...," he couldn't get any more words out.

"Don't worry about it," the aide said. "It's more common than you think."

12

Richard was not yet aware of the fact that he was being drugged, and yet he felt like his mind was slowly disintegrating. The last time he felt this way was when he experimented with nitrous oxide, in other words, "whippets." However, in that case the sensation only lasted a few seconds. This sensation was persistent.

After finishing his meal, he left his room, this time turning left. Around the corner, he saw administrative offices with nameplates such as Director of Admissions and Director of Catering. All the doors were closed, and the hallway was quiet. About halfway down the hall, to the left, was the official entrance to the facility. A large lobby area with significant security made it clear that Richard should not even try to leave. He stared at the entrance. It looked familiar. He had come this way before, but he struggled to recall the details. To his right was the entrance to the community room. He went inside.

As before, the room was buzzing with activity, but most of it nonsensical by nearly anyone's standards. Richard surveyed the room. Most of the patients were downright frightening, either by way of their behavior or their appearance. Only one man appeared approachable, sitting in a wheelchair and staring out at the courtyard. Richard walked to the window, grabbed a plastic chair, and sat down next to him.

"Good morning," he said to the man, hoping for a response that would reveal he was not insane. The man simply turned toward him and smiled. He had silver hair, looked frail, and slouched back in his chair.

"My name is Richard, but for some reason, they call me Mr. B," he continued.

"Very nice to meet you, my name is Dr. Z."

"Why do they call you Dr. Z?"

"I have no idea, you would have to ask Denise."

"Who is Denise?"

"Denise," he replied, "Denise is the director of this facility."

"No," Richard countered, "the director is Dennis, Dennis Something."

"Is that what she told you?" the old man said, smiling.

"Dr. Z, how long have you been here?" Richard said, changing the subject.

"I am not sure," he replied, "but I believe I have been here longer than many people here have been alive."

"That's interesting," said Richard, "how old are you?"

"Denise says I will soon be 110 years old."

Richard figured he was probably speaking to another one of the crazies, as this man did not look like he could be much more than seventy and certainly not older than eighty.

"How is it possible you could be 110?" he asked, deciding to test how the old man could defend his claim.

"Out there," he said, lifting his right arm and pointing toward the garden outside the window. "Because of what is out there."

"Dr. Z!" came a voice from behind the two men. It was a female aide.

"Dr. Z, is this young man bothering you?" she said, smiling.

Richard felt the interruption was intentional, just as he was making some progress.

"It's time for your treatment, Dr. Z, let's go. I'll wheel you back to your room. Say goodbye to Mr. B."

The old man lifted his left arm and pointed it toward Richard.

"Goodbye, young man, it was nice to meet you."

"PLEASE HELP ME." JI-Sung was standing at Emma's apartment door. She grabbed him by the arm and pulled him inside, quickly shutting the door. He looked tired and dehydrated.

"Please," he repeated.

Emma looked him over. He wore the soiled, army green jacket and blue cargo pants that he had been wearing since being pulled from the bathtub. His hair was disheveled, and he had tired eyes. It was clear he was exhausted. And a little scared. He reeked of perspiration.

"Oda," she said, motioning Ji-Sung to follow her. Her limited Korean language skills were not going to help her much with this agent, she surmised, so she positioned him in front of her computer to use its translation capability. Ji-Sung handed her the memory stick he had found in his pocket a day earlier, and Emma pushed it into the USB port of her computer. Before even examining the contents, she copied the material to her hard drive.

For the next hour, they worked at communicating, with Emma providing instructions to Ji-Sung on what he must accomplish on behalf of the Ministry of State Security, China's principal spy agency, as detailed on the memory stick. She gave him a map of the region and a train schedule, then explained the transit system and how to get himself over to The Center for New Beginnings. She showed him on a hand drawn map where she believed that Denise stored her research documentation on how botanical compounds, combined with CRISPR agents, would suspend the process of aging. She never expected that he would be able to get as far as Denise's office, but for the sake of the larger mission, she needed to express optimism. If he did succeed and returned to her as instructed, she could take whatever he stole, and send him back to Beijing.

"How will I get home to my family once this is over?" Ji-Sung asked in various forms during the conversation.

"They have not told me anything about that," Emma would reply. "However," she added, to keep him engaged, "they will take care of you as they have taken care of me."

Then, she gave him a bar of soap and a towel and pushed him into the bathroom. She put out a bowl of fruit, coffee, tea, and water for him for when he would emerge. By the time he did, Emma had already left for her appointment with George Kolins.

Ji-Sung fell asleep on Emma's sofa for several hours.

AS HE MADE HIS WAY back to his room, Richard continued surveillance of the facility that had imprisoned him. Most of the doors to patient rooms were either completely or partially open. This served a dual purpose; patients felt less like prisoners if they could see outside their room, and staff could get to the patients quickly if needed. Richard glanced into each door as he walked past. If the room was occupied, it was usually by an older patient lying in bed or propped up, watching the television that hung from the wall.

As he approached his room on the left, he saw a door partially closed on the right. He slowed down to ensure he could see what or who was inside. What he saw made him stop in his tracks, directly outside the door.

Inside, he saw the backside of a young woman. She was wearing only panties and looking in the mirror above the sink at the far side of the room. She was brushing her teeth, and as she did, her breasts swayed from side to side, briefly revealing themselves to Richard. She had a dragon tattoo on her right shoulder. Richard could not look away; he was captivated by the sight of this woman and significantly turned on.

As she looked in the mirror, Harmony noticed Richard standing outside the room. She had long ago dispensed with any inhibitions of being seen topless and was proud of her figure. So when she noticed Richard staring at her, she took her time finishing the task and, without turning around, shouted, "Are you just going to stare, or are you going to introduce yourself?"

Richard was immediately embarrassed and stepped out of view of the doorway.

"Oh, sorry, I mean, yeah sure. Do you want to put something on first?"

"Would you like me to put something on?" Harmony replied. "Okay, you don't have to answer that."

Harmony grabbed the shirt on her bed, threw it on, and opened the door fully, revealing Richard still standing outside. She leaned against the doorframe, smiling.

"Hi," she said, "my name is Harmony, but for some reason they call me Ms. D." Harmony reached out to shake Richard's hand.

"How do you know your name is really Harmony?" Richard asked, holding her hand gently.

Harmony twisted Richard's hand under hers, revealing another tattoo, on the underside of her wrist, with her name emblazoned across it.

"Let's just say I'm pretty sure," she replied. "What's your name?"

"They are calling me Mr. B, and it's really pissing me off," Richard replied. "I think my name is Richard."

"Well, Mr. B Richard," Harmony said, "I can see why they put you here." She was still holding Richard's hand and looking at the stitches over his wrist. Richard instinctively yanked his hand away.

"Look, I ...," he started to say before Harmony put her finger to his lips.

"Don't worry," she said, "I know. This is some sick, demented circus we've joined."

Richard was whipped. This woman was gorgeous, confident, and clever.

"Why are you here?" he said.

"They told me that I suffered an overdose of oxycodone," she replied. "It's bullshit."

Harmony peeked outside the door frame and looked in both directions before pulling Richard fully into the room.

"Look," she continued, "this place is not what it seems. I think they have been collecting people off the streets for years. The people running this place refuse to talk about what they do here. They grabbed me because I was exposing them on social media. I am not sure what their game is, but when I get out of here ... hey, are you listening to me?"

Richard was having a hard time absorbing all that Harmony was throwing at him. He had a deer-in-the-headlights stare in Harmony's direction. Part of the problem was that the drugs were having an impact, and part was that he was smitten by Harmony, thinking that a thin piece of fabric was all that separated him from the parts of her body that he could not see.

"Yeah, I mean, I'm not sure," he managed to get out. He felt he needed to get back to his room or he might vomit right in front of his new love interest.

Harmony understood. She had streamed enough crime thrillers on her phone to have been suspicious of the food and medicine from the beginning, and worked hard to avoid allowing the drugs in her system. Having a bulimic friend that would routinely purge her stomach helped Harmony to develop her own defense.

"Look, baby, it's the drugs. You need to go sleep it off," she said.

"What are you talking about?" Richard replied, although in the back of his mind he was already beginning to understand.

"You need to avoid eating anything soft, you know, sandwiches and soups that they've laced with drugs. Stick with the cookies and crackers. Trust me, you'll be hungry but you'll avoid the hot mess they want you to step into."

Richard continued to stare at Harmony. He wondered if the drugs were also making him incredibly attracted to Harmony, or if she was just a hot mess on her own.

"Listen," she continued, "I know what room you're in. Go take a nap. I'll bring you something later tonight."

Whatever Harmony had in mind, Richard was all in.

"LET ME SHOW YOU SOMETHING," Kolins said, motioning Emma to the counter where the microscope was sitting. The two stood side by side in the laboratory on the third floor of the Terasaki Life Sciences Building. A few students were milling around the room as bright sunlight pushed past the white venetian blinds that ran across all windows on the west side of the building, protecting the sensitive equipment from the afternoon sun.

This laboratory was quite similar to the lab in San Diego, she noticed, with three long white countertops running parallel across the length of the huge room. Each counter had a similar setup, including microscopes, centrifuges, and pipetting equipment. Sterile petri dishes were stacked between each piece of equipment.

"Take a look," he continued, pointing to the microscope while pulling over a rolling stool in front of the counter where he stood. As she approached, Kolins opened a small container next to the scope, about the size of a dorm refrigerator. He pulled a slide from the inside of the container and slid it onto the microscope's base.

Emma stepped in front of Kolins, sat on the stool, and leaned into the scope.

"What am I looking for?" she asked. For all Emma's talents, she had nowhere near the understanding of what her doctoral studies would suggest. At her core, she was simply a competent spy.

"Do you see those cells vibrating?" he asked excitedly.

Emma concentrated on the image inside the scope, narrowing her eyes slightly to improve her focus.

"Yes, yes, what is causing them to do that?"

"They are recovering from injury, my dear," Kolins replied, not even trying to conceal his pride. "These are liver cells."

Emma knew enough about liver cells to appreciate what Kolins was showing her. The liver is one of the most complex organs in the body, and many experiments were focused on growing a liver from stem cells. In 2022, British scientists announced they had grown a mini-liver from stem cells the size of a small coin. So unless Kolins had taken this work to the next level, he was hardly in front of any important new developments.

"Ah, okay," she replied, waiting for Kolins to expand further. She did not have to wait long.

"We beat the crap out of these cells," Kolins said, trying to reduce his typically arrogant way of talking into something that a student might say. "By all accounts, these cells should be inert, non-functioning, deceased. But not only are they functioning, they are repairing, rejuvenating, and replicating."

"Replicating?" Emma said.

"Yes, replicating," he replied. "We have succeeded in growing an organ larger than it has any right to be. This amounts to germline editing on steroids."

Emma slowly pulled back from the microscope to look directly at Kolins.

"Professor, have you—"

"No, I've not," he said quietly, interrupting Emma and recognizing she could easily surmise the next step to be clinical trials on human subjects.

"This work is not ready for peer review," he said with as serious an expression as he could muster. "We are still validating the long-term viability of the germline editing process we employed. I need you to keep this on the down-low, as they say. I can't have you get into details in the piece you want to publish. Promise me that I did not make a mistake inviting you here."

Emma also changed her expression.

"Oh, of course, Dr. Kolins," she replied. "Your secret is safe with me."

As Kolins pulled back and expected Emma to follow him back to his office, she scanned the lab environment one more time to gather as many clues as possible that could be relayed to her handlers. She noticed a large refrigerator in the corner of the lab, similar to those used at the Salk Institute.

"Is that where you store the CRISPR reagent?" she asked.

Kolins pursed his lips and put an index finger on top of them.

"Shhhh," he said quietly as he continued back to his office.

"SHE'S INCREDIBLE, BUT she's taking too long," Dennis said to Emma over the phone. "And besides, I have all the necessary resources." By "she," Dennis was referring to Martine Rothblatt, founder of Terasem. By "resources," he was referring to human bodies for experimentation.

Born in Chicago in 1954, Martin Rothblatt became an immensely successful entrepreneur and transgender rights advocate. In 1990, Rothblatt founded SiriusXM and multiple other satellite and communications companies. In 1994, at age forty, Rothblatt came out as transgender, changed his name to Martine, and in 1996 had sex reassignment surgery. Rothblatt eventually became the most highly paid female in the U.S. as CEO of United Therapeutics, a $6 billion biotech firm.

In 2014, Rothblatt founded Terasem, an organization dedicated to exploring technical immortality by blending digitization of memories with nanotechnology. The organization's goal was to create a conscious surrogate of a person by combining detailed data about them in a software application. The organization's website claimed its vision was to support creation of "a conscious analog to the human mind that can be downloaded into a biological or nanotechnological body to provide life experiences comparable to those of a typically birthed human."

Rothblatt's Terasem was roundly criticized as a fairy tale, a pursuit more concerned with creating humans that don't exist in the traditional sense rather than addressing the suffering of humans and the animal kingdom today. Still, organizations like Terasem collected several million dollars in donations from generally eccentric industrialists and celebrities, including, ironically, Howard Steele. When Elon Musk declared in 2021 that his Optimus robot could accommodate the consciousness of a human being, the world started paying attention to what was previously the domain of people with overactive imaginations.

Denise had been paying attention to Terasem from the moment that her father started to accommodate various "transhumanists" on the back patio of his Malibu home. Transhumanists believe that the current limitations of human existence could be overcome through emerging technologies. Howard Steele, like many of the uber-rich, took interest in these fringe interest groups. He had already paid for cryogenic storage of his remains in anticipation of "Howard 2.0."

Small groups of believers would sit with Steele on his back patio overlooking the Pacific Ocean, spinning stories of what the future would be like, a future that Steele desperately wanted to be part of.

"Human beings as we know them will cease to exist," said the visitor who was part bohemian and part venture capitalist. "Mr. Steele, your mind is one that needs to be part of this movement. Preservation of your great mind will ensure these technologies, and this movement will sustain itself."

Steele, who built his successful empire on the practical application of cutting-edge technologies, would be a perfect target, or sucker, for investment, as he was arrogant enough to believe his life was worth extending at any cost. He had ample financial resources to put toward the endeavor, and more than one group of transhumanists left his property with a six- or seven-figure check in hand. Steele was counting on at least one of them to succeed and had secured himself a guaranteed transformation if and when these experiments proved successful.

Dennis was understandably impressed by Rothblatt. Apart from her impressive career, she followed her heart and underwent gender transformation therapy. Dennis was doing the same. The fact that Dennis was going in the opposite direction was hardly relevant.

But Rothblatt's Terasem was not pursuing any promising experiments. Instead, it was diversifying into a collection of smaller ventures: a foundation that collected and stored "mindfiles" from hopeful transhumanists, a charity whose purpose was to educate the public on the practicality of extending human life, and a neo-religious entity to bring a measure of cohesiveness and belonging to its "Joiners." To the casual observer, it was like a complex and convoluted science fiction plot.

"It's a lot of stirring but no gravy," Dennis complained. He was not content to merely stir things up, he was bent on rewriting the rules.

"WHAT WE ARE DEALING with here is potentially the most dangerous type of individual," said Dr. Patricia Novicoff, an FBI psychologist who profiled some of the agency's suspects and persons of interest. "Here is somebody that is willing to do anything to keep power and to achieve recognition."

Novicoff was brought in at the request of Ben Klein to assess Dennis Spence and the situation at CNB and for advice on how best to infiltrate the facility without risking potential harm to Richard O'Brien, presuming he was still alive and being held there. Klein and Novicoff were both standing at the front of the conference room in the LA field office. It was now 4 in the afternoon on Monday.

"Thanks, Pat," said Klein, who turned his attention to his agents. "We have learned a lot about Dennis Spence in the past few hours, a man that has no past because he essentially did not exist. Most of his credentials are fabricated."

The agents in the room were taking copious notes. Jordan and McAuley were dialed in from their vehicle en route to CNB. Sarah Goodman had just arrived at the Los Angeles airport and was dialed in via videoconference from the FBI field office inside.

"First of all," Klein continued, "we now suspect that Dennis Spence was formerly Denise Spencer, the daughter of Natalie Spencer, who was married to Howard Steele. She went missing about twenty years ago, and because she did not have any family, there was never much pressure or incentive to learn what happened to her. Nobody ever filed a missing persons report for her."

Next, Klein put up on the screen behind him a picture of Dennis Spence next to a picture of Denise Spencer. The resemblance was undeniable.

"That's her in the picture sent over by Agent O'Brien, next to another woman that we've not yet identified. Your forensics team did an artificial aging analysis based on the last photo of Denise, and the congruence with the image in the photo is over 90 percent."

"Why is she—or he—so dangerous?" asked Sarah, looking to either Novicoff or Klein for a response.

"Well," Novicoff replied, "you have impulsive criminals, and you have those that plan out their crimes, you know, like the Zodiac killer, BTK, and others. Spence is in the latter camp. His motivation is less from greed than need."

"Need what?" came another question.

"That is what we don't know yet," Novicoff replied. "When we cannot derive motive, we need to look at what the suspect is doing and how they are doing it. We cannot presume to understand the motive of someone who is essentially sociopathic."

"What makes you think Spence is sociopathic?" This time it was Klein, who turned to face Novicoff.

"Look, there is speculation that Spence is picking up homeless people off the street, and we don't know why. It's not like he is rehabilitating them and returning them to society. And if this is true, he needs to be taken into custody irrespective of O'Brien's disappearance." Novicoff began to feel like she was not helping the investigation as much as she could. Spence was indeed a puzzle.

A louder-than-necessary announcement came blasting through the speakerphone.

"Maybe he hates homeless people and wants to eliminate them, you know, like a mattanza." It was McAuley, who made the comment because he could never resist the temptation to introduce surfing or nautical terms whenever the opportunity presented itself.

"A what?"

"Mattanza," he repeated as an on-site agent turned down the volume on the conference room speakerphone. "It's an Italian fishing technique where you guide all the fish in one place, you know, to slaughter them."

The other agents looked at each other in disbelief. It was true that many residents of Los Angeles would support almost any policy to reduce the number of homeless people on the streets, but McAuley's idea was more movie plot than reality.

"You know what they say," Novicoff said sarcastically, "for every complex problem there is a solution that is clear, simple, and wrong."

"But what about Occam's Razor?" McAuley pushed back. "The simple theory is the preferred theory."

By now the agents were beginning to wonder what kind of bohemian specimen this rookie really was. Jordan's left hand was cradling his forehead as he shook his head in frustration at his partner, but he was also navigating the car across California Route 60, which required his full attention. "McAuley is a piece of work," one agent muttered under his breath. Agents were typically, by design and behavioral profile, unexcitable: collect clues, assess risk, and complete missions. They were not inclined to engage in extended intellectual banter.

Klein had enough of the back and forth between Novicoff and McAuley. "Look, that's enough," he said firmly. "We have to assume O'Brien is in serious danger and to move with purpose."

Ironically, Klein would never have guessed that Richard was at that moment making out with a beautiful woman.

13

"You captured an FBI agent?" Emma asked incredulously, her voice a tad erratic. "Denise, WHY?"

"I panicked. You should have seen the file they had on me," he replied. "Anyway, I want you to stop calling me Denise. It's Dennis. My testosterone levels have finally normalized. I've a new gender identity. Be happy for me."

The situation was now out of control, and Emma was not trained to deal with such threats. She kept shaking her head in disbelief. Her responsibilities as a spy were becoming more and more ambiguous. What she never expected was that Dennis, emboldened to accept risks from a lifetime of taking them, would jeopardize his freedom with the capture of a federal agent.

"What are you doing with him?" she asked, trying to regain her composure.

"I have him on a similar regimen as the others," he replied, not sharing that the dosage for Richard was close to twice the strength of other patients.

There were two ways in which drugs were administered. After breakfast, certain patients were told to line up outside the commissary, where they were provided their medication and a small paper cup of water for washing it down. An aide would immediately shine a flashlight into their mouths to ensure patients were not hiding the pills so they could spit them out later. An equal amount was added to soups and sandwiches at lunchtime, ensuring that all patients were sufficiently medicated and not likely to become combative or disruptive.

"And you have him on HDACi?" Emma asked.

"Yes, I've increased the dose in his meals, just to be sure."

Emma was aware of Dennis's experiments with HDACi, histone deacetylase inhibitor, a class of drugs originally used in psychiatry as mood stabilizers to treat epileptic patients. More recently, however, experiments had proven that administration of HDACi could reliably cause memories to be erased. A steady regimen of it would slowly cause a subject to lose grip on reality. What was left behind could leave patients in a fog of confusion. Most experiments were conducted on laboratory mice; clinical trials were planned for victims of PTSD but were tied up in controversy when bioethicists learned about them and objected to the idea.

Emma worried that Dennis's encounters with law enforcement could get them both in trouble and that risk was no longer theoretical. She wondered if Dennis was becoming schizophrenic and if the gender reassignment therapy had fucked with his mind. More importantly, she wondered if her own cover would be blown.

The protocol for Emma's work allowed for direct contact with the agency only in emergency situations. Telephone calls were discouraged, texting through encrypted chat programs was permitted. She sat in her apartment and considered the best course of action. Then she reached for her phone and made the call.

"It's not safe to go in there," she said to her superior officer, sharing additional details about the environment inside the hospital.

"Is he mentally stable?" the man asked.

"I'm not sure," she replied.

"What about our agent?"

"I worry about his safety," she said. "This situation is out of control."

FELIX JORDAN AND JEFF McAuley sat in an unmarked black Ford Taurus outside the imposing gates of The Center for New Beginnings. They had arrived at 6:45 in the evening. A steady stream of traffic passed the entrance, but no vehicles were going in or out of the campus. Jordan was sipping from a Coke in his left hand as he held a cheeseburger in his right. McAuley finished up his California burrito. Food wrappers littered the seats and floor. It was now 7:20 p.m.

"So this is it?" McAuley said, breaking the silence.

"*What* is it?" Jordan shot back with a hint of irritation in his voice. He made a mental note to complain to Klein that he was not enthusiastic about having to partner with all the Bureau rookies.

"This," McAuley repeated, holding his left and right hand in front of the windshield as if it was about to fall in his lap. "This!"

"Man, what the fuck you talking about?"

"Like, is this how FBI agents spend most of their time? Just, like, you know, sitting here and staring out the window?" McAuley had officially crossed the line now.

"No grommet-head," Jordan replied as he took the last bite of his burger. "Sometimes we get to take pictures."

Before McAuley could take issue with being insulted, his cell phone rang, playing the tune to *Hawaii 5-0*. Jordan looked the other way to hide his disgust.

"Yeah," he repeated to himself, "Grommet fits."

McAuley answered the phone, welcoming the opportunity to change the subject. It was Ben Klein.

"Yes sir, we are here at the gates," McAuley said. "Just watching the water and waiting for fins to surface."

Klein let the surfing analogy pass and started to describe the planned raid on the facility. McAuley was doing his best to pay attention when he noticed in the side-view mirror a man crossing the street behind the car and walking toward the gates.

"Sir, we gotta go," McAuley interrupted. "We've got some activity here, not sure what it is, but we may need to speak later, I mean, deal with this later, sir, you know, okay?" McAuley was still a rookie and new to the protocols and expectations around reporting to a superior officer.

"That's fine," Klein replied. "Report back if you have something and stand by for updates." Klein disconnected the call.

McAuley continued to focus on the man who was now several yards in front of the car and easily seen through the windshield. He glanced at Jordan, who was doing the same. The man stood in front of the gates, looking in. He turned his body 360 degrees to see in all directions, then returned to face the gate. He began walking around to the side of the hospital property.

"What do we do?" McAuley asked aloud, ready to take his instruction from Jordan.

"Follow me," he replied.

The two men got out of the Taurus and began walking down the opposite side of the street in the direction of the man. Both sides of the street had large, overgrown oak trees that provided significant shade but shielded the view of the man about every twenty feet. McAuley and Jordan picked up their pace to get closer. As they looked to their left, they could see him continuing to walk along the wall that separated the institution from the outside world. The man would disappear briefly as he passed behind oak trees near the curb. Jordan's eyes narrowed, he tried to get as much information about the man as he could.

As McAuley and Jordan continued to walk, they noticed the man didn't reappear after going behind an oak trunk. Jordan crossed the road and moved as quickly as he could toward the tree without breaking into a full run. McAuley followed. As he got to the tree, he saw the man, kneeling down, trying to pick the lock to a side gate.

"Stop!" Jordan yelled. "FBI!"

Ji-Sung instinctively jumped up and grabbed the top of the wall, hoping to scale it before getting caught.

McAuley was behind Jordan, but McAuley was lighter and faster. He leaped high enough to grab and pull Ji-Sung's ankle. The two fell to the ground. Once there, Jordan pounced on him, pushing the side of his face into the pavement. He grabbed Ji-Sung's arms and pulled them behind him as he sat on his buttocks. With his left hand he pushed Ji-Sung's arms into his back. With his right hand he grabbed the handcuffs on his belt secured the wrists. He breathed a deep sigh of relief; the man was apprehended without incident.

"Dude, that was fantastic!" McAuley shouted. Jordan looked up at him in disbelief. End zone celebrations, he believed, were as inappropriate in FBI apprehensions as they were in college football. He backed himself off Ji-Sung and slowly stood up, bringing him first to his knees and then standing upright.

"Sir," Jordan said to him, "you have some explaining to do." He proceeded to hold Ji-Sung upright so that McAuley could frisked him. McAuley confiscated his cell phone, and the notes provided him by Emma earlier in the day. As per FBI protocol, he would not be read his Miranda rights. The discussion of his rights would happen prior to his interrogation.

Ji-Sung was covered in sweat from the altercation, clearly scared and confused. The three men began walking slowly back to the squad car. Ji-Sung was limping.

"Please," Ji-Sung said, turning to Jordan. "I fail. I no go home."

RICHARD WOKE UP FEELING spent and, ironically, content. The time was just before eleven o'clock. He was face down on the pillow and trying to make sense of things before pushing himself up. His right arm was hanging off the side of the bed. His left hand was cupping a women's breast. Harmony's breast.

He lifted his head just high enough to see Harmony sleeping by his side on her back, the sheets covering her pelvis but leaving her stomach and chest bare. Richard put his head back down, trying to remember how she ended up in his bed.

It was earlier in the evening that she had shown up, quietly entering his room and closing the door. She said something about being off birth control since she was abducted and did not have access to her pills, which fucked with her hormones and made her extremely horny. She said she felt the chemistry between them, moved closer, and gently placed her hand on his crotch. Given that both were wearing hospital scrubs, Richard's erection made clear his feelings, whether intended or not, and besides, he had never denied an attractive woman access to his penis. Seconds later, she pulled down his pants, knelt down, and gave him fellatio. The rest of the evening was a fog.

Richard knew what he had done was wrong, but he was not sure why. The drugs were having their intended effect, wiping clean some of his memories, in particular, that he was already in a committed relationship with Sarah Goodman. He was no longer even certain he was an FBI special agent. After all, wouldn't that be the most amusing of stories he could concoct to impress others? It would not be the first time he stretched the truth if it served him a specific benefit. Perhaps he merely dreamed of being an agent but in reality was unemployed. According to his training, today was C-1.

But to Richard, it was the day he slept with a young and incredibly hot woman, nothing more.

As he lifted his head to see just how much of her body was uncovered, her eyes opened.

"Hey, baby," she said softly as she smiled and turned her head in his direction.

"Listen," Richard whispered, reluctantly lifting his hand off her breast, "you had better get out of here. What if they catch us together?"

"Don't worry," she replied, "they won't do bed checks for at least another two hours." Harmony gently took Richard's arm and returned his hand to her breast, holding it there.

Once again, Richard found Harmony to be full of surprises. Good surprises.

"How do you know that?" he asked.

"I've been observing the rhythm of this place," she said. "You know, it has a rhythm. In the morning, you have patients walking around aimlessly, screaming, vomiting their meds, acting out. In the afternoon, things quiet down, a lot of napping going on. In the evening the aides go home. Security guards monitor the exits and do bed checks around 1 a.m. A second shift arrives just after that, relieving the first shift. They do bed checks at 6 a.m. We're good, baby, relax."

Richard let his head fall back down to the pillow. If he was to be Harmony's prisoner, he was not sure he had cause to complain.

"PAUL, WE COULD REALLY use your help on this," Klein said to his counterpart in LA. Klein was standing in front of Michaelson's desk in his office on the top floor of the LA field office. It was Tuesday morning. The rivalry between Ben Klein and Paul Michaelson was legendary within the agency. Both were overachievers in the Academy, respected within their field offices, and constantly in competition for resources. The fact that Michaelson landed the top job in the LA office gave him an air of superiority over Klein, even though they were technically peers.

"Sorry, Ben, I cannot spare any more grown-ups," Michaelson replied, leaning back in his chair and looking at Klein. "Really, can't you keep a better handle on your boys? Didn't we send O'Brien to you in the first place?" Michaelson had read O'Brien's file and knew he had a playboy reputation. He pictured O'Brien hung over in a hotel room somewhere and was already regretting he had been assigned to LA.

Klein did not appreciate Michaelson's attitude, but he expected it. While Klein was generally recognized as an emotionally intelligent leader, Michaelson was regularly compared to authoritarian leaders for his lack of discretion and dismissive attitude. Unfortunately for Klein, no other concentration of resources was available. It was also fair to assume that Michaelson resented that the director allowed Klein to run the mission simply because Kinkade, whose disappearance and abandoned boat triggered everything else, was last seen in San Diego.

"That's uncalled for," Klein replied. "And you know it."

Michaelson knew he had the upper hand with Klein, but he also recognized that to deny Klein the assistance could prove costly later. He waited five seconds before responding, a tactic he used whenever he wanted the other party to recognize who held the best cards. To Klein, those seconds felt like an eternity.

"All right, Ben," he finally replied. "I'll have my deputy identify a small team to assist you. Just remember to bring them back, and O'Brien, when you find him."

Klein realized that Michaelson was using a power play on multiple levels, first through his condescending attitude and then by delegating the matter to a deputy.

Klein walked out of the office in the direction of the temporary office made available to him, deep in thought. *Where is O'Brien? Is he, as McAuley suggested, a lobster in a pot somewhere? Is he suffering? Where the hell is that search warrant?*

JI-SUNG LAY SLEEPING in the private hospital room on the fourth floor at Los Angeles General Medical Center. He was strapped into the bed, and a security guard was posted at his door. He could have easily fallen asleep because of pure exhaustion, but he was uncooperative on arrival and the staff sedated him. He was being administered fluids to combat severe dehydration while a vital signs monitor displayed his heart rate and temperature. The blinds were drawn in the room.

Before he dozed off, Ji-Sung began to mumble in his native tongue, a dialect one of the nurses recognized as Korean. It took about forty minutes for them to locate a hospital employee that spoke fluent Korean and could interpret.

"He seemed to be under the impression that a bomb was implanted into his abdomen," the attending physician said to Klein as the two stood side by side at the foot of the bed, watching Ji-Sung. "And I know this sounds crazy, but there actually was something inside him. He begged us to detonate it."

"Detonate it?" Klein replied, confused.

"Yes, that's right. It seems whatever he was responsible for accomplishing, the fact that he failed meant he could not go home without unbearable shame, or maybe consequences beyond that."

"Did he say where home is?" Klein asked.

"I'm not sure," the doctor replied. "I wasn't here when he arrived. But we can bring back the nurse that he spoke to when he wakes up."

"And what about the explosive device?"

"We were able to get the thing out without any issues, other than a lot of nervous doctors and nurses, but it wasn't a bomb. It was an amateurish job, but fortunately just below the epidermis layer and fairly easy to remove. It was a GPS transmitter. You know, like a primitive Apple Tag."

"An Apple Tag?"

"Yep, whoever wanted to track him will know exactly where he is."

Klein continued to stare at Ji-Sung as if staring would enable him to extract more information. There was a brief silence before the doctor said exactly what Klein was thinking.

"Are you sure one security guard is going to be enough?"

14

Richard woke up around 9:50 in the morning on Tuesday. It was beginning to feel like *Groundhog Day*. The clinical term would be called "situational depression." He had forgotten his training and stopped counting days. He no longer was convinced he was ever an FBI agent; that seemed the type of ruse someone of his character would manufacture. His swagger was gone. He had lost his motivation. More importantly, he was also slowly losing his mind.

What he did remember was the marathon fuck session with Harmony Hutchins from the prior evening. In fact, he was feeling some pain in his groin area, which he attributed to overuse and some unanticipated sexual acrobatics. He lifted the covers and stared down at his penis to inspect it. It was sore but otherwise looked unharmed. In his warped mind, anticipating another late-night rendezvous with Harmony was the only reason for living. And it was worth whatever soreness or injury he might have to endure.

He swung his legs off the bed and stood up. He was still wearing the loose standard-issue hospital pants that he had worn the day before. But looking inside his pants again he noticed he was not wearing any underwear. They must be in

Harmony's room, he decided. It gave him another reason to see her tonight, he thought, not that he needed one.

Richard slid one foot in front of the other in the direction of the sink. There was a small bottle of hand lotion, a travel-size tube of toothpaste, and a small disposable toothbrush on the edge of the sink. The mirror above the sink was a shiny metal plate—the kind that can't be smashed into pieces. The reflection it provided him was not unlike what would be found in a carnival attraction. It distorted his features and only added to his depressed state of mind.

He turned around to look at his immediate environment. He noticed the room lacked anything that could be used as a weapon. Smooth edges, bolted-down furnishings, and anything removable was made of plastic. He was in a cage. He was deep in thought when a sharp rapping on his door broke him free from his hypnotic state of mind.

"Mr. B, good morning!"

Richard turned his attention to the person standing in the doorframe. He just stared.

"Mr. B, it's time for your appointment with Dr. Spence."

"With who?"

"Mr. B, come on, it's nearly 10 o'clock. Dr. Spence is waiting for you."

Richard was still trying to process how it could be 10 o'clock and it felt like he was constantly sleeping. The aide walked toward him with a clean set of clothes. "Here," he said, "please put these on. I'll wait for you just outside the door. Please hurry. We don't want to keep Dr. Spence waiting."

Richard did as he was instructed. At least this day was about to offer some variety. And perhaps Dr. Spence could shed some light on his situation and why he was in the hospital.

"What kind of doctor is Spence?" Richard asked as the two of them made their way down the corridor toward the administration wing.

"He's a psychologist," the aide replied.

Dennis Spence did not have the academic training to be considered a psychologist, but forging the credentials to be considered a psychologist was infinitely easier than posing as a psychiatrist, which would mean he was a medical doctor, maintained a medical license, and be easily traceable. For Spence's purposes, it was sufficient to refer to himself as a psychologist in order to justify therapy sessions with patients and to validate the impact of his experiments on them.

Richard was guided by the aide into the outer office that led to Spence. As he entered the room, it looked vaguely familiar, but this déjà vu experience had become so common throughout Richard's day that he did not attribute anything to it. He was actually looking forward to speaking to Dr. Spence, whose name was mentioned frequently; he seemed to be revered by everyone who worked in the institution.

"Hello Richard, come on in," a voice beckoned from the private office behind the secretary's desk. "Anthony, thank you for bringing Richard to me. Cheryl is not in; you can leave him with me. But please have a seat in the waiting room in case I need you." What Spence did not need to clarify was that patients might need to be restrained at any point during their meeting.

"Yes sir," the aide replied, then disappeared.

Richard walked slowly into the office as Spence came from around the back of his desk, his arm extended to shake Richard's hand. Richard obliged. Spence then held out his hand toward an upholstered chair opposite his desk, motioning for Richard to sit in it. He sat in the same seat as during his last visit to the office.

Richard's head and eyes darted back and forth as he took in the office surroundings. The room looked familiar but as far as he knew, he had never been in this room before. Spence just stared at him, not speaking. He was focused on Richard's eyes and facial expressions and what that might reveal about his state of mind. Richard finally looked straight at Spence.

"How are you feeling, Mr. B?" he asked.

A couple days ago, Richard would have asked, "Why am I here." He had since abandoned that question.

"All right, I guess," he replied.

"Are we taking good care of you? Do you have everything you need?"

Richard's immediate thought turned to Harmony. He needed Harmony. He was not sure what else was needed other than answers. But he was not even sure of the question. He just stared at Spence, and it was clear to the administrator that the medication therapy had worked. Moments like this emboldened Spence. He had succeeded in bringing many men in powerful positions under his influence since acquiring the institution and beginning his practice of mental manipulation and brainwashing. What Spence did not realize, however, was that Richard had already stopped receiving the medication, thanks to Harmony.

"Richard, do you know why you are here?"

"I'm not sure," he replied. The question caused him to reconsider the possibility that he was, in fact, *not* supposed to be there.

"Do you recall claiming you were an FBI agent? Do you recall assaulting a police officer?"

Richard recalled the first part of the question but not the second. He continued to just stare at Spence. But at this point, he started to suspect again that he wasn't being told the truth about the situation.

"How long do I need to stay here?" he finally asked.

"Well, we don't want to keep you here any longer than necessary, Richard, and it seems you've been doing really well here and getting along with our staff and other patients. So, I hope we can discharge you very soon," Spence replied, telling Richard what he probably wanted to hear but not what Spence intended to do.

"Richard, I want you to do me a favor," Spence continued.

"Okay," he replied.

"I want you to tell me that you realize you are not an FBI agent and have never been an FBI agent. This is important to your recovery. Can you do that for me, Richard?"

Richard stared at Spence. If he agreed that he wasn't an agent and was discharged, he would probably lose his connection to Harmony. If he insisted he was an agent, he would continue to be institutionalized. And what would be waiting for him on the outside anyway? He had no clue. He was confused.

Spence could see the anguish on his face. There was no reason to press Richard today. He wasn't going anywhere. It was more important to fully break him from whatever grip on reality he had left.

"Richard, just think about it, okay? We can talk more in a few days." With that, Spence stood up. Richard took the cue and stood as well. As he did, he saw the framed photo of two women behind Spence. The feeling of déjà vu hit him again, retrieving memories from a few days prior, and inching him ever so close to the truth. Spence could see this as well, and quickly summoned the aide by pressing a button on his desk. The aide reappeared.

"Anthony, Richard looks like he could use something to eat. Please take him to the cafeteria. Richard, we will talk again tomorrow. Get some rest. See you soon."

The aide gently took Richard's arm and led him out of the office. They walked in silence from the administrative wing to the cafeteria in the central wing. Richard recalled being in this room the other day when he met the man claiming to be almost 110 years old. He wondered if he would see him again and have the opportunity to dig deeper into his story.

At 11:00 a.m., the cafeteria was relatively quiet. A few patients sat at tables, staring at puzzles or the television hanging in the room's corner. The old arcade games were still lined up on the wall next to the windows that looked out on the garden. The games had familiar names: Asteroids, Super Mario, Pac-Man.

He stared at the Pac-Man machine. *Pac-Man.* A flood of memories started coming back to him about the Academy, the training, the camaraderie, and in particular the technique to keep him grounded in case of capture. *Pac-Man ... Pacman. PACKMEN.* McAuley. Jordan. Sarah. Sarah Goodman. *My god,* he thought, *I am a fucking FBI agent. And I have a girl waiting for me on the outside.* Richard was so excited that he was shaking.

"Richard?" the aide asked. "Are you okay? Is everything all right?"

"Fuck yes," he replied.

KLEIN STOOD AT THE front of the room as the agents filed into the LA conference room that had essentially become their war room. There was a bit of backslapping for Jordan and McAuley because word had spread quickly that they had captured a potential foreign agent on American soil on Monday night, a first for the office. Klein waited until the banter died down. He did not want to deny his agents the opportunity to express respect for risks taken in the field. It was a good thing Ji-Sung was unarmed or the mood in the room could have been quite different.

"Here is what we know about our guest," he started out. "He appears to be from North Korea. He is not particularly cooperative with information, so we used DNA analysis to identify his country of origin, which took some time as our data on North Korea is limited. Anyway, he looks very healthy for a North Korean given that we believe most

North Koreans are suffering from severe food insecurity. Based on his weight and overall condition, it doesn't look like he came here for the food."

There were a few muted chuckles from within Klein's audience.

"What was he after at CNB?" came a question from one of the agents.

"I wish I could tell you that with confidence," Klein replied. "It appears he was on a mission directed by the Chinese and was sent here by them to collect scientific assets. We will be figuring out exactly what he was after once we finish examining data contained on his phone and some documents he was carrying at the time he was taken into custody. When we are satisfied we've learned all we can, we will send him back with intel that his leadership will find quite valuable."

And that probably would happen quickly. Klein described a call he had just received from the U.S. State Department, which was keen to organize a prisoner swap: In return for Ji-Sung, the U.S. wanted safe return of Tom Adler, a journalist being held in North Korea on trumped-up charges of espionage and conspiracy to commit sedition.

"I don't get it, sir," McAuley objected. "You are letting him return with what he came here to steal?"

"Not exactly," replied Klein. "I'll let Jack Reeves from KCBS explain it."

Klein pointed a TV remote control at the monitor hanging in the conference room. CBS's Jack Reeves appeared with a "breaking news" story.

"*Good evening,*" Reeves says, "*This is Jack Reeves. Our top story tonight: U.S. intelligence has found that Chinese laboratories are manufacturing a serum designed to make soldiers impervious to injury...*"

Reeves, with the assistance of the FBI and the CBS affiliate, had pre-taped the news story to feed Ji-Sung the type of information that would make North Korea's leader so further paranoid and threatened by China that he would feel compelled to take action against his bigger neighbor. Klein watched as the agents took in the bogus information Reeves was dishing out.

"*The Chinese government appears to be on the path to create a nearly invincible army,*" Reeves continued. "*The president is in contact with our allies around the world to discuss appropriate sanctions and countermeasures, although the countries at greatest risk are those in Asia and in particular those that have access to coastal waterways. We will be following this story closely in the coming days.*"

"Sir, so this is a ruse, right?" an agent asked incredulously.

"Yes, and it's playing on the TV in the hospital room of our North Korean guest as we speak."

Klein didn't bother to go into all the details of what it took to produce the video, and for a moment it didn't look like the idea would fly with the higher-ups in Washington. But Reeves enjoyed the adrenaline rush of being involved and was successful in gaining access to the studio between regularly scheduled programming. The thirty-second clip took only about twenty minutes to produce. A sharp observer might have noticed that Reeves wasn't wearing his trademark suit, or that he lacked the full makeup of a television anchor, but it was good enough for their purposes.

"Sir, what intelligence are you sending back to North Korea?" an agent asked.

"Something to keep them busy," he replied.

"YOU'VE GOTTA BE SHITTING me," Harmony said, falling back to sit on the edge of the bed behind her. Richard stood there, stoically, determined not to capitulate into another marathon fuck session, which would have been far more satisfying than the current conversation. On top of trying to convince Harmony he was an FBI agent with a steady girlfriend, he had to gain her cooperation for what would happen next. It would have been particularly useful if he knew what that would be.

"I'm sorry," he said, regretting that he didn't know enough to open up to her sooner. At least he was following his training for the first couple of days where it is advised not to broadcast that your employer happens to be the FBI. Adding the part about the girlfriend represented Richard's new determination to be a stand-up guy who has at least an ounce of integrity. He had to dig deep for that confession.

"Well, baby, nobody could blame you for sampling from the buffet," she replied, running her palms from her neck down to her waist. "I am still happy to entertain you for as long as we are checked into this shit show." Harmony never ceased to amaze.

Richard appreciated the sentiment but tried to stay focused on planning their escape. He presumed correctly that the security at the institution was too thorough to allow a single patient to escape. There were no gaps to exploit. However, two patients working as a team would stand a significantly better chance that at least one could escape. All that would be required, he thought, was the right type of deception or distraction. And if Harmony was capable of anything, it was distracting people.

"Look," Richard said, doing his best to couch the plan as a win-win, "the sooner I get out of here, the sooner we can liberate all the others that are basically being held hostage." As the words left his mouth, he realized the offer did not convey a convincing guarantee. Harmony stared at him for a moment, then burst out laughing, rocking back and forth on the bed.

"What?!" Richard did his best to keep his composure. In reality, he was intimidated by Harmony, a woman with such confidence and swagger that she could convince a prince to abandon all his concubines.

"Baby," she replied, "how do I know you'll bother to come back after your girlfriend is done making up for lost time, and, you know." As she said that, she made an "O" with one hand resting on her lap and pushed the index finger of her other hand through it.

"You have my word," Richard replied, feeling as if he was losing control of the negotiation. "I am first and foremost an FBI agent, maybe not a very good one, but I took an oath, and I need to do this. I need to do it now. And besides, I care about you and want to get you out of here." Richard was reaching now, looking for the one thing he could say that would push Harmony over the line.

"And I have a feeling there are plenty of men out there looking for you right now."

Harmony looked down at her lap in contemplation. There was at least one man that she wanted to see again. But her biggest motivation was to get out of the facility that imprisoned her, and Richard offered her the single best option.

"Okay, baby," she said, "I'm in. What now?"

THE CONFERENCE ROOM in the LA field office of the FBI was at capacity with about thirty agents. It was Tuesday at 4 in the afternoon and the search warrant was in Ben Klein's hands. He received it exactly twenty-four hours from when it was requested. The system of obtaining warrants was highly evolved and worked particularly well when there was a compelling need.

Four tables were arranged in a giant square. Standing at the center of one table was Klein. Behind him, the large glass window revealed a bright orange sky giving way to the night as the sun began to set.

"Okay, everyone, please take your seats," he said as loud as possible to raise his voice above the chattering agents. "We have a lot to cover before I set you lose on the target."

The search warrant would allow the FBI to not only seek the whereabouts of Richard O'Brien, but also seize evidence regarding the operations of CNB and the possible culpability of its administrator, Dennis Spence. He had also been successful in securing a dozen agents from Paul Michaelson, who observed from the back of the room, with a look on his face that could only be described as pissed off that he wasn't the one in charge. Klein signaled his assistant to turn on the projector, which lit up the screen behind him with a larger-than-life picture of Richard O'Brien.

"This is Richard O'Brien, one of ours that we believe is being held at The Center for New Beginnings. This picture is being sent to your Bureau phones." He advanced the slide.

"And this is Dennis Spence, the administrator, who we should presume to be armed and dangerous. However, I doubt he will be on the premises when we break the glass."

He used agency-speak for the moment when an operation moved from surveillance to intervention, in other words, no turning back. Klein chose not to share the less relevant information about Spence's past, which would only distract the agents from their main purpose. He advanced the projector again.

"And here is a map of the grounds and the facility based on what has been filed with the county. We assume it to be current based on drone surveillance."

Klein described in more detail the agency's understanding of how the inside of the facility was organized.

"We will enter the facility through the front, and I want two sets of ten agents each to proceed in opposite directions from there, canvassing the side halls where patient rooms are located," he said. "There will be security present, so be sure to identify yourselves early and often. I don't want a single shot fired during this operation. It shouldn't be necessary."

Felix Jordan was happy to hear Klein's assessment that use of force was likely unnecessary, but his recollection of events from when he was there contradicted that point of view, and he would not allow himself to be fooled again.

"The first priority is recovery of Richard O'Brien," Klein continued. "Don't assume he is in one of the patient rooms. Look for a basement or rooms that may be additions, not on the map you see here." Klein surveyed the crowd to ensure they were looking at the map and memorizing what they could.

"Once O'Brien is secured or is determined to be off the grounds, I want agents to search the office of the administrator and bring out any and all documents in his office. Look for booby traps that might be used to protect whatever illicit activity may be happening there."

Klein paused, reflecting on his last comment and seeking any reaction from the agents. The dual nature of the operation was a concern. Most agents were trained to focus on a singular mission goal. Two goals meant that two things could go wrong. The stakes were high.

"I want the operation to kick off at oh-one-forty-five, just before the second shift of security comes in. The guards on duty will be thinking about going home rather than protecting the premises.

"Any questions?" Klein asked.

"Sir," an agent called out with a wry smile, "what if they commit us all?"

HARMONY TOOK ONE LAST look in the mirror before returning to sit on her bed. It was 1:10 a.m. She unbuttoned her shirt just enough that it would be nearly impossible for a bored security guard to ignore her breasts. She pulled down her pants and threw them on the floor near the door, leaving nothing else on but her panties. Next, she pulled on a pair of clear plastic gloves, the type used to mix a salad, which she had taken from the cafeteria. She was ready. Now it was just a matter of waiting for the first bed check of the night. She listened carefully for the security guards.

"Good evening," said the guard, opening the door slowly. He looked down at the floor and noticed her pants lying there. Harmony knew it was showtime.

"Honey, me soooo horny," she said, borrowing a line from *Full Metal Jacket*. "Me love you long time!" She scooted off the bed toward the guard, rubbing her panties. As she approached the guard, she pulled open her shirt further to reveal her chest. Her eyes were focused like lasers on the guard. "Me so horny," she repeated. "Me suck you now."

The guard's mouth dropped open as Harmony closed in on him. She gently grabbed his arms and pulled him toward her, planting her lips on his, then let her left-hand drift down to cup his genitals. She massaged them gently, arousing him further. The guard melted in her arms. He had heard stories of guards assaulting female inmates but not the other way around. This time, he thought, he had won the lottery.

Richard waited patiently under the bed, breathing as shallowly as he could to avoid attracting attention. As Harmony positioned the guard next to the bed, Richard grabbed his ankles as tightly as he could, yanking him hard to the point that he fell forward into Harmony's chest. The guard was forced to wrap his arms around Harmony for balance. She reached into the pocket of her shirt, pulled out a washcloth, and jammed it over his mouth, being careful not to let any of it touch her skin. The guard's grip on Harmony immediately relaxed, his pupils disappeared behind his eyelids, and he passed out. All his weight was now on Harmony's shoulders as gravity brought them both to the floor. Harmony quickly escaped his grip and stood up.

Richard crawled out from under the bed. He and Harmony looked at the guard, who lay face down on the floor, his arms spread out. They were both breathing heavily.

"That was amazing!" Harmony yelled, then covering her mouth as she recognized the possibility of another guard coming by.

"Dr. Z was right," Richard said, still breathing heavily, "that aconite is potent stuff."

The plan worked because the guard visited Harmony's room before Richard's. Or perhaps he did look in on Richard but was fooled by the pillows strategically positioned to make it appear that Richard was asleep under the sheets. It also worked because both Harmony and Richard were able to learn much more about the power of aconite from Dr. Z who told them how to recognize it in the hospital's garden. It was fortunate that the plan worked, because Richard did not have a Plan B. He reached down and removed the guard's pepper spray, taser, and keys.

"Help me get his uniform off," he said. Harmony winced but complied, unbuttoning the guard's shirt and releasing his belt. The security guard was a bit overweight. But a deal was a deal, and there was no turning back. Richard sat at the guard's feet and pulled off his pants. He would soon assume the role of a security guard and be able to walk straight out the front door of the institution.

That's when the building alarms went off.

15

Richard held the taser with his right hand and grabbed Harmony's hand with his left, and the two ran from the room toward the main entrance. Richard was in a loose-fitting, blue security guard shirt, the buttons misaligned because he dressed in a hurry, the tails hanging out of the back of the pants. Harmony looked like she stepped away from a train wreck, her shirt wide open, disheveled hair, and no pants. The two looked like they were acting out a scene in a poorly directed B-movie, running down the hallway en route to the exit.

The alarm was deafening, and patients began stepping out of their rooms into the hallway, confused and creating an obstacle course for Richard and Harmony to navigate. Richard knocked one of the patients over but didn't look back. Bright white strobe lights flashed just below the ceiling on the hallway walls, piercing the otherwise dark corridors as if there were lightning inside the building. It was so loud and chaotic that Richard found himself bewildered when he suddenly faced a phalanx of five armed men in tactical gear blocking his access to the exit.

"FBI! Drop your weapon, NOW," one of the men yelled above the cacophony of the alarm.

Until now, Richard had presumed the alarms went off because a video camera caught him assaulting a security guard. If that were the case, this response was more than a bit over the top. As he considered what he was facing, the alarms were shut off, although the lights continued strobing.

"I'M AN FBI AGENT," Richard yelled, his heart beating so hard he could feel it pulsing in his neck.

"Yeah, and I'm the tooth fairy," the lead agent responded. Even if the agent did recognize Richard, he was not about to break protocol during the most dangerous portion of the mission. Richard wasn't at all surprised by the response anyway. The absurdity of the situation would be comical and ironic if not so frustrating.

"Get on your knees and lay down your weapon," the agent commanded.

Richard was still holding Harmony's hand as the two kneeled down in unison. To signal his intent to cooperate, he pushed the gun out of his reach. As he did so, Harmony released his hand and buttoned her shirt. Two agents approached and guided Richard and Harmony down to the floor, wrapped their hands behind their backs, and secured their wrists with zip ties, the clicking sound signaling the end of the adventure that had started just moments before. They were helped back to their feet and directed toward the lead agent, who was looking down at a photo of the missing FBI agent on his phone. Richard was not prepared for what happened next.

"Hello, Richard," the agent said, raising his head. "It's good to see you."

OUTSIDE THE INSTITUTION, Richard and Harmony, no longer zip-tied, leaned against the edge of a paramedic van's back door, receiving a cursory medical evaluation before their trip to a hospital for blood tests and a more thorough examination. It was about 2 a.m., and a new shift of CNB security guards was showing up. A crowd was forming outside the front entrance of the institution, with FBI agents interviewing patients, guards, and other employees. Silent cherry lights rotated from the top of multiple law enforcement vehicles that had gathered on the scene.

Bright lights on poles were erected to create enough visibility for the agents to function and ensure that nobody tried to leave the premises. An agent brought Richard and Harmony cups of hot tea. Both were as rattled and exhausted as if they had stepped off a rollercoaster that had malfunctioning brakes.

"Richard," came a sound from behind the group of agents surrounding them. It was Sarah Goodman. Richard started to tear up on seeing her and collapsed into her arms. Harmony looked on, slowly putting the pieces together as her heartbeat approached a resting rate.

As Sarah embraced Richard, she looked over his shoulder and noticed Harmony. She knew enough about Richard's past to put her own pieces together. She would leave the necessary conversation about what it all meant for another time.

KLEIN SAT IN A CONFERENCE room at the FBI office in San Diego before most of his staff arrived. With Richard safe and still going through medical evaluation, he decided to head to his own office that morning and to escape, for the moment, the awkwardness of treading on Michaelson's turf.

The sun had started to rise and make its presence known against the full-size glass windows on the east side of the room. An intense yellow glow was gathering around the blinds. It was not so dark that the cold fluorescent lights were necessary, and anyway, Klein welcomed the zen-like atmosphere in his home away from home. Outside the room, he could hear footsteps and light banter of people arriving at work.

He stood in front of a massive whiteboard that was placed on the north side of the room. Typically, this would be used as a screen for presentations from the projector hanging from the ceiling, but it had been repurposed as a place to arrange the intelligence for one of the most important cases of his career. He stared at the material on the board with his arms crossed, his right hand squeezing his chin.

One item was an image showing The Center for New Beginnings. A picture of Dennis Spence, who was still at large, was underneath it. A picture of Ji-Sung, taken while he was sleeping in the hospital, was connected via a line to CNB to the far right. Below Ji-Sung was another line leading to MSS, China's Ministry of State Security. U.S. intelligence regarded the agency as being like a combination of the CIA and FBI.

Klein believed there was a missing link to the case. It would not make sense that Spence was working for China because if he was, sending Ji-Sung to scale the institution's walls would have been unnecessary. Unless Spence had research findings he wouldn't give up? He took a dry-erase marker, drew a line from "CNB" down to the right, and added a question mark. Someone, or something, was competing for the same secrets and technology that Spence was involved in developing.

His concentration was broken by his assistant knocking on the open door to the conference room.

"Sir?" she said in a soft voice, slightly apologetic for the interruption. "I have the State Department on the secure line."

"CAMBODIA?" KLEIN EXCLAIMED. "Are you serious, sir? Why Cambodia? We don't have a good footprint there, sir."

Klein was speaking to Assistant Secretary Roger Jafek at the State Department about the transfer that was being negotiated between the United States and North Korea.

"I understand your concern," Jafek replied. "We don't have a lot of flexibility here, Ben. As you can appreciate, a one-to-one exchange is in itself a victory for the U.S."

Jafek was referring to the long-standing, unsanctioned practice of trading hundreds of prisoners or detainees for just one citizen of a democratically led country. Israel had set the current record, releasing 1,027 detainees in exchange for Gilad Schalit in 2011. The U.S. never came close to that ratio but routinely brokered the release of detainees in exchanges coordinated with the governments of Russia, Venezuela, Cuba, Iran, and Afghanistan. The coveted one-to-one ratio was achieved in only one of the last five exchanges.

"All right," Klein conceded. "But can you explain the reason why Cambodia was selected as the neutral territory?"

"The North Koreans have a close relationship with Cambodia going back to the days of the Khmer Rouge. The DPRK supported the government in exile during those days. When the Vietnamese ran the Khmer Rouge out of the country and the king returned to power, the North Korean government built a museum in the city of Siem Reap to honor the Angkor empire, splitting profits with Cambodia. Hell, the Cambodians have already been serving as intermediaries between DPRK and South Korea. I think we can work with them on this."

This was a lot for Klein to take in. He had never been to Cambodia and was not particularly interested in sending one of his agents into Siem Reap for a prisoner swap. He was trying to unpack all that Jafek told him when Jafek spoke again.

"One more thing," Jafek said, "we have no intention of letting the world see what the real Tom Adler looks like."

"Sir?"

"We want you to select one of your agents to pose as Adler for the media. We have plans to send that agent on a mission in the same region once the exchange has been made public. Posing as Adler."

Klein did not like the sound of this. It was one thing to coordinate an operation with the State Department, it was another thing for them to direct the FBI on sensitive missions, as the agency was accountable to the Justice Department and the Attorney General. Besides, this was the type of mission better suited for the CIA.

"Let me stop you right there, sir—" Klein replied, perfectly confident in his understanding of protocol.

"I understand," Jafek interrupted. "We've got Justice on board. For this one, we are playing for all the marbles."

ROGER JAFEK CLEARED his throat and adjusted the microphone sitting in front of him on the long table, facing members of Congress who had assembled for the Intelligence Subcommittee Special Hearing on the Use of Germline Editing among Adversarial Nations. "I do," he responded when asked if he would tell the truth and nothing but the truth. Jafek had welcomed this opportunity to finally get traction for what he considered a serious threat to national security.

"Secretary Jafek, can you please state, for the record, your current and past positions with this administration?" came the question from the chair of the proceedings, Maxwell Frost, the Democrat from Florida's 10th Congressional District.

"I am currently an Assistant Secretary of State for the United States. Prior to this, I was director of warfare innovation assessment at the Defense Intelligence Agency. And prior to that, I was in the counter-terrorism division of the CIA."

"And for the benefit of the members of our subcommittee, secretary, what was the focus of your work at the DIA?" Frost continued.

"I was focused on understanding the threats posed by the creation of tools to wage biological warfare and what we called 'bio-weapons development' among nations that were not allies of the United States."

In his role at the DIA, Jafek became one of the most knowledgeable people in Washington regarding biological warfare. His elevation to the State Department gave him the megaphone to put this threat on the radar of the current administration. Before this, the U.S. had ignored the activities of China, Iran, and other countries that were keen to exploit this new frontier that combined science and defense, two disciplines that were rarely mentioned in the same conversation.

"Secretary Jafek, how would you describe the ambitions of China with regard to the exploitation of germline editing to support their military capabilities?" This was, of course, the question that would fuel the entire debate about whether the United States needed to take preemptive action against foreign powers seeking to bypass the already clear ethical boundaries established by scientists and their governments across the globe.

"Sir, I have no doubt that China, and potentially other adversaries, are, as we speak, investigating the potential to take their discoveries in germline editing and weaponize them."

There was slight murmuring in response to Jafek's statement that made it clear his concerns resonated with the representatives on the panel.

"And secretary, can you state what specific threats are posed by a country that has exploited this field of science?"

Jafek paused before answering. It would be important to put the most serious and credible threats at the beginning of his response.

"Sir, the government that controls germline editing can essentially design a population with whatever are the most desirable traits they wish to see in their people. They can create a superior fighting force, a self-repairing biological mechanism for all living things, and extend the life of their people indefinitely."

"Secretary Jafek, what can you tell this committee that serves as the proof for your concern?"

"Sir," Jafek said with as deadpan a voice as he could muster, "most of the intelligence we have with regard to the capabilities of China is classified. However, you need only look at the growing list of companies that have been added to the Commerce Department's trade blacklist for their work in the field of genetics."

Much of the purpose of these hearings is to serve as political theater for academics and pundits, the media, and interested members of the public to get insight into the workings of Washington. That is why nobody registered surprise when, just as Jafek spoke, a large whiteboard display was brought forward with the names of Chinese companies that were forbidden to access U.S. technology due to the suspicion on the part of the Commerce Department that they were involved in nefarious activities, possibly at the direction of the Chinese government. One of those companies, BGI Genomics, was the world's largest company working in the field of genomics and was added to the list in 2023. Another company on the list was the less well-known Harbin Bio-Splice Laboratory Company Ltd.

JI-SUNG WATCHED CNN on the television monitor hanging from the corner of his hospital room. He was propped up in his bed watching the subtitles run across the bottom of his screen as Jack Reeves reported the fake news.

The discovery of China's experiments to create a superior race validated everything Ji-Sung knew about his original mission, and he was relieved that he was no longer in possession of his personal phone, or the FBI would know more about him and his role in the North Korean spy agency. He felt confident he had convinced the Americans that he was just in the wrong place at the wrong time during a tourist visit to Shanghai. As he was taking in everything that CNN was reporting, Ben Klein entered the room, accompanied by an interpreter.

"You are going home," he said, trying to muster a smile. The interpreter provided the interpretation. Ji-Sung looked confused.

"We understand you were being forced into breaking the law here," Klein continued. "We mean you no harm. We are sending you back to North Korea. Oh, and we safely removed the device that was inserted into your abdomen."

Ji-Sung just stared at Klein as he listened to the interpretation. He was speechless. Tears started forming in the pockets of his deep-set eyes. Perhaps this nightmare is nearly over. Perhaps he can offer his government valuable intelligence from his unexpected visit to the United States.

"You will be traveling with some of our agents to Cambodia, where we will be handing you off to your government," he said. "And I want you to give this to the people on your side." Klein held up a memory stick. Ji-Sung moved his attention from Klein's face to what he was holding in his hand.

"I understand your government will have concerns about what the contents of this device will do to their computers. They can install it on a dedicated machine that is not connected to a network. They will find the information useful in their efforts to contain threats to their sovereignty. I'll have our agents hold on to this until we return you home. We will hand it to you before we part company."

"Joh-ayo," he replied, still stunned at the good news. The two made eye contact for a still moment, as if to communicate more than words were able to do. Klein smiled again, then turned and left the room.

It is true that Klein wanted more from Ji-Sung. He had many more questions about his guest. The phone they took off him supported the theory that he was collecting scientific data to support efforts in germline editing, and that he was being directed by the MSS, not the DPRK. However, the ability to provide him with details on how to compromise the Bio-Splice Laboratory would be the best reason to send him home.

"RICHARD, I'D LIKE YOU to meet Roger Jafek from the State Department, and I believe you already know Sarah Goodman." Sarah had made arrangements with the Detroit office to remain in support of Klein's ongoing investigations. A round of handshakes followed, including a very awkward handshake between Richard and Sarah.

"Yes, sir," Richard replied. "Pleased to meet you, Secretary Jafek."

The four were meeting in a small conference room at the branch. This was Richard's first day back at work, and since being discharged from the hospital he had only been able to speak to Sarah briefly. They had not yet discussed his escape with Harmony in tow. They took their seats around a large round conference table, Richard and Sarah's eyes focused on one another as their butts hit the seats.

"Richard, how are you feeling?" Klein asked, interrupting Richard's focus on Sarah.

"Fine, sir," he replied, continuing his focus on Sarah, "anxious to get back to work."

"Well, that's good," Klein said, "because we want to talk to you about a special assignment."

Richard tried to hide his surprise and natural curiosity. Having just survived a week in a drug-induced haze, he was not clear what qualified him for a special assignment.

"Richard," Jafek said, "you know from the debrief that we intend to send Ji-Sung, the North Korean agent, back to Asia in exchange for Tom Adler, the journalist for *Rolling Stone*."

"Yes, sir," Richard replied.

"Well, we would like you to pose as Tom Adler once we have recovered him."

"Sir?"

Klein and Goodman both remained silent, watching Richard to determine his capacity for what would come next.

"We've been in touch with the Adler family and have their cooperation. Adler was suspected as a spy, but we all know this is bullshit," Jafek said. "However, the Chinese don't necessarily know much about Adler, and we'd like to have you pose as a spy willing to sell the Chinese the secrets they believe that you, as Adler, gathered in North Korea."

Jafek stopped to allow this plot to sink in. He now joined Klein and Goodman in staring at Richard. For his part, Richard had to repeat Jafek's last words in his head to make sure he got it right.

"So ... you want me to pose as this journalist and to offer myself to the Chinese? Why me?" The question was legitimate. Klein took it.

"Richard, you are one of the few people in the agency to have met Dennis Spence. He's still at large. We have reason to believe he was cooperating with the Chinese in experiments to boost human capacity through germline editing. You are in a unique position to help us capture him. Also, didn't you major in Asian studies at Michigan?"

"Arabic," Richard replied. Klein leaned back in his chair, raised an eyebrow and flattened his lips, as if he didn't think this made a difference.

Richard could not argue with the logic of being selected for this mission, and in fact, relished the opportunity to work at this level. As a child, he had read many books about British double agents who fooled the Germans into believing they were loyal to the Reich. Never in his wildest dreams could he imagine himself in a similar role.

"Sir," he replied, "I'll do whatever I can to help."

"Excellent," Jafek said. "Richard, we really appreciate your support and will start prepping you for the mission. You'll have to memorize some details about Adler, you know, in case you are questioned. And we will want to adapt your appearance slightly so that you will resemble Adler."

Richard was still unsure what he had signed for when Sarah pushed a small box across the table toward him.

"What's this?" Richard asked, looking nervously at Sarah as he reached for and opened the box.

"It's a wedding band," Sarah replied, looking straight at Richard with a deadpan expression. "Adler is married. It might do you some good to imagine what that's like."

16

Richard opened his eyes in the salon chair and took the mirror that the stylist offered. He was nearly shocked at the reflection. McAuley and Jordan were looking on, equally amused.

"Don't worry, O'Brien," the stylist said, wiping the extraneous hair from his apron and the back of Richard's neck. "What you want to grow back will grow back. What you want to shave off, you can shave off. You'll just need to wait until the end of the mission." The makeup artist stepped back to admire his work.

The mission, Operation Free Eagle, was to travel to Cambodia, pose as the freed Tom Adler, and then travel to Thailand to meet with a Chinese spy to offer what the real Adler learned about North Korea's capabilities in germline editing, a story he found unintentionally while working on another article. Encouraging the Chinese to destroy any part of North Korea's scientific research capability was far preferable to involving the U.S. military. And even if that were not possible, passing bogus information to Chinese intelligence that would have them chasing a ghost had its own merit because it would give U.S. intelligence the opportunity to also plant software code that the MSS would download in the process. To pull off the ruse, Richard was transformed into what the agency knew about Tom's appearance, adjusted for the expectation he was unable to shave while being detained.

Richard now sported a healthy beard and mustache, together with a receding hairline. Compared to an older picture of Adler, adapted to include facial hair, the resemblance was not perfect, but satisfactory. They only needed to fool the media that would be on hand to witness as much of the exchange as they were allowed.

"What if he comes back, you know, like Warmbier?" said McAuley, who was now determined to keep a closer eye on Richard. McAuley was referring to Otto Frederick Warmbier, the American college student arrested in Pyongyang in 2016. He was charged with subversion for stealing a propaganda poster and sentenced to fifteen years in prison. He was eventually released after seventeen months because he fell into a coma for reasons that were never made fully clear. He was returned to the U.S. in a vegetative state and died soon thereafter.

"If Adler comes off the plane on a stretcher," Jordan said, "then O'Brien here will be spending a few days in the hospital with him."

Richard hopped off the chair and brushed even more hair off his lap. "Why are they sending me to Thailand?" he quipped, "why not just meet with the Chinese in Cambodia?"

"That's obvious, dude," McAuley replied, "they want you to have a 'happy ending.'"

Richard ignored the gross innuendo, knowing Jordan would offer the more logical answer.

"We don't have an extradition treaty with Cambodia," he replied. "We do with Thailand. In case, you know, you get yourself in trouble. Again."

RICHARD AND SARAH SAT opposite each other at the restaurant. They both knew it was time for "the talk," since he would leave for Asia the next morning. Richard knew it was on him to start the conversation.

"I know how it looked, you know, that night." He did not have to elaborate.

"How did it look?" Sarah replied.

"Well, it looked like I stepped out of a bad movie set in an oversized uniform with a near naked woman."

"Yeah," Sarah said. "That's about right."

"Sarah," Richard pleaded. "It's *not* how it looked." But of course, he realized, it was. "That woman was helping me to escape."

"What's her name, Harmony? How much time did you spend with her?" Sarah asked in a manner befitting a prosecuting attorney.

"Yeah, Harmony. Honestly, Sarah, she means nothing to me. She's just a friend."

The comment "she means nothing to me," in Sarah's estimation, was as close to an admission of guilt that one could ever expect from someone trying to hide something. She had heard enough, but Richard continued.

"Baby, I was being drugged from the day I was captured. I had convinced myself I was not even an FBI agent. Harmony helped me understand what they were doing to me. She helped me escape."

"It's fine," she replied, knowing it was not.

The two resumed eating, and there were no words between them for what seemed to Richard to be a very long time.

"What now?" he asked.

Sarah chewed her food while considering her reply.

"Well, it seems you are going to Cambodia. And I am going back to Detroit."

RICHARD TURNED ON THE iPad that was handed to him as he boarded his flight to Siem Reap, Cambodia, for Operation Free Eagle. On the device, he would find all the material ever published by Tom Adler, his official bio, resume, family photos, and everything necessary to temporarily assume his identity. There was also a brief on what Adler would have experienced as a prisoner of North Korea. Richard realized he could never completely convince someone that he was Tom Adler if he came under interrogation, but he had no plans to find himself in that situation.

He was immediately impressed by the moxie of Adler, who served as a journalist in some of the most dangerous places at the most dangerous moments in recent history. He covered the Russian invasion of Ukraine in 2022, from the front lines in Donbas. Before that, he was in Syria looking for evidence that Assad had used chemical weapons against his own people. And he was thrown out of Israel for covering the nationalist government's efforts to limit the influence of the Supreme Court.

It came as no surprise that Adler was going through a divorce. His work always took precedence, and his travel schedule made him difficult to pin down. He was closest to his sister, who often reminded him the importance of slowing down.

Adler had gained entry to North Korea under the premise of covering the careers of two aspiring Olympic figure skaters and was sending back dispatches to the editor of *Rolling Stone* about the government's efforts to exploit the potential of germline editing. The Supreme Leader, according to Adler, believed that germline editing could solve the problem of the country's persistent food shortages by creating a workforce that could become more productive with less nutrition. Adler stumbled on the story when his only intent was to report on the quality of life for the average North Korean family. He was taken into custody several months prior, shortly after his minders realized that he was not particularly interested in the Olympic figure skaters, and actually represented a perceived threat to their national security. *Now I understand why we want him back so badly and why our office is taking the lead*, Richard thought.

He popped in a pair of earbuds, turned on Spotify, and closed his eyes.

CHINA FACED AN EXISTENTIAL crisis unlike any other developed country. The situation was so devastating in its implications that it overshadowed any concerns about climate change. In fact, it would decimate the country's population long before climate change did any significant damage. People could see the threat every day they left their homes. They could see it in the streets. They could see it in the corporate world. In short, China was producing too many boys.

China's "one-child policy" was enforced for nearly forty years, starting in 1980. Boys were preferred because they could bring more income to the family. What happened to the less valued female babies was a dirty little secret that was never discussed. By 2015 the Chinese government could see the consequences of the imbalance and relaxed the policy, allowing a second child. In 2021 they increased the limit again, this time to three children. By that time the damage was done; decades of messaging and policies, combined with fears about the affordability of raising children, continued to depress birth rates.

The policies had other unintended effects. Second or third children born during the restrictions were often hidden from view and suffered hardships. They were unable to attend schools for fear of being discovered. Many were unable to gain employment. The number of undocumented children was estimated to be in the millions.

As if this were not enough, the population overall was aging. Due to medical advances and low fertility rates, China had a massive population of elderly, over twice as many as India, three times more than the United States, and nearly as many people over sixty-five as all other countries combined.

The internal struggle to solve the demographic crisis caused China to look outside its borders for solutions. China had already established a robust system for stealing trade secrets and intellectual property from developed countries, and scientific advances to address the demographic imbalance rose to the top of the nation's priority list. In 2008 China launched the "Thousand Talents Plan" to recruit 2,000 high quality experts overseas. By 2017, that number swelled to more than 7,000 scientists and other valued professionals.

Under the program, scientists earned a salary and research funding, which often included funding for a "shadow lab" in China. They were required to sign legally binding contracts that contained nondisclosure provisions, preventing them from revealing their participation in the program. References in published papers and online citations were scrubbed to conceal the program's involvement. Academics would often lie to U.S. grant-making agencies to avoid disclosing how their research was previously funded. In 2018, one member of the program used intellectual property created during work in a U.S. lab and filed for a U.S. patent under the name of a Chinese company. That's when the FBI got involved and began intelligence gathering of its own.

Unfortunately for China, many academics were all too willing to take a salary from the program without sharing the details of their discoveries. For these scientists, the arrangement was a marriage of convenience but not conscience. They sent back reports of bogus findings or failures while publishing their work under fictitious pen names or through collaboration with colleagues. Eventually, the Ministry of State Security started to send spies to selected labs to protect the investments they made and to accelerate the gathering of scientific research.

Ben Klein laid down the brief about Chinese espionage on his desk and turned toward his keyboard. He went online and typed into the browser, "Thousand Talents Plan and Human Genetics." The search returned 18.6 million results.

KOLINS SAT IN HIS STERILE-looking office in the Terasaki Life Sciences Building and leaned into his computer screen. It was time to conduct his weekly cleaning of the machine, that is, to clear his browser history and to delete any documents or emails that involved any communication with the Thousand Talents Program. As he did so, he silently cursed the requirement that his work had to be shrouded in secrecy above and beyond his peer group.

Kolins was among the scientists holding back on sharing research with the Thousand Talents Program, which was one reason Emma Lee was sent to check on him under the fake premise of writing a magazine article. What he showed her was only a small sample of the experiments under his purview at UCLA, where nearly 10,000 students were involved in the life sciences.

But time and money were running out for Kolins. He had missed an alimony payment to his wife, and bill collectors were beginning to call on him. He was approaching a turning point, he thought, when his phone rang.

It was Dennis Spence.

17

"Did you see the congressional hearing on C-SPAN with Jafek?"

Kolins had not heard from Dennis Spence in months. He was aware that Dennis had gone into hiding through reports in the local news about the raid on CNB. He was not aware that a North Korean spy attempted to gain access to Dennis's research, and neither was Dennis.

Kolins and Spence had a history, back to when Dennis was Denise and a pharmacology student at UCLA. Back then, Kolins was a teaching assistant. The two dated briefly until Denise's insecurities and anger toward men made the situation untenable. They remained in contact sporadically over the years, sharing research and ideas, although Kolins was skeptical of her commitment to the scientific method. Then, she used her substantial inheritance to acquire the Center for New Beginnings and to experiment on the homeless, following this with transgender therapy. For Kolins, it was a bridge too far to maintain a relationship of any significance.

"Yes, I watched it," Kolins replied.

"And...?" Dennis persisted.

"I don't know," he replied.

"How long do you think you can keep going?"

That was a question that Kolins asked himself every day.

"I don't know," he said again. As an academic, he was already embarrassed at his lack of perspective on the situation. "How is your research going?" he said, determined to change the subject.

"Kumar is doing great," he said, "along with a few other patients on the same regimen."

"And what is your plan?" Kolins replied. "Are you continuing to experiment on unsuspecting patients?"

Kolins's attempt at sarcasm was not lost on Dennis, who ignored it.

"I can tell you what I'm NOT going to do," he replied. "I am not going to share this with the idiots at Bio-Splice."

"I HAVEN'T TOLD YOU everything," Kolins admitted. Following his call with Dennis Spence, he was finally ready to get out in front of the lies he had told the U.S. government until now.

"The CCP is attempting to control the CRISPR market," said Kolins, and just as the words left his mouth, his brain silently added, *there, I said it.*

Kolins felt like everyone he was speaking to would understand that by CCP, an acronym used in political circles, he meant the Chinese Communist Party. He was in the conference room of the FBI office in San Diego. He sat at the far end of the room, in front of Klein's spider diagram. Long tables were organized to create a giant rectangle. Along the sides of the room were Klein, Jordan, McAuley, and other agents who had been following the case involving the missing persons and CNB. Kolins made the appointment with Klein with the promise of providing details on the "money for science secrets" scheme run by the Chinese government.

"What research from the United States are they trying to steal?" Klein asked.

"Well, to be clear, they don't look at it as stealing," Kolins replied. "As far as the Chinese are concerned, they are taking what is rightfully theirs, since they paid for it."

Klein had previously shared the intelligence briefing on Chinese espionage and the Thousand Talents Program with his staff, so Kolins's claim fit the narrative they had been provided.

"We will set aside the fact that what they are doing is against intellectual property laws," Klein said. "Let me ask you this, what do you know about The Center for New Beginnings?"

Kolins was not expecting that question, and the look on his face said as much.

"What about it?"

"What do you know about the kind of research being conducted there on the homeless?"

Kolins detested the use of homeless people in Spence's research; it violated everything he held dear regarding scientific values and bioethics, not to mention it was illegal. When he heard the word "homeless," it was all he needed to overcome any loyalty to Spence.

"They were extending the life of patients through CRISPR technologies." Kolins had conducted experiments with a similar goal, which is what he had shown Emma Lee during her visit. What he lacked, however, was a captive audience with which to apply his discoveries. Spence had conveniently cornered that market, which gave him a huge advantage over his scientific peer group.

"So, let me get this straight," Klein asked. "You've got someone that can extend human life through genetic engineering, China has essentially funded this research, and they are coming after it here?"

"It's not only that," Kolins added. "They are able to produce children without parental gestation."

Kolins explained that China sponsored an experiment that created viable embryos from two men. They took skin cells from these men that they grew in cultures to become pluripotent stem cells that could be reprogrammed into any other type of cell.

"As you know, men have an X and Y chromosome," he said. "In the laboratory, they were able to remove the Y chromosome, and through a drug called reversine, they duplicated the X chromosome. They then reprogrammed the cells to become egg cells and fertilized them with the sperm of another male. They can now replenish the female population, reversing the gender imbalance of the past century."

The room fell silent. The story sounded like science fiction, and yet Klein had already read about similar experiments conducted in Japan on laboratory animals. Since it was well-known that humans and mice share at least

70 percent of genetic sequences, it would only be a matter of time before more experiments would use human subjects, especially in China. And the FBI was well aware that China was using the marginalized Uyghur community as unwilling laboratory subjects, likely the source of cells for what Kolins was describing.

"Where is this happening?" came a question from one of the assembled agents.

"The lab is in Harbin. It's called Bio-Splice."

Again, the intelligence provided by Kolins was coming almost too fast for the agents to digest. Most agents studied criminal justice in college, not science. The topic was a heavy lift for several of them. Kolins decided to give the agency a more profound description of the threats posed by the Chinese.

"Gentlemen, evolution is no longer something that happens to us," he said. "Germline editing is the future."

"What can we do to stop this?" came a question from one of the agents.

Kolins hesitated, then decided he had come this far and needed to pick sides.

"I may have already done that, at least for now," he said, resigned that he had now let the genie out of the bottle and would have a lot more explaining to do. So, he continued.

"To be clear," he said, trying his best to show a level of bravado that would gain the confidence of even a trigger-happy agent, "I had recognized the possibility the Chinese government would make an attempt to come and collect early on the work I was doing. I could never be sure, but I wanted to be ready. I didn't want to be preempted on any discoveries I had been working on."

"And so...?" Klein asked.

"And so, I always had in a vulnerable part of my lab a small freezer that was labeled for CRISPR-adjusted bacteria. If anyone was in my lab to learn about my work, I'd point to it as I explained the research I was doing. They would naturally assume the bounty was in there, even though it was actually stored on another floor of the laboratory in a secure location."

The agents weren't following.

"What was really in that freezer was a toxic reagent that would destroy any living samples it might be combined with. Think of it as a trojan horse."

"And so...," it was Klein again, who was losing patience.

"Well, before I made my appointment to visit you, I found that four vials from that freezer were missing. That, gentlemen, is why I am here."

THE SUN WAS BEGINNING to set on a humid spring day in Siem Reap, and dramatic streaks of pink and purple clouds were everywhere, as if a god had smeared his hand across the sky. The Cambodian city's airport was a busy place even if a high-profile prisoner exchange was not on the schedule. This, after all, was the gateway to Angkor Wat, the temple complex of the ancient Khmer empire that once stretched from southern China in the north, Myanmar to the west, and all the way east to Vietnam, covering most of modern Southeast Asia.

Recognized by the *Guinness Book of World Records* as the largest religious structure in the world, Angkor Wat understandably attracted throngs of tourists. Tonight, the crowded airport included Western media outlets as well, anxious to catch a glimpse of the highly anticipated exchange and the promised return of Tom Adler.

The airport itself was simple and small, a very long structure topped by Cambodia-styled triangular roofs that would curve upward at each end in front of the domestic, international, and freight concourses. Cambodian Air domestic flights would still be flying today, but all other flights were canceled in light of the activity anticipated at the international side of the structure.

While the State Department would normally insist on secrecy to prevent the circus-like atmosphere whenever media outlets converge on a scene, they welcomed it this time. Through security protocols established in cooperation with the Cambodian government, a select number of news organizations, including CNN, NPR, and the BBC, were permitted to set up on the airport tarmac. It was important to amp up the fanfare for this event in order to ensure the Chinese were paying sufficient attention and had a visual reference for Tom Adler.

The unmarked Antonov AN-148 aircraft rolled slowly toward a carpeted area on the tarmac in front of space number seven, where Matthew Cackett, the U.S. ambassador to Cambodia, stood waiting. Next to him was an FBI agent, and next to him, a man appearing to be Kim Ji-Sung. That man was wearing handcuffs, which was standard procedure. The blindfold was not. A makeshift tunnel made from soft plastic had been erected and would be the passage used by Tom Adler and Kim Ji-Sung to walk from the plane, or to it. It was described as a safety precaution. As the plane came to a stop, airport personnel adjusted the tunnel slightly, with enough clearance that the stairs from the plane could be set down nearby.

As the exchange got underway, media outlets that were provided talking points by the FBI began covering the story of Tom Adler, what he was doing in North Korea, and what he discovered when he was there. Among the reporters was Jack Reeves.

"We are looking forward to welcoming back one of our own, a fellow journalist and truth-seeker, Tom Adler," he said. "As we wait anxiously for the exchange, let's take a look at the incredible career of this brave journalist and some of the important stories he has covered."

Reeves would not typically qualify for an international assignment, but the CBS network bigshots took an interest in him given his prior contribution and appetite for adventure, it was not difficult for the FBI to secure his involvement, and besides, he helped identify some of the key assets needed to pull off the ruse in a credible fashion. Reeves knew a lot of people in the news industry, including those who could be trusted and those who could not.

"And finally," he said after reviewing Adler's prior assignments, "he entered North Korea to cover the Olympic hopefuls Ryom Tae Ok and Kim Ju Sik, the country's popular figure skating duo who are training for the Winter

Olympics. What he stumbled on, however, was not only a robust doping program for athletes who compete internationally but a few scientists exploring germline editing."

Anyone following Adler's career closely could have been forgiven for being a bit skeptical, as he would never bother to cover as pedestrian a story as one involving a couple of Olympic athletes.

Reeves continued to explain the implications of germline editing to a largely uneducated and unsuspecting public. His peers from CNN and the BBC were doing the same. It was a well-orchestrated performance, guaranteed to goad China into believing that their trade partners were in an unofficial race with them to exploit this new frontier of genetic engineering.

Reeves tilted his head and placed his hand on the receiver in his left ear. "Wait," he said, "it seems that the plane is about to let down the stairs. We are about to get our first good look at Tom Adler since he disappeared six months ago."

Between the reporters, their camera crews, the U.S. delegation, and the Adler family, there were about twenty-five people on the tarmac. By this time, the sun had set behind the plane, and dusk concealed most features of the landscape, apart from the plane itself. Everyone was focused on the door of the jet as it pushed its way out from the cabin, turned sideways and then back into the plane, revealing the light from the inside. Then, ever so slowly, a man's silhouette appeared in the doorway. He looked thin, as was expected, and Richard was prepared to suck in his gut for as long as necessary once he was introduced to the world as Adler. Camera clicks filled the air as all eyes were on the man walking down the stairs.

The distance from the bottom of the plane's stairs to the tunnel was only about three feet, so Richard, posing as Adler, disappeared quickly. As soon as he did, the FBI agent responsible for Ji-Sung gently took the man by the arm, and the two headed into the tunnel. The crowd was spellbound, as if they were watching a solar eclipse or some other rare phenomenon demanding full attention. Some reporters continued with the coverage.

The FBI agent and the man observers identified as Ji-Sung could be seen exiting the tunnel's far end. The agent removed the man's blindfold and handcuffs and guided him by the arm onto the plane's stairs. Within seconds he was at the top, entering the plane and not looking back. Shadows inside the plane suggested that he was greeted by his comrades before disappearing completely.

The crowd waited for Tom Adler to appear. This was taking longer than anyone expected. As the State Department was provided a picture of Adler in advance by the DPRK, they could anticipate what he would be wearing, so there was no need for the two men to exchange clothing—Richard was wearing the same green jumpsuit as Adler would have been wearing.

A few moments later, a man appeared, smiling tentatively and waving to the crowd. Richard's first stop as Tom Adler was to shake the hand of Ambassador Cackett, whose back was to the cameras allowing him the opportunity to whisper "Good luck, son" to Richard as he embraced both his hands. Tom Adler's sister came forward next and embraced Richard, and the two hurried off to a large black SUV where they were ostensibly going to the local hospital for medical evaluation.

The unmarked jet powered up again and slowly pulled away from the crowd. The deafening noise from the jet signaled to many reporters that it was time to leave.

For a short while longer, a few remained to continue coverage of the extraordinary exchange they had just witnessed, the adventures of Tom Adler, and the implications of a "germline-capable" North Korea.

"And the SUV is now making its way to Royal Angkor International Hospital where Tom Adler will undergo extensive tests," said Claire Monroe from CNN. A natural concern would be that he had contracted HIV or hepatitis or suffered from intestinal worms due to contaminated food.

BY 2:45 A.M., LONG after the airport had officially closed, three black SUVs and a fire engine remained on the tarmac, idling in the dark. The still air of the night did not indicate that anything else of importance would happen, the members of the media left hours before, and most of the city's residents were fast asleep. A few bats roamed the skies in search of food.

The Approach Lighting System was suddenly turned on and began blinking its alternating pattern of red and white lights. Floodlights hanging off the terminal building were illuminated, piercing the darkness below. Insects attracted to the lights began circling above.

Then, an AN-148 that bore the markings of Air Koryo, the state-owned airline of North Korea, descended through the clouds and aligned itself with the runway at Siem Reap International Airport. It landed and made its way to space number 1 at the far-left side of the terminal. As it slowed to a halt, the SUVs turned on their lights and came alongside.

Four agents exited the first SUV and stood at attention, two near the front of the aircraft and two near the rear. Next, three men exited the back of the second SUV. In the middle was Kim Ji-Sung, whose arms were being held by an agent on either side. One of the men held a walkie-talkie allowing him to communicate directly with the air traffic control tower. Shortly after he spoke into it, the door of the aircraft opened and the stairs were deployed. The two agents holding Ji-Sung moved toward the bottom of the stairs.

A clearly disheveled man, the real Tom Adler, came walking down the steps, holding the guardrail carefully for extra support. Two steps behind him was a North Korean soldier. Adler stopped halfway down the stairs, as commanded by the soldier.

Next, it was time for Ji-Sung to make his way up the stairs. Once he reached the halfway mark, Adler was permitted to walk down. Ji-Sung was escorted onto the jet by the soldier, and both quickly disappeared. The exchange was complete.

As the stairs to the plane were brought back up, the engines started to rev up once again. The third SUV's doors flew open and Adler's wife and children appeared, along with two more agents. Under the supervision of eight federal agents, but without any members of the media present, Adler was reunited with his family.

18

Denials from North Korea came quickly. By the time most Americans were waking up, their newsfeed included details of the dramatic prisoner swap, followed by Pyongyang's condemnation that argued claims of a doping program and germline editing laboratory were fabrications of a "Western society looking for an excuse to attack a sovereign nation." They were not far from wrong.

The negative press attention did little to improve relations with North Korea in spite of the promise of valuable intelligence that was being provided to Ji-Sung. The promise of that intelligence persuaded the DPRK to be silent over the staged exchange of prisoners, but in reality, even if they called out the charade, nobody in the West would believe them. It was decided that the extensive media coverage made it too risky that Richard's true identity would be revealed during the exchange, effectively scuttling the mission.

Richard spent the morning with Tom Adler in a closed-off wing of the hospital. They met with other FBI agents who had flown in from the American Embassy in Bangkok, where they have a permanent office. The purpose of the meeting was to learn as much as possible about the areas that Adler visited in North Korea so that Richard could accurately describe them as if he had been there himself. While the North Koreans had not come close to matching the advances in germline editing being made in other countries, Adler was able to describe some of the industrial sites that, based on satellite photos, could convince someone that a large scientific laboratory was indeed there.

"You're not going to sully my name, are you?" Adler asked Richard. It was hard to tell if Adler was being facetious. It was not hard to feel sorry for him; he had a rolling IV pole attached to him in order to address his severe dehydration.

"Well," Richard replied, smiling, "not intentionally."

Adler was required to participate in the meeting because he was now considered an asset to the mission and besides, it was too dangerous for him to be seen with Richard in public. The movements of the two men had to be carefully coordinated in the event members of the media were still hanging around, looking for a story or the opportunity for a one-on-one interview with Adler. Such a scoop would be quite a coup for any reporter who made the trip to Cambodia. Adler would have his beard shaved off in a few hours, which would significantly reduce the risks of being discovered.

"Richard, we will be booking you a ticket to Bangkok, and then on to Los Angeles," said Marty Friedman, the lead agent. "You will spend three days in Bangkok first. We have you set up to do an interview with Stephen McDonnell of the BBC. MI6 helped set this up as they are cooperating with us. We expect that you will be contacted by a Chinese agent while you are there. We'll be sending you a specific meeting location shortly."

"Okay, but why exactly will they be looking for me?"

"We are circulating the narrative that you are not happy with the way you were being treated by *Rolling Stone*," Friedman replied. "We filed the paperwork last week through the New York County civil court to sue for lost wages, where the magazine is based, just in case anyone tries to validate it." This was the second time in recent weeks that the FBI needed the cooperation of the media to stand behind a bogus story in the interest of national security. In the case of the fantasy reported by Jack Reeves there was an audience member of only one person. But asking *Rolling Stone* magazine to play along with the scheme was an extraordinary step for the intelligence services and had the potential to infuriate American free-press advocates.

In reality, Adler had already decided after nearly losing his life in a North Korean hard labor prison camp that he was done with journalism and would officially retire once he got back to the States, and work on saving his marriage. Besides, suing the magazine for any reason was not his style, and had his editor not signed on with the plan he would have had serious objections.

"Look," Friedman explained, "if we show you to be disgruntled, the spies out there might be more inclined to believe you are willing to share some of what you saw in North Korea *before or instead of* giving the story to the magazine. Anyway, that's the narrative we created, and we have our agents pushing it in the region as we speak. That you are looking for someone that is willing to not only pay for the story but to pay for specific intel about the location of the laboratory."

The two "Adlers" now looked at each other. If anyone knew how to bring a spy out of the shadows, it was the FBI.

"Also, give me your tablet," Friedman said to Richard, who reached into his backpack and handed the device to the agent. As he did, Friedman passed him a brand new iPad.

"Obviously, Tom came back empty-handed, so if you are asked, you picked up a new iPad in Bangkok and downloaded all your documents from the cloud," he said.

Richard nodded as he thought about getting into his new character.

"We've loaded this up with some of Tom's drafts and added some editing apps that a journalist would use," Friedman added. "There are photos in there of a fake laboratory, maps to indicate its location, and some unpublished scientific papers," he said. "Let me be clear, Richard, we want them to get their hands on this, but please don't make it so easy to sell or steal that they become suspicious."

Richard nodded, looked at the iPad briefly, then put it in his backpack. He then had a delayed reaction regarding Friedman's last statement.

"What's in the scientific papers, and why are they unpublished?" he said. He was not particularly in the mood to read a bunch of dense copy that he wouldn't likely understand.

Friedman was hesitant to go down this path, but he knew Richard needed the best preparation possible.

"Okay, so, have you ever heard of tardigrades?"

Now that was a word that Richard felt he should know but didn't. Rather than appearing cliché, he waited for Friedman to continue.

"We wanted to find a narrative that the Chinese could not resist because we need them to fully dissect the iPad and to ensure we deliver our camfecting code in the process. So, the unpublished papers describe North Korean experiments on tardigrades."

That wasn't helping, so Friedman continued.

"Basically, tardigrades are these tiny eight-legged creatures that are nearly indestructible. They can exist in the hottest temperatures anywhere; we're talking three hundred degrees. They can survive freezing, like being totally frozen, and NASA even sent them into space, and they survived there. They can live thirty years without water and can go into suspended animation whenever conditions threaten them. They can even survive radiation from a nuclear blast.

"Believe me, I've learned far more about tardigrades the past few weeks than I've ever wanted to know. Go ahead, google them, you'll see. There is a lot of interest in learning how the tardigrades do what they do and figuring how the human race can tap into the tardigrade's mojo."

Richard and Tom looked at each other again and broke out laughing.

"So, you are basically laying down catnip for them? And tardigrades are the catnip?" Adler said. It was phrased as a question but was more of a statement of fact.

"We believe the Chinese will find it irresistible to gather this intelligence from North Korea," Friedman replied, "and it would be very believable that North Korea would place a high degree of value on exploiting tardigrade research and learning how to create a more sustainable population that suffers from a tainted water supply and serious food insecurity. Oh, and given the lack of sanitation in the country, they will have a near infinite supply of tardigrades. Trust me on this."

It was clear that Friedman had done his homework, and he convinced Richard to read up more on the whole tardigrade thing in case he was asked about it.

After another hour or so of discussions, with Tom sharing intimate details of his personal life, it was time to cut Richard loose into the world as the "new" Tom Adler. Richard and Tom embraced as if they were identical twin brothers, departing in different directions. Tom would be going to the operating room for a shave and a haircut. He would remain in the hospital another two days, then be unceremoniously discharged in the evening, when nobody would notice. He would be escorted to the airport where he would board an FBI-owned Gulfstream jet, with no external markings, for his trip back to the States where he would undergo intense debriefing regarding his time in North Korea.

Richard would head to the airport separately for a short fifty-minute flight to Suvarnabhumi Airport. He fully expected a small contingent of media correspondents following him and meeting him there and was provided a script of approved talking points for any encounters with the media, including the statement "I've already told everything I know and saw to the FBI."

"Make me proud," Tom said as the two took one last look at each other.

"You are a tough act to follow," Richard replied.

Richard left the hospital with Marty Friedman. As they stepped out of the hospital doors, all Richard could think of was *game on*.

EMMA LEE FINISHED TOUCHING up her lips with deep red lipstick, then pulled back to look at herself in the mirror of her room at the Banyan Tree Hotel. Her medium-length black hair lay perfectly on her shoulders. She leaned in again to curl her eyelashes, then assessed the effect. She was as attractive as she needed to be. She was still in her underwear, preparing for her next mission.

At twenty-eight, Emma was much more comfortable in the role of naive college student, but if called upon to seduce a man to obtain intelligence, she knew she had the talent. And being back in Asia made her that much closer to her family. She was promised an extended leave from her many employers once Tom Adler's iPad was stolen.

There was another reason that Lee was chosen for the mission. Among the agents in her division, she had the best English skills, a credible profile already established in the States, and she could most effectively establish the veracity of information she was directed to acquire. Emma Lee had become one of the agency's most valuable assets.

Having Lee steal the iPad was deemed a safer alternative to buying it, where the source of funding might be eventually traced by the Americans, leading back to the CCP. And Adler was considered an easy mark: potentially going through a divorce, disgruntled, and yet willing to meet up to do a deal.

She moved to the bed where she had two outfits laid out. On the left was a slim red dress that she would wear with a pair of fuck-me pumps. *Too cliché*, she finally thought to herself. She reached instead for the sheer blouse on the right, which she paired with a black leather skirt. With the black bra underneath, she would be sure to get the necessary attention. She stood in front of the full-length mirror on the front of the bathroom door. She was ready.

She pulled her phone from her tiny purse and took a selfie in front of the mirror, just in case Tom failed to show up and she needed something provocative to persuade him to eventually meet her. She dropped her phone and lipstick inside. She then turned off the lights and headed for the elevator that would take her to the fifty-ninth floor and Vertigo, the rooftop bar. As the elevator rose, Emma put her hands under her breasts and pushed them up a bit, ensuring maximum cleavage was revealed behind her near transparent blouse.

Since moving to New York, Richard had prided himself on being a man of the city, able to power walk across town when the moment called for it, and the Banyan Tree Hotel, where he was told to go, was only about 1½ miles from his government-approved Marriott. So he naturally thought he could leave early and get a feel for Bangkok, a city he had never visited before. Then he stepped outside. Even though the sun had set about a half hour earlier, he still felt the smothering ninety-four degrees and 100 percent sticky humidity.

What Richard saw as he navigated down the crowded street was a city full of contradictions. Street food was ubiquitous, even near glamorous hotels. He walked past makeshift religious shrines displaying fresh fruit that were erected in the corner of practically every parking lot, near cannabis stores and hookah bars. Massage parlors offering the unadvertised special, a "happy ending," seemed to appear every few hundred feet. And a seemingly random collection of electrical wires hung haphazardly from light poles, lining the sides of every street in the city.

Taxis, scooters, and motorcycles swarmed the streets like stampeding wild animals. Neon lights that rivaled Time Square and Piccadilly Circus demanded his attention and overwhelmed his senses. The smell of noodle soup was everywhere. Bangkok epitomized everything that Richard loved and loathed about dense urban environments.

Richard felt he needed a new shirt after walking only a few blocks. Sweat was beading on his forehead, escaping from his armpits, and running down his back. After convincing himself that walking was not the way to go, he stepped aside from the stream of pedestrians and used the Uber-like Grab app to hire a ride. Moments later, a young boy on a scooter swung into the curb and onto the sidewalk, startling him.

"Banyan Tree?" the boy said through his face mask.

Richard would have felt like a wimp to send the boy away, so he hopped on. The next ten minutes were pure terror. As the bike took off, Richard nearly fell backward on the pavement.

The boy quickly joined the swarm of scooters buzzing in the same direction on Thanon Sukhumvit, the city's main artery. When they approached cars stopped at a traffic light, the boy snaked between them, leaving precious little room between Richard's knees and several side-view mirrors. The boy even hopped the bike onto the sidewalk and threaded it between light poles, street signs, and people.

The boy wore a helmet, Richard didn't. At one point, as he was traveling at ninety-three kph, Richard was about to tap his shoulder to say "no más" when he saw an even younger boy flying past them. On the back of his bike was a girl who couldn't have been more than twelve years old. She was looking down and texting on her phone. Seconds later, another scooter whizzed past, the female passenger sitting sidesaddle in a dress behind the young operator. Richard decided to suck it up and go the distance.

Stepping off the bike, Richard was a bit wobbly but still standing. His first instinct was to kiss the pavement, but he settled for squatting down to loosen the muscles in his legs that had tensed up on the ride. He then stood, took a deep breath, and started walking.

He entered the lobby of the Banyan Tree Hotel, took the elevator to the fifty-ninth floor, then climbed several winding staircases up to the top. When he finally reached the roof, he looked down on the lights of Bangkok and thought that after a couple of drinks anyone could be convinced that they were looking down on his adopted home of New York. The spectacular view had Richard believing what the travel magazines said: This was one of the best rooftop bars in the world.

Richard had been informed in an intelligence briefing that the Banyan Tree was a favorite of wealthy American businessmen and MSS agents, so he was wary as he walked around, looking for a place to sit. Some agents posed as prostitutes, looking to score a meeting with an American where the mark would be oblivious to any scheme.

He noticed a large pole with a camera looking down on the entire area, so he picked a spot where he would have his back to the camera. He chose a spot overlooking the bridge over the Chao Phraya River that bisected Bangkok.

Richard understood why the agent would want to meet him at the Vertigo bar. The environment was subdued, but pulsating music was just loud enough to frustrate eavesdroppers. Tables lined the perimeter of the roof, allowing guests to enjoy a panoramic view of the city lights. The lights on the roof were kept low to avoid spoiling the intimate atmosphere. A warm breeze flowed across the roof, offering relief to his sticky skin and slightly moist shirt.

Richard cradled his spiced rum and Coke, looking out on the city lights, wondering how many tourists were silently screaming on the back of a scooter down below. He reflected on how incredibly lucky he was to have survived detention and drug-induced schizophrenia and to have a role now that he felt destined to play. Then he realized what would happen next: He was about to meet face to face with a Chinese agent! His right thigh began to vibrate. It was all happening so fast.

The iPad Richard was provided was resting under his left arm. He was assured by Marty Friedman that he would be contacted at the bar tonight, and he would simply need to be there between 2000 and 2200 hours until contact was made. Just then, he felt a gentle hand rest upon his shoulder.

"But I thought Tom Adler drank gin and tonic?" said the voice behind him.

Richard turned around and stood. He was face to face with Emma. He was always attracted to Asian types, and Emma pulled off the look of a femme fatale perfectly.

"He does?" Richard replied, forgetting for that moment that he was operating undercover as Tom Adler. "Well, he also likes to mix it up sometimes, especially when traveling abroad. After all, rum is a drink of the tropics, and if feels pretty damn tropical out here tonight."

Of all the preparations made to ensure Richard could pass as Adler, knowing what he drinks would have been one of the more important things to know. And it was apparent that Emma did her homework.

Richard smiled, but it was not authentic. He was too nervous.

"Please," he said, holding out his arm. "Have a seat."

Emma placed her purse on the table, ran her hand under her skirt, and took the seat opposite Richard.

"My name is Elisabeth," she said, looking directly at Richard with an intimate gaze that could make any man feel unsettled.

Richard stared at her for longer than either expected. He had an uncanny feeling that he had seen Emma somewhere before.

"Tom, Tom Adler," he finally replied in a slightly tentative tone. "But it seems you know that already."

"Tom, it's so wonderful to finally meet you," she said, smiling broadly. "My people are very interested to learn more about your research."

This elicited a modest smile from Richard to serve as acknowledgment.

"May I buy you a drink?" he replied, forgetting that Tom Adler was probably not as promiscuous as he would be, but then again, not really caring either way. He was having too much fun playing make-believe with a sexy woman, and he knew that as far as being an undercover agent, he was sure he was destined to be good at it.

Emma did not need to be specific about what she was after, nor to run the risk of their conversation being overheard in a country that was already teeming with foreign agents of various governments. The two agents knew why they were there and what they were supposed to do. If it went any further than that, their secret would stay in Bangkok.

"Tom," Emma continued, moving her hand on top of his. "I'd rather continue this conversation in my room. We'll have more privacy there. What do you think?"

Richard did not need to hear that twice. He pulled a 500-baht bill from his pocket and laid it beside his drink. He stood and again extended his arm to encourage Emma to walk ahead of him.

As she moved ahead of him, he gently placed his hand on the small of her back, just to signal that he was up for anything she might propose. He could not help but think of

Sean Connery, as James Bond in *You Only Live Twice* when Bond removes the dress of his adversary just as the camera cuts away from the scene.

"Oh, the things I do for England," he whispered in a voice nobody would hear.

Emma and Richard didn't speak as they headed down the elevator to Emma's hotel room. *Whatever she proposes, don't drink anything*, he thought to himself, remembering his training and what happened to him the last time he accepted coffee from a suspected adversary. Emma may have been interested in using her sex appeal to take advantage of Richard, which he would enthusiastically welcome, but it did not mean he could let down his guard.

The elevator doors opened to the forty-ninth floor. Richard followed Emma down the hallway to her room. As she stood at the door, she turned and flashed a smile at Richard, signaling that the evening was about to get more interesting. She placed her key card against the door, and a green light signaled it was unlocked. She pushed open the door and walked in.

As Richard stepped inside after her, he was hit hard from behind and fell to the floor. The blow hurt, but while he did not black out, he did drop the iPad, which was scooped up by whoever had hit him. The attacker was out the door before it even had an opportunity to close. He was gone in seconds.

Emma rushed to Richard's side as he lay in the fetal position on the hotel room floor, holding his head.

"What the fuck was that?" he cried aloud.

"I'm so sorry," Emma replied, "I have no idea. I don't know how he got in here."

As if. The agent working for the Chinese Ministry of State Security had entered Emma's room shortly after she left it, just as planned. It was important for Emma to appear innocent of wrongdoing, but she strongly objected to harming anyone who was more than willing to give up what he was offering.

"Are you all right? Let me see where he hit you." Emma was kneeling next to Richard, massaging his scalp.

"Fuck," he said, cradling his head with both hands, "he took my iPad, didn't he?"

"I don't see it, so yes, I'm afraid he did."

As he ran his head over his scalp looking for signs of blood, Richard considered the possibility that he had accomplished the mission already. Certainly, the iPad was now in the hands of the adversary, presuming the narrative spread by Friedman's local resources got to the right audience. He actually felt relieved.

"Let me get you up," Emma said, feeling slightly guilty about her part in the assault. She did her best to pull Richard first to his knees, then to his feet, and got him to the foot of the bed. Richard looked at the slim red dress that was still lying there. Elisabeth was an intriguing character, he thought to himself, and he wondered if, in the service to the agency, he might still get lucky tonight. As unbelievable as it was that his mind would even venture in this direction, Richard was being Richard, and given the ambiguity of his relationship status with Sarah, he saw no problem with this stream of consciousness. It's like getting a hole-in-one on a golf course when playing alone; nobody would believe the story anyway. He would regret that sentiment a few moments later.

"Tom," she said, "I need to report to my superiors that we lost access to your story," telling yet another lie. She looked with sympathy at Richard, who was now standing opposite her. He felt the opportunity for a more interesting evening slipping away.

"I can still assemble some coordinates for you, you know, of the lab," he replied, a bit desperately. "I just need to get on the web and pull down the files from my iCloud account."

What Richard was offering was essentially useless information, but given the circumstances, and the fact that Emma herself did not appear dangerous, he wanted to see just how much bogus information he could pass along. He was fully invested in the ruse, behaving like a man trying to save a relationship that was already lost.

Emma did not want to send the signal that she already had everything she needed on the stolen iPad, so she acquiesced.

"All right," she replied. "How about we meet tomorrow morning, shall we say, 10 o'clock in the lobby?"

Richard could not believe that he was about to be ushered out of the room of a beautiful Chinese agent in a see-through blouse. But his head was aching, and he finally realized that chivalry and integrity were more important to his identity than the ability to engage in gratuitous sex. He slowly moved toward the door and mustered a smile.

"Are you sure you'll be okay in here by yourself?" Richard asked, allowing himself one last chance to salvage the evening.

"Oh yes, I'll be fine, don't worry. I'll see you in the morning, Tom."

With that, Emma opened the door and held it open for him. Her eyes looked up at his, but she was no longer smiling. She was too ashamed.

"Good night, Elisabeth," Richard said, and he walked out the door. He would ask the lobby concierge to ensure it would be a four-door sedan taking him back to his hotel.

BACK IN HIS ROOM, HE pivoted back to thoughts of the assault. While he couldn't identify the assailant, he did want to alert the branch that the iPad was likely on its way to China.

"Elvis has left the building," he texted via Signal, indicating that the iPad was taken. He did not feel the need to elaborate on how the device made it into the hands of the Chinese. This detail could be provided later.

He fell backward on the bed and stared at the ceiling. He listened to the pounding rain, a near constant part of the Bangkok soundtrack this time of year. The night ended much earlier than expected, he thought, but there was one thing he had not resolved, and that was why Elisabeth looked so familiar to him. He opened the photo app on his new phone, which was restored with files he had stored on the cloud before being taken hostage at CNB. He began thumbing through the photos, many of Sarah Goodman, until he landed on the picture sitting behind Dennis Spence's desk. He zoomed in.

"What the fuck, it's her!" he said aloud. "She's working with him!"

Images started flashing through his mind, back to when he first met Dennis Spence. The identity of the other woman in the photo was never established. His heart rate started to increase. His breath became shallower. He was not sure what to do in that moment.

He jumped off the bed, started for the door, placed his hand on the doorknob, then stopped. *What am I going to say when I confront her? What's the plan? What do I hope to achieve?* Clearly, he wasn't ready to take full advantage of his discovery. He released the doorknob and began pacing the room.

No, he thought, he is not going over there tonight. In fact, he won't reveal what he knows when he sees her the following morning.

"I am one step ahead of her!" he thought to himself. He concluded that he could gather information without her knowing what she was giving up. This evening turned out even better than he expected.

Between the bruise on his head and the new intelligence dancing across his mind, Richard was exhausted. He laid himself back on the bed, this time face down, breathing heavily into the pillow. What he didn't understand is that it can take a full week to adjust to travel across the international date line. He fell asleep, fully clothed.

RICHARD WOKE AT 7:25 the next morning. Already the humidity was fogging the windows and making it difficult for him to look out on the city of Bangkok and the cars, bicycles, scooters, and motorcycles that jammed the eternally busy Sukhumvit Road below. Horns and sirens complemented the chaos.

Richard wanted to catch "Elisabeth" off guard by arriving a few minutes early to her hotel room, just in case he could catch her doing something that might further expose her. He took the elevator up to the forty-ninth floor. As he approached her room, he saw the housekeeping cart outside it and the door open. He moved faster, and his heart started keeping pace with his footsteps. He reached the room and looked inside. She was gone.

Richard walked into the room. A housekeeper was stripping the bed. He instinctively pulled his badge, realizing that he had no authority on the premises but hoping the housekeeper would get the message. She did, bowing slightly, then walking past Richard into the hallway. She pushed the cart down the hall. Richard closed the door.

He stood in the center of the room, trying to understand why Elisabeth would commit to a meeting, then disappear. He did a 360 turn to look for any clues she may have left behind. He walked into the bathroom and did the same. Elisabeth may have cleaned the bathroom herself, he theorized, because there were no clues that the room was ever occupied. The toilet was hissing as if the interior seal was defective.

As he was about to leave, he noticed a small piece of shiny copper at the bottom of the toilet. It was a SIM card for a cell phone. Maybe she flushed it in the dark and didn't notice that the water pressure failed to carry it into the sewer system. Richard reached in and pulled it out.

It was still early. If Elisabeth was on her way back to China, she may be headed to one of the two main airports in Bangkok or already there and waiting to board her flight. He could still catch her. But he remembered that the last time he tried to do something like that, at Dulles Airport in Washington, he ended up in the hospital and arrested for impersonating a federal official. He held the SIM card above his eyes to allow the sun to shine on it. No, he thought, he had everything he needed between his thumb and forefinger.

EMMA LEE BOARDED THE China Eastern flight to Harbin wearing a UCSD hoodie, torn jeans, and Converse sneakers. She played every bit the part of a student returning home to visit family. She carried an iPad just like many other passengers. As she took her seat, she sent her mother a text in her native tongue, "Ma, I'm on the plane. I'll see you soon."

She pushed the small cooler underneath the seat in front of her. Getting the samples through security was simple; nothing was in a container of three ounces or more. On the contrary, each vial held only about 0.5 ml of live

CRISPR-altered bacteria, six vials from UCSD and four from UCLA.

What Emma was bringing to China represented the missing raw materials necessary to create the closest thing to an indestructible human being.

19

Even though the deputy chief of the Intelligence Section of the MSS had issued multiple memos to alert staff to the risks of "camfecting," it was inevitable that some would forget to replace the piece of tape on their computer camera after a videoconference. Camfecting is a hack that allows remote activation of a webcam, lets the hacker see whatever the camera sees, and, depending on the code installed, the contents of what the user is viewing on the computer screen.

The FBI had employed camfecting as far back as 2012, and since then had discovered how to activate the camera without the user realizing that it was recording. More recent advances extended the technique to security cameras and mobile phones.

The MSS deputy also had warned staff to refrain from using public charging stations in airports, hotels, and other places where they were becoming ubiquitous. This was because of yet another security risk, called "juice-jacking," where connecting to such networks could allow the delivery of a virus or other malicious software. It was always a challenge to communicate such directives to field agents overseas, and often these instructions would arrive too late or fail to reach the intended audience.

The deputy's concern was reasonable. The CIA, through some arm twisting and promises of security assistance via the State Department, persuaded Thailand's National Intelligence Agency to tap into the Banyan Tree Hotel's wi-fi network to juice-jack Emma's phone. A package was delivered to her device, which she would later pass to the lab, allowing the Americans to eavesdrop via camfecting. Just in case she didn't use the charger in her hotel room, the same software code was installed on the iPad she had helped steal from Richard, offering the FBI a tactical advantage that would be the cornerstone of any effective mission: *redundancy*.

"We are online," said the young technician in the basement of Bangkok's U.S. Embassy. The scale of the FBI operation, an extension of Operation Free Eagle, required the embassy to procure several extra monitors, which were now set up on banquet tables in the dimly lit room. The tables were positioned against the wall; a series of folding chairs were on one side, and a tangled web of HDMI and power cables, extension cords, and other wires emanated from the monitors on the other side. Windows at the top of the walls were blacked out to conceal the room's activity.

As the technician made his announcement, six monitors began to pop with the images being projected from Bio-Splice. A small piece of white tape at the top of each monitor indicated the view being provided: Lab 1, Lab 2, Hallway 1, Hallway 2, and Entrance. The technician focused on the sixth monitor, its specific focus not yet identified. Marty Friedman looked over the technician's shoulder, a cup of coffee in his hand.

"Anything yet?" he asked.

"Sir, this one has been a challenge," the technician replied. "There is a lot of fog that is making it tough to see. Also, the camera is panning back and forth. So, we need to record the screen, then slow it down if we want to look at something closely."

"Fog?" Friedman asked. "So, it's a walk-in refrigerator, right?"

"Yes, sir, I think so," the tech said. "If we are watching when someone enters, the fog will likely dissipate outside the room, giving us a better view."

It would have been helpful to know exactly what they were looking for.

"SIR, I THINK YOU SHOULD see this."

The technician was leaning into the sixth monitor again. He was excitedly tapping a pencil on the table. He was on his fifth cup of coffee and had been staring at the various screens for the past three hours.

Friedman sat at a table in the corner where he had been waiting for something to pop.

"What've you got?" he replied, not looking up from his laptop.

"Someone opened the door to the freezer, and I recorded the video feed just after. I think it's a morgue."

Friedman wasn't surprised to hear that a morgue existed within a scientific laboratory. The intelligence community had already conceded that China was likely experimenting on human subjects, especially the Uyghurs. The topic infuriated most democracies and added to China's poor human rights record, but it was not new information. Friedman continued working.

"All right," he said, his head still buried in administrative details.

"But sir, I think these people were frozen alive or are being kept alive."

The technician had slowed down the recorded video feed to reveal information on each body stored in the freezer. The fact that it was recording various vital signs indicated that the bodies inside were being stored as cryogenic subjects.

Again, Friedman continued his work. Nothing yet merited further attention. Cryogenics had expanded significantly in the past few years, and the FBI investigated many of them to ensure they were operating legally. It would stand to reason that the Chinese would be experimenting on Uyghurs and using them to perfect the process of freezing patients now and recovering them in the future.

"But sir," the technician said again, his voice raised to communicate the urgency of his discovery, "The names of the people . . ."

Friedman reluctantly put his hands on the table to push himself up. He couldn't ignore the technician any longer. He turned toward the bank of monitors and stepped over to the technician. He put his hand on the tech's right shoulder, leaned down, and peered into the monitor.

"Sir, look."

As the camera panned slowly across the room, the names of the people inside the freezer were slowly revealed while Friedman read the names aloud.

"Steele, Escobar, Jobs, Musk . . ."

"THINK ABOUT IT," SAID Dr. Patricia Novicoff, the agency's expert in psychological profiling. "If you had an idea that was going to outrage society, would you broadcast it to the world?" Novicoff was meeting by secure videoconference with the agents assigned to Operation Free Eagle, a mission that had morphed from the prisoner exchange that freed Tom Adler to the investigation into Dennis Spence's experiments and his possible connection to the Chinese Ministry of State Security. Novicoff was asked to join the call to help the agents understand the motives of Dennis Spence in running a clandestine operation that involved kidnapping, medical malpractice, wire fraud, and probably more felonies.

"I understand why he was operating under the radar, but why is Spence so eager to work with the CCP?" asked Klein, hoping Novicoff might provide some clues.

"Spence's behavioral profile suggests the need for absolute control," Novicoff said. "But if he doesn't have access to all the resources necessary, he may be cooperating with China out of necessity. I would expect that from Spence's perspective, he believes he is using the Chinese, and not the other way around."

Since the raid on CNB the agents had a fair amount of information on Spence's prior activities, which included experiments on the homeless people that he collected off the street. The experiments were intended to extend the lifetime of these subjects while providing for their care and comfort. Spence could justify the effort on moral grounds since, although the subjects didn't have the option to leave, they were much better off than before. According to his notes, multiple iterations of his experiments and subsequent fine tuning resulted in Spence doubling the lifespan of his subjects.

Until this point, the agents had been busy with the disposition of patients from CNB to family members or shelters and in general shutting down and securing the facility. They were only now digging into the notes, medical records, and lab documentation recovered in their raid.

"Do we understand why Spence was grabbing candidates for cryogenesis?"

"It may have been a purely commercial enterprise," Novicoff replied. "However, my expectation is that there was some collaboration going on since Spence had an intense interest in the field of germline editing. We found an article on that topic published in *Science* under his former name."

Among the documents recovered were legal forms Spence had prepared for some of the wealthiest people in the world, people who could afford to be frozen when they were on death's door and arrogant enough to think the world would still want them hanging around.

The agreements were comprehensive and provided for the body to be collected immediately when the individual had expired, but before officially pronounced dead, by an ambulance company partly owned by Spence's corporation. A fake death certificate would be generated as the body was transported from wherever expiration had occurred. Doctors, nurses, clergy, and others would be duped into believing they were standing over the right body. A swap with a homeless person was easily provided by Spence's seemingly endless inventory.

A refusal from any member of the "supply chain" to cooperate fully would be documented and generate a replacement. The customers would have already made clear to family and friends their intent to be cremated, sparing the need for a fake funeral or open casket ceremony, and producing the right amount of ashes when required was never a problem. The ruse was impressive in its scope, but buyers like these could afford whatever Spence chose to demand, and there was never a logistical challenge that money couldn't solve. Immortality, or something close to it, was the ultimate prize for people who had amassed more wealth and power than they could exploit in one lifetime.

"Something I don't quite understand," Novicoff mused, "is why these powerful people chose to put their faith in Spence when there are so many alternatives for cryogenic preservation out there."

What the FBI had yet to piece together was that the cutting-edge technology, combined with breakthrough advances in pharmacology and germline editing, were now exclusively available only from Bio-Splice. While the CCP intended to use these resources to become the world's only invincible superpower, they could not resist the opportunity to fund the operation from the deep pockets of American celebrities and industrialists.

"Dennis Spence must be one hell of a good salesman," Felix Jordan said.

"I think Spence liked to think he was playing God," said Jeff McAuley, who was shifting restlessly in his chair, anxious to discuss the next steps.

"That's a reductive argument," Jordan said in a sarcastic tone.

"Did you just insult me?" McAuley asked.

"No," Jordan replied, "I am agreeing with you, you idiot. You're the one spouting off about Occam's Razor and all that esoteric shit."

Klein had little patience for the nearly constant bickering between Jordan and McAuley, which began shortly after they were teamed up. After working together for just a few weeks, they had become like a married couple who soured on each other.

"Okay, people," he interrupted, "that's enough."

"We believe that the laboratory is housing the bodies of Pablo Escobar, Steve Jobs, David Koch, and Howard Steele. But what about Elon Musk? He's obviously alive, or are we to believe that the Musk we know is not the real Elon Musk?"

"According to the data we have been able to read on each chamber," said the technician who was dialed in from Bangkok, "that chamber is currently vacant, without any life-support being provided. We think it's simply reserved for him. There is another chamber we found with Spence's name on it, presumably reserved for him as well."

"If there was anyone that would fit the profile of someone seeking preservation at all costs," Novicoff chimed in, "it would be Musk. And likely Spence as well."

Those conclusions about Spence would prove true. As the agents continued to pore over the documents in Spence's office, they found that his calendar included an appointment with a wealthy businessman in Hong Kong in four days. He was about to slip away.

A CLEAN-SHAVEN RICHARD O'Brien, who no longer bore a resemblance to that journalist recently released from a North Korean prison camp, boarded the Delta Airbus A330 bound for Los Angeles. The storm that had been hanging over Bangkok had not yet moved on, and the tarmac was covered in puddles of standing water. Although it was only 9:20 in the morning, the overcast skies made it look like dusk. Richard peered out from his window seat, reflecting on his role in the mission in which he played a starring role. In his front pants pocket he carried the prize, the SIM card from Emma Lee's mobile phone, wrapped securely in anti-magnetic tape.

He had mixed feelings, however, about how his moral compass was performing. He would have readily slept with a Chinese agent and used the "all in the line of duty" excuse to justify it. Was there any hope for him?

The reality is that he wanted more than anything for Sarah to have accepted him back after he fought his way out of CNB. He closed his eyes and tried to remember what she looked like naked that night in New York when they first slept together. His daydream was interrupted by a voice from above.

"Sawasdee, Mister Richard, may I offer you water, coffee, or tea?"

Richard looked up at the young flight attendant leaning over him and smiling. She was of Thai descent and had the exotic look that always pushed Richard's button.

"Hello," he said, smiling. It would not be the first time that Richard thought about seducing a flight attendant. In fact, he used to treat the seduction of attractive flight attendants as a hobby or sporting event. He was proud that he was a two-time member of the "mile high club" from past LA-to-New York flights. He quickly decided this would not be one of those times.

"You know what," he said, "I'll just have a bottle of water."

The flight attendant smiled again, handed him a six-ounce bottle, and moved on to the next row.

Richard pulled out his phone and texted "I miss you" followed by a smiling emoji to Sarah Goodman. Then he pulled a cannabis edible he had smuggled into a box of Altoids and began chewing it. Finally, he put down his phone, closed his eyes, and prepared himself for the fifteen-hour flight home.

BEN KLEIN'S CHART WAS nearly complete. At the top was Bio-Splice, which anyone in the FBI would recognize as being controlled by the Chinese Communist Party. Lines below it led to George Kolins, Emma Lee, and Dennis Spence, a kind of three-legged stool, as Klein would later describe it. To the right was DPRK, with a line below that leading to Ji-Sung. Another line linked Emma Lee and Ji-Sung.

"All right, everybody, please settle down, and let's get started," he said to a packed room of agents. "We have a lot to cover this afternoon."

Klein laid out his theory of how all the bad guys were related.

"We have the CCP using the company Bio-Splice as a laboratory to exploit germline editing well beyond the recognized ethical limits of the practice," he said. "In fact, they are conducting research, both in China and through academics in the U.S. and possibly other countries, to understand how to extend life organically while building replacement organs as needed. We don't see any evidence of this falling under control of the People's Liberation Army, but we can't discount the value this would have to their military capabilities."

He continued, "They are using their agents in the MSS to steal intelligence from U.S. institutions and academics. And thanks to the SIM card that Agent O'Brien brought back from Bangkok, we've connected an MSS agent to a North Korean agent, the one we captured outside The Center for New Beginnings. We believe, based on examination of the chip and our own interviews, that the North Korean agent was attempting to gather intelligence from Dennis Spence, who had made significant progress on extending life via pharmacology."

Klein said the situation presented two undeniable concerns.

"First, that the Chinese could be sharing their findings with the Russians. Second, that Spence is still missing."

"Sir," an agent complained, "what about the bodies, you know, the fact they have American bodies on ice?"

"There is nothing inherently illegal about that, no matter how violated we may feel about it," Klein replied. "The fact is, a few hundred people around the world have submitted to being frozen. Hell, Ted Williams is frozen somewhere."

SARAH GOODMAN WAS STILL at her hotel in Los Angeles, finishing up paperwork on a routine investigation into the interstate drug trade she was working on in Detroit. Students were found taking fentanyl from Ohio into Michigan, and it was showing up more frequently on the campus of U of M. Every time she saw a reference to the University of Michigan, her thoughts turned to Richard, who attended before joining the FBI.

Since the two last spoke, Sarah had done some serious soul-searching, careful reading of the case reports on CNB, and analysis of the drugs its operators used to subdue the unsuspecting people they captured and presented as patients. The institution conducted a range of experiments, most including some form of memory replacement or eradication, and a lucky few were given treatment to dramatically extend their lifespan, research that Bio-Splice was funding. Spence kept comprehensive notes and produced many unpublished manuscripts.

Sarah also read the medical evaluation of O'Brien following his liberation from the facility. As it turns out, he was also seriously doped up and, according to his testimony, was not only in a state of confusion, he had abandoned his belief that he was ever an FBI agent. His condition had deteriorated rapidly as he tried desperately to hold on to his identity. It was like he was strapped to a time bomb.

In her heart, she decided to forgive him, but she didn't have the courage to initiate contact. Remaining in LA when she intended to return to Detroit was her way of keeping the door slightly open. Then she saw the smiling emoji.

"WHAT AM I LOOKING FOR, Captain?" asked John Nathanson, assistant director of counterintelligence for the CIA. Nathanson was dialed into a secure videoconference with Capt. David Antczak of the aircraft carrier Ronald Reagan, which was operating near the South China Sea.

The Reagan was awarded the first opportunity to test one of the Navy's newest weapons: the MQ-9B, a short-takeoff-and-landing drone built on the original design of the highly successful Reaper. The manufacturer, General Atomics, also created a kit to convert a standard Reaper to the STOL version, allowing them to operate on aircraft carriers. The kits were already making their way across the fleet. Drone footage was highly valued by U.S. intelligence because military satellites could only produce vague images of what was happening on the ground.

"Watch closely, sir," Antczak replied. The two were examining surveillance footage taken just hours before by the MQ-9B launched off the Reagan.

"There, sir, wait, I'll freeze the frame."

The video feed, in grainy black and white, plainly showed troops assembled in formation on a man-made island just two hundred nautical miles from Taiwan. Judging from the barracks and related infrastructure he had been studying, Antczak estimated that 1,500 troops were on the island. The video provided the best proof yet that recent tensions had escalated beyond the point of no return.

"See what I mean?" Antczak said. "They are organizing. We've never seen this much manpower, and we believe that an attack on Taiwan is imminent."

Antczak was not exaggerating. Over the past few years, visits between U.S. and Taiwanese diplomats, criticized by China as "conjugal visits," had enraged the CCP. The final straw was when the president of Taiwan traveled to Washington and stood side by side with the American president in the White House Rose Garden. From that point forward, the Chinese military shifted its policy from conducting aggressive drills over the skies of Taiwan to secretly initiating plans for a full-scale invasion. This was consistent with intelligence reports that Nathanson had been gathering over the past several months. Conventional wisdom in Washington suggested this was not a matter of if but when.

As part of its global strategy to claim jurisdiction over the South China Sea, the CCP had authorized the dredging of the seabed in that region, piling it on top of reefs that were exposed during low tide to effectively create about a dozen islands, though an accurate count required constant monitoring by American and Australian satellites and surveillance aircraft. According to intelligence reports, the military infrastructure, missile systems, and fuel storage across 3,200 acres of new bases didn't leave enough room to plant a tree.

Taiwan was only 100 miles from the closest Chinese shore, but now the Philippines and Vietnam were threatened more than ever by China's aggressive claim to sovereignty over the South China Sea. Many analysts believed the region could explode with the slightest provocation, pulling American forces into the conflict.

"Thank you, Captain, this is very helpful," Nathanson replied, anxious to take this information to the CIA director.

"Sir, there's something else you should see," Antczak said.

"What's that?"

"We've not had too much time to improve the resolution on this with the equipment we have onboard, but we did blow up the images to give us a pretty damn good look at the enemy."

Antczak pushed a new image to the screen.

"And?" Nathanson was losing patience. He had seen plenty of images of Chinese military formations.

"The crazy thing, sir. All the troops look like spitting images of one another. Like 1,500 identical twins."

20

The impetus for creating "test tube soldiers" followed from the July 2009 riots in what is known as the Xinjiang Uyghur Autonomous Region of China. A violent dispute broke out in a factory between Uyghur and Han Chinese workers. Many Uyghurs disappeared in the aftermath of these riots. The internment camps followed.

During this time, the U.S. relied heavily on informants to gain a better understanding of what was happening on the ground in China, and many risked their lives trying to obtain information on what was specifically going on in Xinjiang. According to an investigation in *The New York Times*, between 18 and 20 CIA sources in China were either killed or imprisoned between 2010 and 2012. All that could be confirmed by the report was that the size of the camps were growing exponentially, soaring to an estimated 1.8 million detainees by 2022.

Human rights organizations presumed that the camps were growing from an increase in detentions. Nobody would have suspected that it was due to forcing women of child-bearing years to be surrogates for genetically modified embryos, designed according to standardized specifications, that were being grown on a massive scale in secret Chinese laboratories. Bio-Splice operated one of these "egg factories" in Harbin and was building a second laboratory in Shenzhen.

The cloned babies were hidden from view in dormitories until they reached an age of four. They started their vocational education and training when they reached eight years of age and were shortly thereafter transferred to farm field work to help feed a growing camp population.

Children born to surrogate parents were not given traditional names. The first two numbers indicated the year of birth, followed by the surrogate mother's serial number, followed by a number indicating whether the child was the first, second or later birth from the surrogate. The children would never meet their surrogate mother as the camp had security fences which prohibited adult detainees from interacting with the clones. Although the clones were taught to speak Mandarin, they were also provided military-style training which included the protocol to speak only when invited to do so. And because each clone was essentially identical in every way to the others, it was not possible to develop real connections to one another. Any discussion between clones was a discussion between strangers.

The official age to join the People's Liberation Army is stated as being eighteen years of age. However, the compliant behavior of the clones, combined with their excellent hereditary characteristics and lack of familial connections, persuaded the CCP to make an exception and to begin their combat training when they reached fifteen years of age. As tensions between China and U.S. increased over the sovereignty of Taiwan, the new test tube soldiers would be pressed into service as soon as they could handle a rifle.

IN 1998, INTELLIGENCE analysts from the CIA told their FBI counterparts that two known terrorists, members of the group that eventually attacked the World Trade Center, were involved in the bombing of the USS Cole and had recently obtained visas to enter the United States. The FBI filed the report in its threat-assessment files but never acted upon it. The FBI denies being provided the information, and the finger-pointing will likely never end.

Why would the FBI have reason to ignore the warning? As with most CIA intelligence products, it did not include sources or methods used to acquire the information, as that would jeopardize the CIA's ability to continue collecting intelligence. As far as the FBI was concerned, vague predictions without names, sources, or methods are useless and do not warrant an investigation. Thus a summary of the mistrust, wary collaboration, and occasional missed opportunities in a relationship between two stubborn, bureaucratic bedfellows.

More recently, the CIA and military analysts worldwide established broad consensus that a Chinese invasion of Taiwan would fail, based on the assumption of U.S. military support shortly after first contact. However, due to the dense urban geography of the island, casualties would be enormous, up to ten times the number of military and civilian casualties Ukraine had absorbed in defending itself against Russia. But as the intelligence agencies were about to learn, that calculus was no longer accurate.

Ben Klein and his team sat around the "war room" conference table in the LA field office, staring at the large monitor on the northern wall. It was 5:30 a.m. on the West Coast, the only time they could agree on with their East Coast counterparts. At the other end of the secure transmission sat John Nathanson and three CIA analysts from SATA, the agency's Sino-American Threat Assessment section.

"According to agents we have embedded, the PLA is pretty confident they can accomplish their objectives within a week of the invasion," said the lead analyst from SATA. This was a dramatic shift from intelligence estimates available earlier.

"And this is why." The analyst put on the screen an enhanced version of the photo taken by the drone. The image was chilling in its detail: A row of identical-looking soldiers at attention in crisp, dark green uniforms, with row upon row of other identical soldiers behind them. Their gaze and lack of expression made them appear artificial, like mannequins in a store window. They all had brown eyes, thin eyebrows, taut skin, and olive complexions. It was a verified intelligence photo, but it would be easy to convince someone that everyone in the image was photoshopped and duplicated from a single person.

"Holy shit," Jordan said. McAuley's mouth dropped open. Klein and others in his department just stared back at the soldiers who were staring at them.

"Where did these dudes come from?" Jordan wanted to know.

"These soldiers do not bear the facial characteristics of Han Chinese," another analyst from SATA contributed. "The Han is the majority ethnic group in China, representing 92 percent of the mainland's population. We've concluded that these soldiers are not Chinese."

"What the fuck are they?" said McAuley, forgetting that his low status didn't permit profane expressions in meetings like this, even if the expression fit perfectly.

"What we see in the nose bridge and color tones is a mix of Caucasian and East Asian characteristics," the analyst said. "Consistent with what would be seen among Uyghur populations. Based on facial analysis, we estimated these soldiers to be between fifteen and seventeen years old."

Both sides at this point were speechless.

"How is this possible?" Klein said, asking the question that was on everybody's mind.

"We don't know, Ben," Roger Jafek replied. The assistant secretary at State was on the call from Washington. "Frankly, this may be a matter of shooting first and asking questions later. Taiwan is running short on time and options."

Again, the San Diego team was muted.

"Gentlemen," Jafek added somberly, "we've got to figure a way to support Taiwan's defense with a single, secret, and decisive game-changing act. Emphasis on secret." What he didn't have to say was why.

Unlike the war in Ukraine, which Americans supported on moral grounds, the defense of Taiwan would probably be viewed by the American people as a proxy war, and the last version of that kind of war with China did not end well, with the fall of Saigon and more than 58,000 servicemen dead.

RICHARD RETURNED TO the States, landing at LAX at 6:26 p.m. He was spent, not only because he was traveling over eighteen hours, but because he made the mistake of popping an edible on an empty stomach. As he deplaned, he felt like a zombie, and he couldn't walk much different from one. He remembered what his dad once told him, "Never check your luggage, and it will last forever." This was one of those times he was grateful for that advice, as all he could think about was lying flat for an indeterminate amount of time. He coasted through passport control and called up an Uber. Within forty-five minutes, he was walking through the door of the home he rented with Jeff McAuley.

"There he is, the man!" yelled McAuley, who popped off the sofa immediately and raced to give a bear hug to his favorite partner. McAuley was wearing his signature surfing board shorts under a Hawaiian short-sleeved shirt.

"Hey man, it's so good to be back. What a trip."

"Wait, wait, don't tell me," McAuley said as he pulled back from embracing Richard. "We've got a special guest here that's been waiting for you."

Richard half expected a puppy to walk out of the kitchen. Instead, it was Sarah Goodman.

THE TEMPERATURE IN the room shot up a few minutes after the newly prepared FBI briefing document was handed out to Klein and his team.

According to the report, progress in cloning sentient species went largely unnoticed unless you were in the academic community of biological sciences. Within just a year of a failed bid by Costa Rica to ban human cloning across all members of the United Nations, South Korea announced it had successfully cloned a series of human embryos. Bioethicists in countries that had already banned human cloning immediately had something to talk about. Countries not so constrained by the moral and ethical considerations of human cloning amped up their efforts. Many used the excuse that such methods could cure life-threatening disease, although the connection between the two was ambiguous at best.

The South Korean study in 2004 appeared in the respected journal *Science* and claimed that 242 eggs from 16 female donors yielded 30 viable embryos. The same South Korean researchers announced another milestone a few years later: They claimed to have created a streamlined process that uses far fewer human eggs to produce usable embryonic stem cells, "a major step toward mass production," according to experts who followed the work. Chinese spies wasted no time in infiltrating the scientific community in Seoul.

It took four more years for any significant progress to be made. In the meantime, the Chinese press slow-walked announcements of progress in cloning animals to distract from the country's real intentions. In 2022 they announced they had cloned an Arctic wolf to demonstrate science's ability to sustain threatened populations, and, a year later, cloned "super cows" that would produce 70 percent more milk than typical bovine species. Around the same time, U.S. intelligence confirmed the Chinese were cloning monkeys.

One of the advantages of cloning in the laboratory was the ability to select for the most desirable traits, giving rise to the phrase "designer babies." And China had the most robust resource for raw materials anywhere on the planet: the Xinjiang internment camps.

The report continued:

> *The Xinjiang camps have been routinely criticized by the UN for alleged abuses including rape, torture, assault, and execution. It is suspected that many female prisoners have been subjected to forced sterilization. Others have been placed into so-called baby factories and to act as surrogate hosts for "pre-packaged" embryos.*

"Are you fucking kidding me?" Richard blurted out as he slapped the report down on the table. It was his first agency meeting since returning to the States. "That's what this is all about?"

"Settle down and do the math, or if you can't do math, just read it here," Jordan replied, pointing to the second page of the report, and reading it aloud: "The camp has between eight hundred thousand to 1.8 million prisoners. If half the prisoners are female and merely 15 percent are of childbearing age, it would produce a minimum of sixty thousand women capable of giving birth to a genetically engineered embryo. And each of those embryos could be identical in composition. It would be reasonable to expect that, if this was the intention of the CCP, that the byproduct of this effort would produce the optimal human subject for conscription into the PLA, and that further, these conscripts would be considered disposable."

"This is outrageous," Richard continued. "They are fucking monsters."

The report went on to discuss the various methods used to support the suspected operation, including injecting stem cells from their optimal subject into embryos and implanting them for further gestation by a female host. One of the most significant findings from the report came at the end.

"If the process began in earnest based on the timeline we have estimated, starting with capitalization of the methodology used in South Korea, the first line of cloned human beings would have reached an average age of eighteen by 2025, the minimum age to serve."

"But the photos obtained don't look like eighteen-year-old soldiers," an agent observed, stating out loud what everyone else was thinking.

"The report stops there, simply stating the PLA policy," Klein replied. "That doesn't mean the Chinese are playing by the same rules they wrote when they formed the army. Besides, if these troops have no formal connection to family, there's nobody to complain about the fact these kids, or whatever we want to call them, are too young."

THE TAIWANESE FOREIGN minister was on the phone with his American counterpart, Secretary of State Adam Hunt, after learning about the troop formations on a man-made island approximately 200 nautical miles from Taiwan.

"We have a couple options we are working on at our end," Hunt said. "We will be presenting them to you in the next forty-eight hours. We just want you to be prepared to mobilize resources on your end."

"Of course," replied the minister. "Mr. Hunt, we are most grateful for American support. We will follow your guidance."

There were, in fact, several possible responses. One option would be a preemptive strike, as Israel pulled off in marvelous fashion in 1967 when it recognized that the Arab countries surrounding it were poised to attack and sent its new warplanes to the skies to destroy the Arab airfields and many of its aircraft.

The problem was that any option would merely represent temporary setbacks for the Chinese. At this point, there was no response that would put a permanent end to the capability established by the CCP to produce an endless supply of soldiers. And the fact that the laboratory was further improving the viability of embryos, including the ability to rejuvenate damaged organs and to sustain themselves indefinitely, would require creating thinking on a whole new level.

Hunt understood all of this as he hung up the phone. It was going to be a long night.

THE FBI MOVED QUICKLY to collect an impressive and eclectic group of scientists. In the interest of time, the meeting was held over videoconference. As the participants signed onto the platform with the web address and credentials they were provided, the first thing they saw was a large FBI seal covering most of the screen, and below that the words,

"YOU ARE ABOUT TO ENTER A SECURE MEETING. PLEASE CONSIDER YOUR IMMEDIATE ENVIRONMENT TO ENSURE YOU CAN MAINTAIN CONFIDENTIALITY. FEDERAL LAW PROVIDES SEVERE CIVIL AND CRIMINAL PENALTIES FOR THE UNAUTHORIZED RECORDING AND DISTRIBUTION OF CONTENT FROM THE USE OF THIS PLATFORM."

The scientists invited to the meeting represented some of the most experienced researchers in the field of genetic engineering. Some were quite pragmatic, which might help the group overcome the roadblocks that egos can place in the path of progress.

"Okay, everybody let's have some quick introductions," said Roger Jafek, as he watched five miniature headshots on his screen.

"Justin Egrin, lab director, Salk Institute."

"Dr. George Kolins, pathology and laboratory medicine, UCLA."

"Diane Gayle, professor of molecular and cell biology, UC Berkeley."

"Ethan Underwood, UCSD Health Sciences."

"Kim Su-Young, principal investigator, Seoul National University."

Several agents monitoring the call remained silent, their initials in tiny circles at the bottom of the screen providing the only indication that the meeting was much larger than it appeared.

Egrin was contacted by the FBI a few weeks earlier because his contact details were found on Emma Lee's SIM card. And Kolins had proactively contacted the FBI and recommended Gayle, who had worked with Jennifer Doudna on the research that led to her team winning the Nobel Prize for discovering the CRISPR gene-editing tool. Underwood was the last member to be found by the FBI. He held an academic appointment at UCSD, but he also had collaborated with Dennis Spence on the experiments that led to the remarkable life-extending therapies for patients at CNB. He chose not to mention that to his peer group for fear of being judged.

Kolins had also lobbied to include Gil Kumar, the botanist rescued from CNB, but Klein felt his mental state was too uncertain to be a reliable asset, and he couldn't afford to let the group put too much confidence in his contributions. Kumar was still being treated for potential psychiatric trauma while physicians were trying to understand how he could be over 100 years old but look not a day more than 70.

"We appreciate you all coming together here to help us understand and address an imminent threat, especially you, Doctor Young, thank you for participating so late in your evening," Jafek told the scientists. The truth is that every person in the room felt an immense sense of pride to be chosen by the FBI for the call, with the possible exception of Underwood, who was facing potential charges in connection with supporting Spence's research.

"Look, we don't have a lot of time," Jafek said. "You will be on this conference call until a viable solution can be recommended to us. We will have agents monitoring the discussions that can answer any questions where the information is not privileged. But you will not leave the call until you can present your recommendations. And please remember that you've committed to nondisclosure of anything discussed here today."

This was not going to be an entertaining, free-for-all discussion. Jafek looked so serious that the phrase "life-or-death" was unnecessary.

"I will return in three hours and we will keep the line open at least until that time," Jafek added. "Are there any questions?"

If Jafek waited long enough, he expected there to be many questions, but nothing that this group of highly educated people could not figure out on their own. So he cut to the quick.

"Good luck," he said as he left the call.

DENNIS SAT OUTSIDE with his iced coffee at the Bird Rock Café in Del Mar, a half mile from Interstate 5, with a pleasant view of the ocean. He was more than halfway to Tijuana and exhausted from the terror of driving on the freeway from LA. This was the first time he had driven a significant distance on the highway, having avoided driving most of his life. The stop-and-go nature of the route between LA and San Diego was notorious and would exhaust anyone after an hour or two.

It was four o'clock in the afternoon, and the sun was beginning to make its way down to the western horizon, where beachgoers would gather to see it disappear. Dennis could see the backs of about twenty-five tourists from his table.

He wore sunglasses and had put on a scarf even though the temperature was about seventy-eight degrees. He wore a light shade of lipstick. He didn't care if people wondered about his gender identity because those concerns evaporated long ago. The important thing now was to avoid being recognized. He would easily reach the border before nightfall and use the pedestrian bridge that stretches from San Diego directly into the Tijuana airport.

Since going off the grid, Dennis was not able to keep up with his medications and ran out of anabolic steroids necessary to sustain his transformation. While he would still pass as a male with relatively soft features, it was not the result he wanted. A trip overseas offered him opportunities to get his life back on track.

However, his financial situation had worsened because the bank froze the assets of CNB, and he had limited funds parked elsewhere. He refused many offers from the Chinese to sell his research to them, and vowed never to cross that line. He was highly leveraged on credit cards he carried under an alias. *I should have opened that Swiss bank account*, he thought to himself, angry that he could neglect something so fundamental to his strategy.

He had not heard from Emma Lee or anyone from the MSS via Signal or Threema. He did not know who among his contacts he could trust anyway, and in all respects felt like a persona non grata.

If ever there was a time to consider the choices he had made, this was it. Everything was going well until the visits by the FBI. Did that necessarily mean it was over? Could he have sent them away without incident? Did he really need to drug Richard O'Brien and assault Agent Jordan? He played the scenario over again in his head and came up with the same conclusion: His destiny as a fugitive was decided long ago when he murdered his father and caregiver, for starters.

By 4:45, he decided it was time to leave for the forty-five-minute drive to the border. He checked his backpack to make sure he had ready access to his fake passport and the pepper spray he always carried, at least until he got to airport security. He got up and walked toward his rented vehicle for the last leg of his journey in the United States. He would soon be at the Tijuana International Airport boarding an Aeromexico flight to Hong Kong. Of the places that did not have an extradition treaty with the United States, it was one of the few where he could see himself living.

THE SCIENTISTS GATHERED on the teleconference didn't need much time to arrive at a consensus on how to address the immediate and long-term threat from the Chinese.

"It's really quite simple," Dr. Young told Roger Jafek when he was called back early. "You just need to raise the temperatures of the incubators where the samples, embryos, and CRISPR agents are stored. They are highly sensitive to fluctuations in temperature so you don't even need to cook them."

Jafek was underwhelmed. He was expecting ingenious but got obvious.

"And how do you suggest we raise the temperature?" he asked, a bit of peevishness leaking into his voice.

"We assumed that was something your men could figure out," Professor Gayle offered, "but we talked about how Operation Olympic Games accomplished essentially the same thing through, you know, Stuxnet."

Now Jafek was impressed, and a little embarrassed, that the scientists had to remind him about the legendary attack by Israel on centrifuges operating within Iran's "air-gapped" nuclear plant. An air-gapped facility is cut off from the internet to avoid penetration by malware. The Israelis recruited a Dutch agent to join a team of technicians that would service the Dutch-designed equipment. Once inside, he installed the virus, which not only caused the centrifuges to malfunction and break but simultaneously sent messages to the operators that everything was functioning properly. The mission was a success, set the nuclear program back several years, and ushered in a new era of cybersecurity that would now have to include monitoring not just amateur hackers but nation-states conducting comprehensive cyber warfare.

"Okay," Jafek said, "that's impressive and plausible, but we would need to get somebody inside the laboratory."

"Secretary Jafek," Kolins said, "you've probably learned that I had samples from my lab stolen about a week ago, right?"

"Yes, I'm aware," Jafek replied.

"Right about now the Chinese laboratory staff is probably trying to figure out why many of their samples are decomposing," Kolins said, "and their first suspicion before considering contamination is that the equipment has failed. They are not designed to last forever, you know, and need regular calibration."

"Okay." Jafek thought he might know where Kolins was going.

"So, you have an agent posing as a technician go in there to service the equipment, and voila, you have access to plant the virus that will tell the lab managers that everything is fine, even though it won't be."

Jafek thought this was brilliant. Exactly what he hoped for when he sequestered a group of highly intelligent people.

The challenge would be finding a technician who could get past building security.

"Okay, we'll need to find someone that understands this environment, could be trained in the mission quickly, and ready to go. Any ideas about that?"

"Secretary Jafek," Kolins said, "certainly you can find such a person. The academic community in Southern California alone is filled with anti-communist scientists that fled China and would readily volunteer for such a mission. I can put you in touch with a dozen of them."

Jafek appreciated that Kolins was probably right but dispensed immediately with the idea of bringing in an outsider for the mission. No, he thought, he would find the right asset from within the CIA later that afternoon.

"All right," Jafek replied, ready to pivot to the other topic on the agenda. "What about these cloned soldiers that are an imminent threat to the security of Taiwan?"

This time it was Su-Young's turn to speak.

"This is also pretty simple solution," he said. "In South Korea, we came to value the security of a 'panic button' in case we found that we couldn't control certain outcomes."

It was beginning to sound like science fiction again to Jafek and the other participants in the room.

"We included a marker for the gene, in other words, a specific genetic sequence, that when subject to an audio frequency of 60 kHz would generate symptoms similar to what you in the U.S. call Havana Syndrome."

Jafek was intrigued. "Tell me more about that."

"So, humans can detect sound in the range from about 31 Hz to almost 20 kHz," Su-Young said, "but rats and other animals can hear up to around 70 kHz. We encoded some lab rats with a gene that would theoretically disable their motor functions if they were subjected to tones 60 kHz and above, sounds we couldn't hear. When we run those audio frequencies in the lab, these rats become confused, sick, and some would even attack each other.

"From this point on, we included that marker in all our CRISPR reagents, including ones we believe were stolen by the MSS after we published our paper," Su-Young concluded. "It's not something we talk much about."

"And so," Jafek inquired, "if the clones are based on the genetic code you created, they would be affected by the same frequencies?"

"They definitely should," Su-Young replied. "And so would a number of other animals that can detect sounds on that portion of the audio spectrum. Think of it as a dog whistle but with strong disorientation and behavioral effects."

Jafek was again impressed. Havana Syndrome was a near obsession among those in Washington connected to foreign service. While it was never confirmed that the debilitating impact of the disease was the work of a foreign adversary, scientists at the National Institutes of Health were able to produce similar effects by running experiments on laboratory animals. So exploiting Su-Young's idea to effectively debilitate the Chinese clones had great potential.

Jafek thought to himself, *it's beginning to feel a lot like Christmas.*

21

O nce the president was briefed and gave the go-ahead, things accelerated quickly. The director of the CIA dictated the timeline. The deployment of a virus to destroy the inventory of embryos in the Bio-Splice laboratory, combined with the use of a high-frequency signal to disorient and essentially disarm the army of clones would both happen within seventy-two hours and as close to one another as possible. It was daunting in complexity but not outside the capability of the U.S. agencies working in cooperation with Taiwanese authorities. One of the president's requirements, however, was that the CIA and FBI cooperate and share resources to maximize the probability of success. Such directives had been ordered in the past and did not always work as intended.

"Sir, we don't have enough time to plan this out properly," said Richard, pleading his case with Ben Klein. Since his return from Southeast Asia, Richard was placed into an Assistant Coordinator role for Operation Carbon Paper, the codename given to the mission to destroy the Chinese cloning program. It was a small reward for his performance in Cambodia and Thailand, and one that was intended to keep him relatively safe for now and out of public view. He was given the opportunity to name the mission and chose the near obsolete special purpose paper to symbolize the agency's intent to make Chinese human copies obsolete. Even as an Assistant Coordinator, however, he had to report to multiple senior officers.

"We don't have a choice, O'Brien," Klein replied, "wheels are already in motion."

"Sir," Richard said, "hear me out. Designing and testing that code can't be done on that timeline, and we'd be sending an agent in there to perform an act that probably won't do what's intended." Richard did not have a deep background in technology, but he had friends in the software industry and had heard enough about "best demonstrated practices" in software design, development, testing, and release to know that a seventy-two-hour timeline was ludicrous.

"Focus on staying in contact with the Navy and making sure those clone blasters are deployed," Klein replied. "Don't concern yourself with the CIA action in Harbin. Let them deal with it."

Richard felt there was something he didn't know about the plans to infiltrate Bio-Splice. Perhaps it was above his pay grade, or perhaps the agencies were stepping into an enormous blunder.

A CALL CAME INTO THE procurement office of the Bio-Splice Laboratory from a sales rep in the Chinese distribution office of Thermo Fischer Scientific, offering to supply the latest thermal cyclers to the facility. Thermal cyclers are used to amplify segments of DNA in the laboratory. They have heating, cooling, precise temperature controls, and require regular maintenance. Thermo Fischer Scientific, Biobase, and Guangzhou Medical Equipment are three of the biggest companies that produce them.

"We are not interested," the procurement officer said. "We use Guangzhou." The same is true for our new facility in Shenzhen so no need to call them either."

"Thank you, sir, I am sorry for any inconvenience."

The caller, working for the CIA in Beijing, passed the information along to his handler. The next call, originating from Harbin, came into the laboratory director.

"Good afternoon," the caller said, "My name is Li Chen. I am the new regional customer service manager for Guangzhou Medical Equipment. I would like to introduce myself and to offer my services. Would you have a moment to discuss the performance of our equipment at your facility?"

The laboratory director was distracted and more than a little irritated. For the past week the lab had been on lockdown, trying to understand if it was contamination or faulty equipment that was the reason for so many embryos that had decomposed.

"I am very busy right now, this is not a good time," the manager replied.

"I understand," said Ms. Chen. "It's just that we've discovered some of the thermal cyclers among our customers have a fault. The software that runs these machines needs to be updated. It may be producing a high rate of false positives.

But we are unable to update your equipment remotely because you are not online."

The caller now had the lab director's attention.

"What is the nature of the problem?" he asked.

"It's the temperature control," Chen explained. "We've found about 20 percent of the machines in use are unable to maintain strict temperature compliance. Again, we cannot assess your equipment because you operate off the grid. I understand your work is important. If you haven't seen any problems, then perhaps we can meet at your convenience some other time."

"How soon can you get here?" the director asked.

"Will it work for you that I come the day after tomorrow?"

"Yes, please have security call me when you arrive."

"Very well, thank you," she said. "I will see you in a couple of days."

The CIA operative sent an encoded text to her handler. *We are in. Send the 'technician' in 2 days' time.*

"IS IT FEASIBLE?"

Roger Jafek had wasted no time assembling the best minds from marine science, the Army Corps of Engineers, and the U.S. Naval Research Laboratory to discuss the deployment of remotely operated signaling devices near the three man-made islands that the Chinese had militarized.

"The tectonics of the South China Sea have a complex character," said Anthony Lawrence from the Naval Research

Laboratory. "The continental slope in that region has a stepwise block structure, descending in a staircase-like pattern to the bottom of the basin, which occupies the central part of the South China Sea."

Lawrence was one of those military officers with a science background who insisted that his statements be completely unambiguous even if it took a while to get to the point.

"At an average depth of 3,950 meters," he continued, "we cannot secure anything to the ocean floor, it's too deep, but there are seamounts that come up as high as 3,875 meters, so their peaks would be accessible by any number of means, including technical divers."

"So," Jafek insisted, losing his patience.

"So, in theory, yes," Lawrence replied. "We could secure a remotely operated device to a seamount. We just need to find the ones that will optimally carry the signal across to the islands."

"Okay then," Jafek replied. "You have until tomorrow morning to find them and another twenty-four hours after that to deploy the devices."

Jafek left the room with Lawrence staring at his back.

Jafek didn't have the need nor inclination to explain this to Lawrence, but it was important that the mission offer plausible deniability. As designed, the operation would probably deflect any charge of responsibility from the Chinese that the U.S. was involved in a preemptive strike against their assets. U.S. intelligence would have to be satisfied that the mission go down in history as part legend and part fact. First, however, it needed to be successful.

IT WAS ESTIMATED THAT it took up to ten coders three to four years to develop the Stuxnet cyberworm. Once it was discovered, it took over three months to reverse-engineer the code to understand how it ultimately destroyed several centrifuges in an Iranian nuclear facility that was suspected of producing nuclear weapons. The Cyber National Mission Force, operating under the U.S. Cyber Command, was given forty-eight hours to produce a cyber worm that would perform similarly to Stuxnet when installed on the IT network within Bio-Splice.

Anyone who understood data forensics and coding would recognize this as an unreasonable expectation. However, the team of professional coders and hackers working within the agency had a few advantages: first, they were some of the best coders in the world, and second, they had more advanced tools to quickly create sequences of code based on latest-generation algorithms that made Stuxnet look like the Betamax of the VCR industry.

The worm had to do at least two things simultaneously: slowly raise the temperature in thermal cyclers while keeping the temperature displays exactly as the Chinese operator had set them. A secondary goal was that the worm would travel within the secure network and cause other temperature controls (incubators, freezers, and such) to do the same thing. The agency quickly activated an electronics lab in the basement of its headquarters at Fort Meade, Maryland, to test the effect of its prototypes.

"GINA, DO YOU THINK you can pull it off?" Jafek asked. "They are expecting you tomorrow."

Genji Wang, known as Gina Wang in the United States, was born in China to a pair of university professors dedicated to democratic causes and fiercely anti-communist. They sent their daughter to UC Berkeley, where she obtained a degree in biology. To her parents' delight, she joined the CIA in 2014 and was stationed in Taiwan, close enough to China to access it when necessary without the risk of being outed and captured there. Her work for the agency was a closely guarded secret.

"Yes, I think so," she replied, always careful to manage expectations. However, in this case, not achieving expectations would mean that Gina might spend the rest of her life in a prison cell.

Gina's identity in Taiwan was already carefully cultivated. She worked as a pharmacy aide during the day and in her off hours conducted various reconnaissance missions when directed by the agency. She made multiple visits to China without incident where she would always visit her parents, and she became a valuable source of intelligence for the CIA. This mission would raise the stakes for her, but it might also reward her with a position of greater importance in the agency, something that drove her ambition.

"Okay then," Jafek said. "We are having a new Chinese passport and credentials sent over and you'll receive them today by courier. Good luck, Gina, and thanks."

The credentials would position Gina as a customer service regional manager for Guangzhou Medical Equipment by the name of Li Chen. The documents would be immaculate in their preparation because, after all, this was something the CIA was actually quite good at, and it maintained current pictures of their field agents for just such an occasion.

"Oh, one more thing," Jafek added, "we are also getting you the memory stick which contains the virus. This might not be ready until this evening as we are finishing it up here. We'll send it over to our embassy at the American Institute; they will load it on the physical device which you'll take with you."

Gina hung up the phone and went to her bedroom to pack. The flight from Taipei to Harbin was nine hours. She would need to catch a flight tomorrow morning. She hoped the memory stick would be available in time. The mission was operating with a very thin margin for error.

22

The USNS Effective edged to within two hundred nautical miles of Scarborough Shoal, or what China calls Huangyan Island. As a noncommissioned vessel, the Effective was not equipped for military conflict and was therefore the ideal ship to support Operation Carbon Paper, as its movements would typically not be interpreted as aggressive. Although the Chinese still considered *any* American vessel in the South China Sea to be spying on them, the Effective is categorically described as an ocean surveillance ship. These research vessels are principally focused on monitoring and mapping the oceans. While they carry radar and sonar equipment to detect specific threats, they cannot defend themselves.

In broad daylight, eight dinghies left the Effective equipped with mobile depth finders and digital NOAA maps to help locate the pinnacles and seamounts on which the devices would be secured. Operating in daylight would help deflect any concern that the many Chinese vessels in the region might have as they tracked the small boats. Still, six of the dinghies were merely decoys and mimicked the action of the two others without deployment of any devices.

The devices were a simple adaptation of equipment the Navy had used in multiple applications: a buoy supporting a small speaker that could broadcast in a specific direction. The buoy was also outfitted with a device that would enable the Navy to destroy it remotely. Either one device could be detonated or all of them simultaneously. When floating on the surface, the buoy looked no larger than a dinner plate and would be very difficult to spot from any airborne surveillance. Still, it was decided they would be destroyed at the end of Operation Carbon Paper to conceal U.S. involvement.

Each targeted location was approximately seventy-five nautical miles from the islands the Chinese had created. It was confirmed through experiments that the sound waves could travel this far, however, in a storm or high winds, there could be significant interference with the effectiveness of the signals. This was an unavoidable risk, but it was also known that such weather patterns were usually transitory, whereas the audible signal, once turned on, could operate 24/7.

Two divers from each dinghy did the work of securing the devices. They did backflips off the dinghies, and once ready, they submerged at the same time. According to U.S. Navy diving tables, the divers would have up to twenty-five minutes at a depth of one hundred feet to find the seamount and secure a line before beginning the decompression phase of the dive, in which they would have to remain in more shallow water until the absorbed nitrogen in their body could escape. This would be in addition to safety stops at twenty feet.

When the divers secured lines to the pinnacles, the floating device remained topside. A minimum amount of slack was desired so the device would remain right side up and not drift too far. Each diver had a waterproof drill, eye hooks, and carabiners to attach the line to the reef. These divers had done the procedure dozens of times before for different purposes. For them, it was just another day at the office.

AS THE COUNTDOWN BEGAN for the dual operations in Harbin and off the coast of Taiwan, Richard's pulse began to race. He had been on his phone constantly since the approval of Operation Carbon Paper, ensuring that everyone involved felt supported and knew what was expected of them. He took a red-eye flight to Taipei and was working in an office at the American Institute in Taiwan on Jinhu Road to be closer to the operation and in a time zone that aligned better with the planned activities.

Richard was "in the zone," multitasking like never before, fully engaged in the mission. He implored the CIA to ensure that the agent going into Bio-Splice had all the proper documentation and a working copy of the cyber worm. He had the Naval Research Laboratory run two tests and provide two separate confirmations that the sound wave frequencies emanating from the buoys would have sufficient amplification to reach the islands. He had Kolins explain, for the fifth time, how stolen samples would cause havoc in the Bio-Splice laboratory, enough so that they would accept outside help. He had Underwood recreate the experiment to demonstrate the impact of the high-frequency sound waves on laboratory rats. When he visited Underwood's lab at UCSD via Zoom and witnessed a laboratory rat kill and cannibalize another rat in its cage, he was both nauseated and convinced. He didn't sleep much in the run up to the mission's break-the-glass moment.

It was 9:30 a.m. in Manila and 9:30 p.m. in Washington when the secretary of state spoke to his counterpart in the Philippines. He had already completed calls to other key allies to inform them of the U.S.'s intent to neutralize the growing threat to the sovereign rights of nations in the South China Sea to have free and unfettered access to the international waters in that region. In the case of the Philippines, there was a risk that the high-frequency sound waves would hit part of their coast as well and that wildlife might be adversely affected. It was a small price to pay, the secretary argued, to reign in Chinese ambitions that already caused the Philippine government considerable concern.

"Really, building a new airport would be easier than this," Richard said to Sarah Goodman, as the two lay in separate beds, he in Taipei and she in LA. "There are so many moving parts to this mission, I am feeling like I've missed something."

"I'm sure you have it all covered," Sarah offered, smiling through the phone at him. "But you know what they say, experience is the hardest kind of teacher. It gives you the test first and the lesson afterward. Remember your training, babe. Second-guess all your assumptions."

"That's good advice, actually," Richard replied, silently rejoicing that he could be relaxed with Sarah once again. "Hey, remember when I took you for 'XLB' in New York?" he said, reminding her of the soup dumplings they shared when they first met. "Meet me in Hong Kong, and let's get authentic. I can't handle another bowl of noodle soup out here."

"Hong Kong?" Sarah replied, surprised that Richard could be so spontaneous at this very moment, with so much on the line.

"C'mon," Richard egged on. "We deserve a break after this is all done, and I need to connect through there anyway."

"Well," Sarah replied, not able to come up with a strong objection at that moment but feeling there must be a good reason out there somewhere.

"It'll be great," he added. "We'll get massages at one of those spas together. Please say yes!"

"What, didn't you have a happy ending in Thailand?" Sarah replied, trying to delay any commitment.

"I'll let you in on a little secret," Richard said, looking at her through the phone. "That wouldn't happen without you."

GINA SAT IN THE BACK of the cab outside Bio-Splice Laboratory. It was time to assume the role of Li Chen, regional customer service manager of Guangzhou Medical Equipment. She looked down at the badge hanging around her neck, designed to be a replica of the equipment company's employee badge. She looked down in her purse for other official documents provided by the FBI that would establish her identity and the memory stick she would push inside the USB port on a computer that provided access to the internal network. She closed her eyes briefly to prepare herself.

"Is this it?" the driver asked, looking at Wang in his rearview mirror and wondering why she was still in the back of his car.

"Yes," she replied, "thank you. Can you wait for me, please? I will pay your fare for holding here, and I expect to be no more than twenty minutes."

According to her training, spending more than twenty minutes incognito significantly increased the chances of being discovered. Agents slip and give their identity away, or someone recognizes them. She set an alarm on her phone that would remind her that, should she not succeed in the mission by that time, she would make some excuse about a personal emergency and abort it.

"Fine," said the driver. "I'll wait over there." He pointed to a parking lot reserved for employees and official contractors, as the facility rarely had visitors.

Wang left the cab and walked into the lobby of the facility. She approached someone sitting behind a small desk that would examine the documents of anyone that was not wearing an official Bio-Splice badge. Two security guards were standing nearby. One was watching a show on his phone. The other was staring off into space, as if in a trance.

"Li Chen, regional customer service for Guangzhou Medical," Gina said, in an official tone. "I am here to see

Yuze Zhang." She handed her identity papers to the woman behind the desk.

What Gina did not realize was that a camera hanging from the ceiling was trained on her face. It was connected to MSS facial recognition, and she was identified as a suspected spy, an agent they had known to be operating in the Chinese provinces for several years. Someone they desperately wanted to catch. The person who was supposed to be monitoring the camera, however, was nowhere to be found at the moment Gina was standing at the desk.

As Gina bent over to fill in the visitor log, the elevator door opened and two men walked out. One was a security guard. The other was a technician. For Guangzhou Medical. As it turned out, another lab employee, one whose job was on the line due to the decomposed embryos, had called Guangzhou Technical Support the day before and summoned a technician who arrived earlier in the day. He was finishing up and confirmed that all equipment was operating according to published specifications.

"Who are you?" the technician asked as he approached the desk to log out and noticed Gina's badge.

Gina looked to the right and was face to face with the technician. Each looked down at the other's badge.

"Hi," she said, aiming to remain calm. "I'm the new customer service manager for the company."

"No, you're not," the man said angrily, his eyebrows coming together at the center of his face.

"Excuse me?" Gina replied, fully intending to talk her way out of the situation.

"You are not the customer service manager for Guangzhou. I know the customer service manager from Guangzhou. He was the groomsman at my wedding. And you are not him."

Things escalated quickly. Gina stepped away from the desk and turned halfway around, hoping she could make it to the cab. The woman behind the desk raised her arm and pointed at Gina while looking at one of the guards. The technician stepped away as the guards closed in. Within seconds, each guard held one of Gina's arms. She would be taken to a back room as security called in the police.

It would only have required one squad car to take Gina into custody, but five of them sped onto the laboratory campus, their sirens loudly announcing their arrival and their lights rotating for the duration of their visit. Gina's purse was confiscated, but not before she was able to touch the single button on her phone that sent a distress signal to the agency. She had been captured and had no means of escape. She was in serious trouble, and she knew it. It took less than three minutes for her cover to be blown.

As word spread that a spy was captured on the grounds of the building, employees crowded windows to look down on the activity, and people who were entering or exiting the lobby as the scene unfolded stayed exactly where they were, as this was the most exciting thing that anyone could remember happening at the lab. As Gina was escorted out of the facility with zip ties holding her wrists behind her back, a disheveled-looking man quietly entered from the loading dock.

"WELL, IF YOU THOUGHT security was bad before this happened, we can only imagine what it is going to be like starting tomorrow." Yuze Zhang, the lab manager at Bio-Splice, was speaking to his wife, who had just heard from him about the agent being captured. Gina Wang had been transported away about thirty minutes before, and things were getting back to normal.

"Does this mean you will be late tonight?" his wife asked.

"Probably," he replied. "A couple of police are still here. They will probably want to ask me some questions."

As they spoke about various options for dinner, a jolt the magnitude of a large earthquake shook the building, the window outside his sixth-floor office shattered, and a bookshelf came crashing down, books scattering everywhere. Zhang dropped the phone, stood up, and made for the door to his office so he could see what was going on. Within seconds, a second jolt, this time even stronger, rocked the building, setting off alarms and the automated sprinklers. Zhang fell to his knees. Others who were still standing ran for the exits. The building was on fire, and people were screaming. A bomb attached to an oxygen tank in the facility's basement guaranteed that the fire would have enough fuel to overcome any resistance. The sprinklers were not nearly capable enough to protect people or property.

Meanwhile, the man who had entered the facility from the loading dock when all attention was on the front lobby, a North Korean agent by the name of Kim Ji-Sung, was walking away from the building. He continued to look ahead and didn't bother to look back at the building as he walked away, even as it was consumed in flames, destroying nearly all life inside.

Yuze Zhang had just barely enough time to get back on his feet to recover the phone handset hanging by its cord from the desk, and to tell his wife that he would not be coming home.

"SIR, THIS IS A CLUSTERFUCK inside a train wreck that is about to become a major shitshow," Richard blurted out in a video conference call with Ben Klein. "How are we expected to recover from this?"

Richard was angry. He had foreseen the likelihood that the Bio-Splice portion of the mission might turn to failure, and he had raised his concerns often. He had predicted the cyber worm, which was so new that nobody had the opportunity to name it, would fail to affect the required temperature controls. Instead, the agent carrying it was captured. With the seventy-two-hour timeline set down by the CIA, the FBI's reputation was on the line, people's identities were in danger of being revealed by the agent's inevitable interrogation, and the viability of the entire mission was now threatened.

As Richard waited for Klein to reply, a very excited young aide came running into Klein's office. Richard could see him enter the frame of the video.

"Sir, we are getting reports of a major fire at the Bio-Splice Laboratory," the young man said, "it started about ten hours ago, mid-day in Harbin. Sir, the building has been destroyed."

"Thank you, Bill," Klein said.

Klein watched the aide leave and then turned his attention back to his monitor, and Richard, who had a look of disbelief on his face.

"How did you . . . How did . . . you do that?" O'Brien managed to say.

"One word," Klein replied dryly. "Redundancy."

23

At 6:05 in the morning, just before the sun began to rise above the horizon, a bird was resting on a floating plate out at sea. Suddenly, it jumped off and started to fly, but it lost its way and dove straight into the water. Bats on the nearby islands started to screech. Shortly thereafter, rats that had arrived on the islands from supply boats began to scatter around in the open, in different directions, as if they were trying to escape something. Some ran directly into the ocean and drowned. A cacophony of horrific sounds began to emanate from what would otherwise be a quiet pre-dawn morning.

Cadet 07-8556-03 was one of the first clones to experience symptoms. The cadet was born in 2007, gestated to birth by surrogate prisoner #8556, the third child she produced for the Party while serving in the Xinjiang camps. He was urinating in the latrine before he was expected at the morning formation when he felt an overwhelming sense of nausea. He realized that if he reported this to his commander, he would be put in detention, so he initially ignored it. Then, he slowly fell to his knees and started vomiting directly into the urinal.

Symptoms in other cadets started to appear rapidly. Some who did not exhibit nausea instead demonstrated unprovoked aggression toward other soldiers, assaulting them in fits of rage, which created a domino effect and led to riots on a massive scale. Some soldiers wandered aimlessly on the base in violation of curfew. Still others just lay in bed, unable to get up.

The officers, none of whom were clones, were baffled. Many cadets were shot for attacking officers or put in detention for insubordination. Soon, the situation became unmanageable. Within thirty-six hours from the beginning of the broadcast from the nearby buoys, a cadet shot and killed his commanding officer. He was shot and killed seconds later.

Because the cadets vastly outnumbered the officers, the officers abandoned the island in order to consider what happened and what could be done to restore order. By the time the last officer left the island, Cadet 07–8556-03 was dead from a self-inflicted wound.

Rumors about the cadets began to reach the mainland and other soldiers in the PLA. They saw several officers returning and heard many things they were not supposed to hear. While the PLA on the mainland included only a few clones, word spread fast that something bad was happening on the islands and that going there would mean disease or death. This was translated into a superstition that the islands harbored a deadly virus or were cursed and that nobody was safe there. It became clear to the leadership in the PLA that the situation was unsustainable; they would not be able to maintain an effective presence on the islands until they understood what had happened to the clones. They certainly could not plan any movements on Taiwan.

The state media, which dictates the truth in China just as the sun dictates daytime, was determined to avoid any news about what was happening on the islands from the outside world. They were only partially successful.

THERE ARE WELL OVER 250 companies in the United States owned by Chinese corporations. This is simply the number listed on the various U.S. stock exchanges; the real number is likely much higher. However, if you wanted to count the number of American-owned companies based in China, you would need only a few fingers. And the three largest American companies based in China are BeiGene, Zai Lab, and Bio-Splice Laboratories.

BeiGene was founded in 2010 by American billionaire John V. Oyler and Xiaodong Wang, a Chinese American scientist. All three companies focused on the discovery, development, and commercialization of biological therapeutics. After 2019, when He Jiankui was jailed for undertaking germline editing experiments on human subjects, the companies went silent on discussing their own research and ambitions in this area. Howard Steele saw that Oyler could launch a company in China and outside the regulatory purview of the United States, so he became one of the early investors in Bio-Splice. His shares in the company came with a reservation in a freezer.

For Steele's part, he wanted to commercialize products outside the U.S. because he had an enormous distrust of the FDA, NIH, and other regulators. And the CIA similarly wanted to grab and exploit discoveries before commercialization, and patents gave the winning pharma company a limited-term monopoly.

Bio-Splice, like other companies with significant foreign ownership, employed operating agreements to create a virtual barrier between the management, finances, and strategic activities of each enterprise. This protocol functioned for a time, but it did not consider the ambitions of some within the CCP to exploit Bio-Splice's most groundbreaking discovery, or the CIA's determination to either control it or capture and kill it.

In spite of the outcome, this was not the FBI and CIA's finest hour, but instead, it was another case of the left and right hands operating in completely different worlds. It all began when the CIA recognized the potential of germline editing for its own military purposes and began to gather (steal) intelligence from American universities, Chinese companies, and anywhere else that progress was being made.

This would not be the first time the CIA acted as if the rules didn't apply to them. When Edward Snowden revealed that, in spite of it being illegal, the act of spying on Americans was actually happening, the CIA accepted the blame but then adopted the position that the boundary protecting individual liberties did not extend to U.S. corporations. When it was revealed in 2017 that the CIA had been spying on Apple for over five years to better understand how to access the content of locked phones, it prompted a protected source to say, "If the government can spy on Apple, what's next?"

What *was* next was Bio-Splice. The company was on the CIA's radar long before they discovered that George Kolins was supplying the company with information that would accelerate its ability to successfully clone human embryos. In a perfect world involving world-class intelligence agencies, the CIA would have shared what it had with the FBI. Like an overplayed soundtrack, this would not be the first time the United States had all the information necessary to prevent something from happening but waited so long to move that irreversible damage was done.

In fact, it would be reasonable to expect that U.S. intelligence agencies would ask for the cooperation of American companies rather than steal their discoveries. However, when you consider the logistics of entering into agreements with these companies, making and keeping promises to protect their intellectual property, and ensuring that there are no moles and no leaks, then the alternative of simply grabbing the discovery makes infinitely more sense. To be sure, it's a nuanced situation.

That said, the decision to end Bio-Splice's operation was made many weeks before the fire, when Ji-Sung was in U.S. custody. The memory stick he brought back to North Korea had all the information necessary to end the Chinese threat, compelling enough to persuade them to destroy the laboratory rather than to merely steal its secrets. And if China chose to pin the intervention on North Korea, all the better.

24

Russia had Kim Philby. Germany had Mata Hari. First Germany, then England, had Eddie Chapman. The U.S. had too many double agents to mention, and many continue to operate undercover today. But in the modern age, few were as valuable to the U.S. intelligence apparatus as Emma Lee.

Emma Lee's career as a CIA agent began while she was a sophomore at UCLA. She was specifically recruited because of her ties back home, her background in biological sciences, and evidence from her Instagram account that she was popular, charming, and outgoing. She checked all the boxes. The process of seducing and recruiting her took several weeks and included meeting with the CIA near the UCLA campus, followed by intense training while she maintained the appearance of being a full-time student. At the urging of the CIA, she took a job at the Salk Institute when she later enrolled at UCSD.

To prepare Emma Lee for her role as a double agent, the CIA turned to the case history of Eddie Chapman, also known as Agent Zigzag for his proclivity for playing one side against the other. Chapman started to spy for the Germans during World War II because he was already a convicted criminal in England with limited prospects. However, once he landed in England as part of a plot to destroy a British airplane factory, he gave himself up and, after significant interrogation and more than a few raised eyebrows, joined MI5. He would go on to be involved in multiple acts of espionage on behalf of the Allies. He and Emma remained loyal to the country they admired most.

Emma was instructed to approach the MSS while visiting her parents and explain that she could not afford to pay for her education at an American university. She would embellish the story by explaining how, due to her struggles as a Chinese student who had recently arrived in America, she had plagiarized many papers and feared she may soon get thrown out of the university. The image of a petite, intelligent, and determined young woman fit the MSS profile. She checked all their boxes, too.

Although it was at times difficult to remember which side she was on and equally stressful, Emma had the attention to detail and rock-solid demeanor to pivot seamlessly from one character to another. At times, such as when she had to plug her cell phone in at the Banyan Tree Hotel to download the camfecting software code, she had to do so pretending that she didn't know the consequences of her actions. This constant role playing, where a simple misstatement could land her in a Chinese labor camp, would take its toll on her eventually. Although the legendary reputation of "Agent Zigzag" had already been claimed, Emma embodied it perfectly.

BY THE TIME DENNIS walked off the flight in Hong Kong, Chinese state media was broadcasting that Bio-Splice Laboratories was destroyed by "a fire of unknown origin." Dennis stopped and watched the coverage. By now, he thought, his Hong Kong customer would also have seen this news. His last prospect for a significant infusion of cash was gone. This was not the most alarming thing to happen to him in his lifetime, and he would get through it. For now, he needed to sleep because of the torturous flight from Tijuana.

As he arrived at his hotel, his phone slid a notification across the bottom of the screen: "Patient Nearby." This was an amateurish but effective phone app that Dennis created to notify him if a patient was approaching. It was another one of Dennis's paranoid obsessions to ensure that he would never be attacked from behind by one of his victims. Patients had a chip installed in their wrists, similar to what animals received to aid in their recovery when they went missing. The stitches would be explained to patients as an attempted suicide that they had blocked out of their minds, probably because they were ashamed of themselves. Dennis opened the alert and saw that the patient ID belonged to FBI Special Agent Richard O'Brien.

Dennis believed that Richard O'Brien in Hong Kong could only mean one thing: He was coming after him. *It's always something*, he thought to himself, *always one more crisis to solve before I'm free and clear to enjoy the path I chose.*

He surmised that the agents had looked at his calendar and sent Richard after him.

Dennis knew there was no extradition treaty between Hong Kong and the U.S., but he didn't realize that no law enforcement agency from the U.S. would send an agent into a foreign country without the country's consent to apprehend a suspect. Such a move was too dangerous, and only the Israelis were competent at it. The ability of the U.S. to operate in Hong Kong was essentially terminated when it reverted to Chinese control in 1997.

The island of Hong Kong was only thirty-four square miles, and the app Dennis designed had a range of twenty-five miles, so Richard must be on the island and close. But Dennis had the advantage, he thought; he could see Richard before Richard could see him. And that would make all the difference. The hunt would begin in earnest in a few hours.

IT FELT GOOD TO BE holding a woman's hand again, and the fact that the hand belonged to Sarah Goodman was particularly blissful for Richard. He had moved from his standard-issue Marriott Hotel in Kowloon, where he had stayed the evening before, to the exclusive Mandarin Oriental on Hong Kong Island. He had gone to the airport earlier to meet Sarah and guide her back to the city, arriving at the hotel around 5:10 in the afternoon.

Massive cumulous clouds hung over the entire region all day, following torrential thunderstorms. While the Hong

Kong skyline and Victoria Harbor are immediately recognizable on screensavers, those views would not be emerging for a few days. For now, it was wet, dark, and foreboding.

"We are already checked in," Richard said, smiling broadly to reflect how proud he felt for the arrangements he made in anticipation of this important evening. "And we have massages scheduled at 5:30."

"Oh . . . okay," Sarah said, still a bit jet lagged from the flight but grateful she didn't need to make many decisions for now.

"We'll dump your luggage and then head to the spa. They offer a 'couples experience' in adjoining rooms, followed by a private tea service for two," he said. "We'll see how you feel after that."

The idea was to unwind after the long flight before they began exploring the island and looking for the best XLB. Richard ordered the traditional Thai massage; Sarah looked at the various options and ordered the aromatic body massage. The two walked behind the spa counter and into separate rooms where the massage therapists were waiting for them. They were each wearing the robes offered in their hotel room.

"Hello Richard, my name is Angelina, and I'll be taking care of you this afternoon," the masseuse said to Richard. "Please take off all your clothes and lie face down on the table, and I'll be right back. Just cover your butt with a towel." Richard smiled at her, but he couldn't see if she was smiling back because she was wearing an N95 mask.

He was always confused about this part. *Undies on or undies off?*

"Undies off," she said as she left the room and gently closed the door behind her.

After removing his underwear, he put his head down on the table and pulled the towel over his rear end. A few moments later the masseuse returned.

"You're American," Richard said, hoping to start some small talk.

"Yes, I came here to study Theravada," she replied as she started arranging her oils on a nearby table. "I fell in love with Hong Kong and decided to stay. I'm originally from Orange County."

"Oh yeah?" Richard replied, his face firmly planted in the face pillow, looking down at the floor. "I'm in LA myself."

"Really? That's great. Now, please, just relax."

The masseuse started to rub oil on Richard's back, applying just enough pressure to demonstrate to him that she knew what she was doing. It felt really good. As she ran her hands up and down from his neck to the small of his back, she increased the pressure. She momentarily lifted her hands before starting up again. Richard was starting to zone out.

He didn't realize that when she reached over to her table, she poured several ounces of pure aconite oil on his back and applied it with her gloved hands, up and down his arms. Suddenly, he felt a sharp blade pressed hard against his neck, and the palm of her hand pushed firmly against the back of his head. It hurt. A lot.

"You've ruined everything," Dennis said. "You and that slut Harmony." He applied much more pressure to Richard's neck, drawing blood.

Richard immediately made the connection and wasn't fully surprised to run into Dennis again, he just didn't expect it to happen while he was lying on a massage table. He remembered Dennis sitting across the desk from him at CNB and thinking that the man was of a fairly small frame at the time. *I can take him*, he thought.

Richard tried to take his fist and jam it against Dennis's waist. If he hit him hard enough, he could pop off the table and either attack him or run. There was one problem: He couldn't move his arms. He needed another plan.

Richard rolled his body in the direction opposite the knife and fell on the floor. Dennis laughed, realizing he was in control and there was nothing Richard could do. Dennis wasn't a sociopathic murderer, but he did insist on having the upper hand and could not afford to be captured by Richard. This was the last piece of remaining business, one of the only people in law enforcement who would recognize him. He had a few options for dispensing with Richard but wanted the aconite to take full effect, and there was no great hurry since the massage was scheduled for forty-five minutes.

While Richard's arms were paralyzed by the drug, he still had his legs. Within seconds of crashing down on the floor, he kicked a small stand near the massage table that held massage oils. The stand flipped, some bottles shattered, and others just lay on their sides, their contents pouring out. Puddles of oil and broken glass were everywhere.

Dennis stepped around the broken glass to stand over Richard but hadn't counted on the noise. Sarah, whose instincts were spot on, heard the commotion and came running into the room wearing only her panties. When she stepped on the oil in her bare feet, her legs flew forward and she landed hard on her butt. Dennis jumped back. Having a second agent trying to apprehend him was also not in his plan.

Shards of glass were scattered across the floor. Sarah tried to get up but the oil on her hands, knees, and feet made it difficult. She rolled around and was on all fours. But she startled Dennis enough that after he unwittingly stepped backward, he also slipped on the oil. All three of them were on the floor, with Richard and Sarah crawling over and trying to subdue Dennis, who still held the knife. Sarah pinned down the arm holding it.

Richard managed to get up first, completely naked, his penis flying back and forth as he jockeyed for position vis-à-vis Dennis. He had the presence of mind to think that one of the worst outcomes would be for Dennis to sever his penis, so he tried to cover it with his left hand as he prepared to fend off Dennis with his right.

Dennis had managed to shove Sarah aside and both were standing as well, panting. It would be difficult to say which team had the upper hand; Dennis had the knife, but Richard and Sarah had training in hand-to-hand combat. And they were blocking the door that would provide Dennis with an exit. Time seemed to hit a speed bump. The three stood facing each other, desperately trying to catch their breath before the next round. Dennis spoke first.

"Is it true what they said on CNN?" Dennis asked. "That Howard Steele's body was destroyed in the Bio-Splice fire?"

Sarah and Richard looked at each other, neither expecting a conversation to emerge.

"Yeah," Richard said, "I think so."

Dennis looked at the floor, thinking. Richard and Sarah had eyes trained on him, squatting slightly to strengthen their stand, their hands extended. Richard was not sure he could contribute to the ongoing battle as the aconite had affected his eye-hand coordination. Meanwhile, Sarah was running combat scenarios through her mind.

Just then, Dennis looked up, and stared at the two agents. "Then it's a happy ending after all. I'll see you on the other side."

He dragged the knife hard against his neck. Blood came squirting out. His eyes went up and fell into the back of his head, and his body fell straight down until he was on the floor, lying in a fetal position and face up.

Sarah and Richard stood side by side, naked or nearly so, looking at the body of Dennis Spence lying on the floor of the massage room, blood flowing from his neck and forming a dark red pool around his head. They were surprised to be the last two standing.

Sarah burst out in a combination of nervous laughter and tears. She embraced Richard, arms intertwined, and for a moment, two oily bodies became one. The tension and emotion triggered something inside Richard, who said something he meant but did not necessarily intend to blurt out.

"I love you," he said, "let's get married."

Sarah pulled back and looked at Richard, her expression revealing a moment of emotional vulnerability. She noticed some blood on Richard's neck, probably from the knife's pressure, and touched him gently around the injury. She looked down and finally realized he was naked, with an erection. She covered her mouth and started laughing again.

Within seconds, the masseuse that had been looking for Sarah to start her treatment came bursting into the room. She wasted no time in rushing to Dennis's side, applying pressure to the wound with a towel. She called out to her coworkers to call for an ambulance, although Dennis's body remained lifeless. More and more employees from within the spa began to crowd the room, forming a circle around Spence's body. Sarah and Richard remained off to one side.

The two FBI agents looked down at Dennis Spence a complex, tormented character, now dying before their eyes. They had so many questions about him that would now go unanswered. Richard realized they would probably need to leave Hong Kong quickly. As that sentiment entered his thoughts, Sarah said with urgency, "We need to go home. NOW."

The hotel staff were quick to respond to the incident. They did their best to provide comfort and apologies to Richard and Sarah while they simultaneously called the police. As they did so, Sarah contacted the U.S. Consulate General in Hong Kong to request they make an unannounced visit, allowing just enough time for Richard and Sarah to give the police their statement.

The Chinese police were persuaded that the assault was a case of mistaken identity because Richard had arrived in the country just a few hours before. They found the spa employee that should have been assigned to Richard recovering from a propofol-induced sleep in a nearby closet. Richard and Sarah assured the police they had never seen the perpetrator before, and cooperated with several hours of recapping over and over the same information. Their specific professions might have eventually come up, but a high-ranking officer from the U.S. Consulate General's office appeared to request they be permitted to leave, and without any further reason to detain them, the request was granted, with the understanding that they would not leave the country until the investigation was completed.

Then, they grabbed their bags and were taken directly to the airport.

25

As intelligence reports began to flow into the FBI and CIA about everything China hoped to keep secret, relief spread across the agencies. The secretary of state shared the good news with his counterpart in Taiwan that, at least for now and the foreseeable future, China would be consumed with domestic affairs and investigations instead of focusing its armies on invading the island nation. China abandoned efforts to produce additional human clones from Uyghur surrogates, much to the relief of human rights organizations and related NGOs. Recognizing their inherent vulnerability, the CCP did not want the continued burden of feeding and sheltering them.

The brief and uncomfortable cooperation between the DPRK and the United States returned to the frigid relations that characterized their relationship since the country declared its existence in 1948.

However, there would be an investigation into the handling of Operation Carbon Paper, specifically the decisions that led to the capture of a valued agent, Gina Wang. There would be finger-pointing, second-guessing, and a lot of explaining to do. It would take another five years before the U.S. could present China with an acceptable prisoner swap. When she returned home, Gina would leave the agency, settle into the San Francisco Bay Area, and start a family.

RICHARD PRESENTED HIS report on Operation Carbon Paper in Washington DC in a top-secret briefing, laying out the full scope of the Chinese plot to exploit the potential of germline editing. His audience included senior staff in the branches of the NSA, CIA, FBI, and the State Department. The tension in the wood-paneled conference room was amping up even before the most disturbing intelligence on the work of a foreign adversary was introduced.

The breathtaking scope of what Richard promised to cover gave him full command of the room. On a screen at the front of the room, a complete diagram was presented based on Ben Klein's sketch, illustrating the complex web of actors and organizations involved.

"We discovered the creation of a virtual industrial complex with the aim to clone humans, endow them with self-healing properties, extend the lifetime of some individuals and cryogenically freeze others," Richard said. "Cryogenic commercial operations funded much of the ongoing research, some of it conducted here in the U.S."

"The first phase of the clandestine project began in 2004 with the theft of embryonic material from a laboratory in Seoul, taken then to a laboratory in Harbin," he said, using a laser pointer to identify Bio-Splice. "What the Chinese did not realize, however, was that South Korean scientists embedded a form of 'kill switch' within the DNA of the embryos, affecting any human clones that might originate from them, which we exploited to debilitate clones that were deployed in the South China Sea."

"Their second phase included endowing subjects with the ability to regenerate injured organs based on science that was already pretty advanced by labs around the world, but not yet applied to humans."

"Why did we conclude this was a specific military threat?" came a question from the director of the NSA. "Do we have proof that the Chinese intended to weaponize these technologies?"

"Sir, we absolutely do," Richard replied. "Our asset in the CIA was able to penetrate deep into the organization and provided evidence that the Chinese had created a facility to clone humans that could accommodate these self-healing organs, with the aim of creating an army that they believed would be nearly invincible. Sir, those clones were battle-ready off the coast of Taiwan."

Richard had many more slides to show, but at this point advanced to a series of images taken from the drone and later magnified to show identical looking PLA soldiers. Some members of the audience looked at each other with a hint of disbelief, others took notes.

"If I may continue," Richard said, determined to remain within the twenty minutes he was afforded on the agenda, "a more recent activity, involving research conducted at The Center for New Beginnings in Southern California, was to significantly extend human life. We uncovered an alliance between an American scientist and the CCP to illegally experiment on human subjects. Documents seized from his office corroborated much of what we were able to learn from our own investigation," he added.

"Is that the suspect that . . . ?"

"Yes, Dennis Spence committed suicide in Hong Kong after assaulting an FBI agent." Richard did not clarify that he was the agent that Spence tried to murder, as this was already well understood by his audience.

The remainder of the meeting was spent unraveling the remainder of the mission's findings, then discussing exactly how much information from the presentation would be made public. It would not amount to much.

Later that afternoon at an event open to the press, Felix Jordan received the Medal for Meritorious Achievement while Richard received the highest honor, the FBI Medal of Valor. References to their specific contributions were left vague enough that the press could only refer to achievements made in the past by each of the agents. The four would have dinner that night to celebrate. Jordan, McAuley, and O'Brien would work together in the FBI for the next several years. Ben Klein would retire at the end of the year after an illustrious career.

RICHARD FELT HE NEEDED closure with Harmony Hutchins, so he reached out to her the following week and found that she and Jack Reeves had been seeing each other regularly, their age difference having been conveniently treated with indifference. Richard suggested they meet for dinner, deciding it best that Sarah not be involved. That happened a few weeks later, and the three of them managed to have a wonderful evening without any reference to Operations Free Eagle or Carbon Paper.

Sarah and Richard would never marry, in fact, they eventually started to drift apart. Sarah was convinced that the ecosystem of the FBI left little room for anything else. In the next two years, she would be promoted to special agent in charge of the Detroit field office. Many years later she would marry a local prosecutor specializing in white collar crime who she met on a case she was investigating. Ironically, the range of topics they could discuss was only marginally better than had she married within the agency.

Richard leaned into the Southern California lifestyle and found a place of his own in Manhattan Beach. He continued his promiscuous lifestyle and never found the kindred spirit he had in Sarah Goodman. His expanding network of local married couples rallied around him and encouraged him to focus on sustainable relationships. He became a frequent dinner guest at the home of Felix Jordan who, like his other friends, simply wanted to see Richard succeed and settle down. In time, he would come to recognize this and place less priority on sexual escapades.

George Kolins would be free from the constraints of his NDA, or at least that was his presumption once he learned about the demise of Bio-Splice Laboratory and the end of his private funding. He didn't wait for permission to publish. Kolins's research on regeneration would be published in *Science* and *Genome Biology*, and he would later join the board of directors of Genegineering, a trailblazing American company focused on a broad range of genetically focused discoveries. He would receive a handsome stipend from the company for his services that significantly reduced his financial liabilities.

JI-SUNG WAS WELCOMED back to North Korea after he successfully completed his last mission. He was awarded the Order of Kim Il Sung medal and thereafter retired from the service, enjoying a reasonable pension for the remainder of his days. He would never speak of the dangerous missions he undertook to serve his country and would take the secrets of Bio-Splice and his role in destroying it to his grave. On recognizing that he was most likely captured during his mission to the United States, the MSS designated him a lost asset. They would never make the connection between Ji-Sung and the fire at Bio-Splice.

While the CIA confirmed that the MSS received and downloaded the fake information on North Korea's genetics research laboratories, it never determined whether the Chinese did anything with the material. If they were as competent as the FBI and CIA in sharing information, then it's possible that nothing was done with the bogus intelligence.

THE FBI CLOSED ITS case file on Spence. Examination of his personal papers would reveal he was aware that Howard Steele had invested in Bio-Splice, and that's how he connected to the company in the first place. It was only when he started working with Bio-Splice that he learned Steele had never died from drowning. Per the contract with Bio-Splice, Steele's body was transported at very low temperatures the moment he was loaded into the ambulance. From there, he was transported to China at great cost, an expense that was little more than a rounding error in Steele's corporate balance sheet.

IN HONG KONG CEMETERIES, uniform, rectangular tombstones are positioned so close together that barely any daylight passes between them. Hong Kong's cemeteries are full. It has long been acknowledged that, when it comes to real estate in Hong Kong, it is more expensive to be dead than alive. Already 90 percent of the 48,000 people who die each year in Hong Kong are cremated.

The process of finding a resting place for Dennis was something Emma felt obliged to manage. She realized it wouldn't be easy, particularly as he would have been arrested for assault and attempted murder had he survived. Emma understood Denise's early feelings about cremation. "A colossal waste of raw materials and spare parts," she once said. Given this, Emma had hoped to give Dennis a traditional burial, perhaps also for selfish reasons because it would allow her the opportunity to say goodbye.

Unfortunately, the Hong Kong police eventually made the unilateral decision that his body, once processed at the morgue, would be cremated.

Dennis had no next of kin, and the intended resting place for his body, the Bio-Splice Laboratory in Harbin, no longer existed. His family did not subscribe to any faith. For his stepfather, Howard Steele, capitalism was the only religion worth practicing. Cremation seemed as good an option as anything else.

The world would never come to appreciate Dennis's genius or his potential. Dennis's research into the combined potential of pharmacology and botany to extend human life would not be fully understood until the passing of his mentor, Dr. Kumar, whose life he greatly extended. Once Dr. Kumar was transferred from CNB to an assisted living facility in Pasadena, he began to circulate to his university contacts many of his unpublished papers on his early work and experiments, research that Spence took to the next level and kept secret.

ASHES FROM CREMATED bodies can be stored in a columbarium in and around Hong Kong alongside the urns of others who chose the same path, or had this path chosen for them. Of course, there are fees for storing ashes. Alternatively, you can scatter the deceased's ashes in designated areas off the coast and be free from ongoing expenses. The government offers a free ferry for mourners who wish to pursue this option. Curiously, this activity is managed by the Food and Environmental Hygiene Department. Emma Lee consulted the ferry schedule before picking up Dennis's ashes.

On a Sunday morning when clouds were finally giving way to sunshine, Emma boarded the ferry with a cardboard box. The box was small and square and could be confused for a box containing croissants for a Sunday brunch. In spite of the promising good weather, the wind was making the water a bit rough, so Emma began holding the box with both hands.

She had so many questions left unanswered by Dennis's death. Even the thought of him killing himself was completely inconsistent with her understanding of how he would respond to pressure. Perhaps he was tired of running or realized that a transgender person would never survive in prison. She wondered if she had alerted her CIA handler before Richard was captured, perhaps the unraveling of Dennis's entire existence, his *raison de vivre*, could have been avoided.

She began to reflect on the closing comments made by Dr. George Kolins at the UCSD lecture, *there is a difference between making people better, and making better people.* She thought, if the latter trumps the former, then the human race is on a dangerous trajectory and that, for her part, she was in the right place at the right time and would be on the right side of history. Then her thoughts returned to Dennis, and she looked down at the box on her lap.

Emma was delinquent in her responsibilities as a federal agent to allow Dennis's criminal behavior to remain unreported for so long. "Why did you have to do it?" she whispered to the box. She remembered their early years at UCLA, skipping class and hanging out on the grass in the common areas, discussing philosophy and other heavy topics. She regretted the day that her report to the CIA about the activities at CNB would place her in the uncomfortable position of betraying a close friend. Then, as her body began to spasm, she brought her hands to her face, and started to sob. As tears flowed down her face, the magnificent skyline of Hong Kong reveal itself on the waters of Victoria Harbor. It was wasted on her.

The wind was running across Emma's face, caressing it. Looking around, she realized for the first time that she was not alone. Several other people mourning loved ones were also sitting on benches, similar cardboard boxes on their laps. Others were walking around the boat, holding their little boxes, with expressionless faces making it obvious that they were experiencing the kind of grief that can only come from profound loss.

Emma had more that she wanted to say to Dennis's ashes when she felt her cell phone vibrating in her pocket. She did not recognize the number but answered anyway.

"Hello, is this Ms. Emma Lee?" the lady at the line inquired.

"It is," Emma replied. "Who is this?"

"Yes, Ms. Emma, I am sorry to bother you," the woman said. "I am in charge of customer accounts at Bio-Splice 2, here in Shenzhen. We've just taken receipt of Dennis Spence."

"Excuse me?" Emma said, trying to process what she just heard and thinking until that point that Dennis's ashes were in the box on her lap.

"Yes, as I said, we have Dennis Spence's body here. You are listed as next of kin and beneficiary of his financial accounts," she said. "I'm very sorry to bother you, Ms. Emma, but we need you to sign some papers and arrange payment for ongoing support and maintenance."

ABOUT THE AUTHOR

I an Rodney Lazarus has been publishing technical articles and opinion pieces in various magazines since 1989. *Cease to Exist* is his second novel, the sequel to his first book, *Con & Consequence*, which is available from most online book retailers.

A native of Detroit and graduate of the University of Michigan, he now lives in San Diego with his wife, three children, and occasionally a cat. He is a certified sailor, advanced scuba diver, and "Six Sigma" blackbelt. He is also an active member of the U.S. Coast Guard Auxiliary.

ACKNOWLEDGMENTS

A project is only as good as the team leading it, and I had a superb group assisting me on this novel that I'd like to recognize. First and foremost, my sister Diane, who committed herself to unvarnished and sometimes painful feedback. Diane was on my advance reading team along with her husband, Larry, a retired professor of American literature. The team also included my cousin Jeff Rosoff, childhood friend Gregg Nathanson, dive buddy Robert Jafek, and colleague Jerry Kolins, MD.

Finally, I could not have produced this novel without the tireless efforts of my editor, John Cannon.

Also by Ian Rodney Lazarus

The Richard O'Brien Series
Cease to Exist